HOT AS HELL

JESSA JAMES

GET A FREE BOOK!

Join my mailing list to be the first to know of new releases, free books, special prices and other author giveaways.

http://freehotcontemporary.com

PROLOGUE

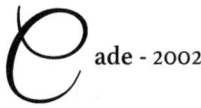 **ade - 2002**

CADE TOOK pleasure in every leaf crunch beneath his beat-up Converse shoes, the faded Fall Out Boy lyrics etched across the toes in EJ's slanted print. "Sorry, dude," EJ said. "I can't believe my dad's making us babysit. For free, too."

Lily shot him a look. "Don't be mean," she said. "Or I'll tell Dad." In her little eight-year-old hands, she clutched her Lizzie McGuire lunchbox that rattled with leftovers.

Aiden tagged along beside Cade to distance himself from Lily as much as possible. In his last year of elementary school, he was desperate to be seen as one of the middle school kids like Cade and EJ. "So," Aiden said. "How are the girls at Walker? Hot?"

"What do you know about hot?" EJ asked his little brother. "But actually, Cade thinks there are some hotties," EJ said as he elbowed Cade in the ribs. "Right?"

"Shut up," Cade said. He kept his eyes on the ground, an explosion of gold and orange under his feet.

"What? I saw you staring at that redheaded girl in

homeroom." Cade could feel EJ's eyes as they bored into him, but he refused to look up. "C'mon, we've been best friends since we were in diapers. You think I can't tell?"

"Not in front of the kids," Cade said in the most adult voice he could muster. *Thankfully, this time it didn't crack*, he thought.

"I'm not a little kid!" Aiden piped up. "It's my last year—"

"You're still in elementary school," EJ reminded him. "And need us to escort you home!"

"Whatever," Aiden muttered under his breath.

"Well, if you're not going to talk about your future wife, what about the field trip Mr. Stroh was talking about? You think you're gonna go?"

Cade sighed. "I dunno. I'm not sure if my foster parents will sign off on it."

"What? Why wouldn't they?" EJ asked. "It's gonna be awesome. Like, they let you feed bears! And since it's a drive-through safari, rhinos could totally charge the bus—"

"You know how they are," Cade said. He rolled his eyes. "They think they can turn every kid they take in into Jehovah's Witnesses. I'll probably be knocking door-to-door while you all are getting impaled by wild animals or something."

"That sounds like child abuse, dude," EJ said as he made a face. "You should call CPS on their ass."

Cade shook his head. "The Parkers are alright, they're just strict. After the Carters, I can't complain."

"Yeah, they were crazy," EJ said. "I can't believe they freaking locked you in the bedroom every night! Thinking you were going to steal their crappy china or whatever."

"The getting locked in part wasn't so bad. It was the totally forgetting to have any food in the morning for any of us part that sucked. Not that it happened all the time, but still ..."

"I don't know, dude, going door-to-door doesn't sound much better. Hopefully you get a decent family soon."

"I'd just be happy staying somewhere longer than a year,

honestly. So, I gotta be on my best behavior. Make sure the Parkers think I'm a 'good kid' and all."

EJ laughed. "Good luck with that."

The group turned onto Fairgrounds Road and Lily squealed as the firehouse came into view. "Are we going to get to ride the truck?" she asked.

"Don't be stupid," EJ said. "You know what Dad says."

"It's not a toy," Lily said with a sigh.

"Yeah. But guess what? Dad told me he has a surprise for all of us." EJ shot Lily a smile Cade knew he thought nobody noticed. EJ always acted like his little sister annoyed him, but the love he had for her always snuck in.

"Really?"

"Yeah. But only if I tell him you both were good on the walk home."

Cade watched the towering man appear from behind the glistening red truck. "Mr. Hammond," he said with a nod. "Thanks for letting me come by, too."

"Of course, Cade. You know you're like another son to me." Mr. Hammond pulled off a pair of gloves and shoved them into a cargo pocket. He ruffled Cade's hair. Cade felt himself bristle unintentionally. It had taken him years to stop flinching every time Mr. Hammond did that.

"This your whole brood, Hammond?" one of the newer firefighters asked. "Been busy at home, huh?"

Mr. Hammond laughed. "Something like that."

Cade nodded hello to the crew that had watched him grow up over the years. They were like a little family of their own, even though they weren't related by blood. *Maybe that's how it's supposed to feel in foster care,* he thought. But so far that hadn't been his experience.

"How's third grade treating you, Flower?" Mr. Hammond asked as Lily hugged her dad's leg tight.

"It's *exhausting*," she said. "We're supposed to memorize a new times table every week. Like, what's the point? When are we going to use that?"

"What do you think, Aiden? You agree?" Mr. Hammond asked as he squeezed Aiden's thin shoulders.

Aiden sniffed. "It's not exhausting, it's too easy. I shoulda skipped a grade."

"Be careful what you wish for," Mr. Hammond said. "Middle school's no picnic. Right, EJ? No more recess, no playground—"

"Yeah, but the food's a *lot* better. And there are vending machines."

"Well, if there are vending machines ..." Mr. Hammond laughed and gave EJ a hug.

Cade felt the familiar tug of jealousy as he watched his friend embrace his dad. *Things are so easy for him, and he doesn't even realize it,* Cade thought. *EJ has it all, the whole all-American family and everything.*

"So, what's the surprise?" Aiden asked.

"Eager, huh? Come around front with me and I'll show you."

They raced behind him as Mr. Hammond turned the corner to the small patch of perfectly landscaped greenery outside.

"Kites!" Lily exclaimed. On the lawn were four colorful triangles of fabric. "This one's mine," she said, and stood triumphantly beside the My Little Pony pink one.

"You bet it is," Aiden said. "This one's mine." He knelt down beside the Teenage Mutant Ninja Turtles fabric.

"Spider-Man?" EJ asked Cade. Cade nodded immediately. *Be grateful for what you get,* he thought. But he felt another tug of envy as he watched EJ pick up the Batman kite and admired it. *Shouldn't my best friend know Batman's my favorite?*

"You okay, Cade? That one's for you," Mr. Hammond said. Cade realized he hadn't rushed to claim his kite like the others.

"Are you ... are you sure?" he asked. *Obviously, idiot. Why else would there be four kites?*

"Of course I'm serious! Go on," Mr. Hammond said.

A grin spread across Cade's face and he raced for the kite. *It is pretty cool,* he thought as he admired it.

"Damn, yours is actually shaped like a bat—" EJ started.

"EJ, language."

"Sorry. *Dang.*"

"Thanks, Mr.—" Cade started, but his mouth clamped shut when he saw his biological dad across the street. His excitement over the kite was momentarily forgotten.

Maybe I can finally *go home.*

"Dad! Hey, Dad! Look what Mr. Hammond—"

His dad reached the group before Cade could finish, but Mr. Hammond stood between them.

"Bill, you need to go," Mr. Hammond said, his voice low. "You know you're not allowed to see Cade, and I don't want any trouble. Especially here."

"You can't tell me what to do," he slurred. Cade could smell the whiskey from five feet away. His heart sunk. "You can't tell me I can't see my own son! Cade, c'mere—"

"Stay there, Cade," Mr. Hammond said. Cade couldn't have moved if he wanted to. "Bill, you need to go home and sober up. Do you need me to call a ride for you?"

"I don't need any goddamned charity from you. Cade's, his —his whore of a mother up and left in the middle of the night again. Fucking bitch—"

"You need to go right now."

"Hammond? You need some help?" one of the crew called from the sidewalk.

"Do I?" Mr. Hammond asked Cade's dad.

"Ah, forget it," Cade's dad said. "You all go on playing Captain America or whatever the hell you do."

He began to stagger off, but Cade was stunned. *Mom is gone?*

"Cade, come on," his dad said, as he turned again.

"Kids, you all go inside," Mr. Hammond said. EJ, Aiden, and Lily raced for the firehouse, but Cade was torn.

I need to help find Mom ...

His dad lurched toward him, but Mr. Hammond held him firm. "I'm going to have to call the police if you don't—"

Suddenly, Cade's dad lunged forward and broke free of the grip. He snatched Cade up, and the kite ripped apart between them. The stench of alcohol overpowered him. "It's okay, son. I'm here," his dad mumbled. "We're gonna go to Santa Monica. The... the beach. Sounds nice, right?"

California? A shot of panic raced through him. There was no way he could leave the Hammonds. Never see EJ again—

"No!" Cade screamed. His cry came from the deepest part of him.

He felt his father's fist against his jaw, but the shock dulled any pain. Somewhere in the distance, he could hear and see Mr. Hammond and the other firefighters as they pulled his father away.

Cade turned toward the firehouse. His head rang with yells and his father's drunken threats.

"You're bleeding!" Lily said as he tore into the firehouse.

Cade couldn't speak. The tears that ran down his face blinded him, and the sobs inside filled his throat.

"Don't cry," Lily said. He felt her warm hand wrap around his.

Shame filled him, though he couldn't have said why. He held her hand and cried.

CADE

2013

"Hey, what'd you get on question twenty-two?" EJ asked.

"You still trying to copy off me?" Cade asked with a laugh.

"Just trying to make sure, dude," EJ said. "They didn't tell us training to be a recruit involved so much *homework*. I should have gone into professional baseball or football or something."

"Yeah, completely realistic," Cade said. He finished up the last of the quiz. EJ reached his beer across the old scratched-up firehouse table and they clinked. "Cheers to another day of training done."

"What? I could have done it. I mean, if I got accepted to be a firefighter—"

"Yeah, I think nepotism had a little something to do with that," Cade said with a wink.

"Because my dad's the fire chief? Nah, dude. Totally got in on sheer merit. And because they could really use a boost in the annual hot firefighter calendar."

"I don't think that's a real thing in Salem," Cade said.

"Not yet, maybe," EJ said pointedly.

"You guys done?" Chief Hammond called from the doorway. "You're on kitchen cleaning duty."

EJ groaned, but they both headed to the commercial-sized kitchen and started scrubbing the chili pots from lunch.

"So, how was the date last night?" EJ asked.

Cade cracked a smile. "A gentleman never tells."

"I know, but I was asking about *your* date."

Cade laughed.

"I saw her sneaking out of our place at the crack of dawn. I'm assuming this wasn't an innocent sleepover with popcorn and separate sleeping bags."

"You can do a lot with popcorn," Cade said with a smirk. "Especially the buttery kind."

"Okay, Mr. Morningside Manwhore."

"Don't throw those high school names at me," Cade said. "This is 2013, not the North Salem High days."

"Well, the girl I saw walking out barefoot was brunette. What happened to the blonde from earlier this week? And that poor girl's shoes?"

Cade shrugged. "She has three roommates. And probably other shoes."

"So?"

"Well, the brunette from last night is one of the roommates. So ... I assume I won't be seeing the blonde again?"

EJ groaned.

"Hey, I could be wrong. Depends on whether or not she's the jealous type."

"Which one?"

"Either, I guess."

"I'm honestly not sure if I should be proud or disgusted by having a manwhore as a best friend. And roommate."

"Proud, probably," Cade said. He paused and pretended to reflect into the distance. "How's uh ... Kelsey?"

"It's *Courtney.* And everything's just like it has been for the last month. Not all of us have a rotating selection of women. Some of us have just one. And she's doing great. She's still doing that dressage stuff—"

"You're still jealous of that hot horse trainer, huh?"

"Not jealous. Just ... you know. Concerned for Courtney's safety."

"Afraid she might slip and fall on his cock? It happens. Happens to a lot of girls I meet, in fact."

"She's not like that," EJ said and shot him a look.

"I don't know, man. When we all went out to that bar last week, she was *really* touchy. With, like, every guy there."

"She's just Southern. They're all like that."

Cade nodded and scrubbed the pot. He didn't want to say anything, but he couldn't forget how many times Courtney had touched his dick through his jeans beneath that bartop table. When her hands hadn't been all over him, she'd stared at him and the message had been clear. *I'm yours if you want me.* Cade knew better than to say anything overt to EJ. They'd been down this road before. All that would happen was he'd end up getting blamed for something he never did. *Just keep your trap shut,* he told himself.

"This is what I like to see. Men in the kitchen." Cade turned at Lily's voice and gave her a smile.

"Hey, Lily," Cade said.

"Hi. EJ, do you have a minute? I wanted to ask you about those scholarships at Oregon State you said I should apply to..."

As Lily grilled EJ about applications, Cade stole glances at her.

Damn, she's really blossomed in the past year, he thought. *Verified bombshell.* Her short skirt and white Keds were the perfect combination to show off those long legs.

Cade felt a sudden sting on his arm. "Hey, man," he said. "That hurt."

"That's my sister, dude," EJ said. His voice was playful, but there was a current underneath it that told Cade to back off.

Lily blushed and looked at her feet.

"Ah, I shouldn't even bother," EJ said. "Lily's too smart to fall for you, anyway, you bastard. She's saving herself for her future husband. Right, Lil?"

"Uh, no," Lily said. "You guys are weird. Anyway. Have you seen Dad?"

"Probably in his office," EJ said.

Cade did his best not to stare as she left, especially with EJ's eyes on him. EJ hit him again, harder this time. "Why don't you try thinking about that brunette? You know, the one you actually have a chance with—and won't get killed for hooking up with?"

"First of all, I'll have you know that I'm irresistible to all women."

EJ chuckled as they wrung out the cloths and tossed them into the laundry bin.

. . .

Lily

2015

Lily stood in the parking lot of her favorite coffee shop and let the rain wash away her tears.

Former favorite coffee shop, she reminded herself. It was where Tim had taken her on their first date. *And now it's all over. Who dates someone for three years and then dumps them like that?*

She searched for her keys that jingled at the bottom of her bag.

"Asshole," she said aloud.

Lily couldn't stop going over their last conversation. When they'd started dating as freshmen, Tim told her he was totally okay with her being a virgin.

"I think it's cool!" he'd told her.

However, in the past three years, she had started to get the idea that he was more excited about being the one to "pop her cherry" as he put it, rather than being impressed with her morals and values.

"I want to. Eventually," she'd told him numerous times.

She just didn't know when, and she wanted to be absolutely sure about it. Lily knew it wasn't cool or sexy to be a virgin, especially by her senior year in college.

But she hadn't cared about that, and didn't think Tim did either. Not until he dumped her at the exact same place they'd had their first date.

Now, she was *heartbroken.*

"Lily?" She jumped at the voice and looked up. Cade stood over her, dripping wet. "Are you okay?"

She sniffed.

"Fine," she said. Lily hoped with everything in her it just looked like she was soaked and not crying.

You look freaking pathetic, she thought to herself.

"You don't look okay," he said.

"My, uh. My boyfriend just dumped me," she admitted, her eyes downcast.

Of course I'd run into Cade, also known as the longest crush ever.

"What an idiot," Cade said. "Come on, get in the truck. You're getting drenched out here."

He took her elbow and ushered her toward his baby blue vintage Chevy.

"Can't find your keys?" he asked as he turned on the heat and slid onto the bench seat beside her.

She shook her head. "I don't... I don't know..."

"Let's go to my place," he said. "EJ has a spare key to yours, right? He's not home, but I'm sure we can find it."

"Oh, um. Okay," she agreed.

The ride to the apartment was fast, and thankfully quiet.

"Here you go," Cade said as they walked into the small two-bedroom. He pulled a t-shirt and shorts, both with emblems of the Salem Fire Department emblazoned on them, out of the basket of freshly laundered clothes on the couch.

"Thanks," she said, and took them gingerly.

Lily changed in the shared bathroom and rolled up the shorts numerous times to get them to stay on.

"Hey, you look good in my clothes," Cade said with a wink when she emerged. Something about the way he said it made her burst into tears. "Lily, I'm sorry!" he said. "I didn't mean anything by it."

Cade jumped up and embraced her. "Do you want to talk about it?"

He pulled her onto the couch next to him and pushed the laundry basket aside. Lily picked at her peeling pink nail polish.

"He ..." she started with a sigh. "I don't know. We've been together three years, you know? Since the start of freshman year. And I thought—God, I don't know what I thought. That we'd get married, and all that. Not that we talked about it or anything."

She could hear herself rambling but couldn't stop.

"And then there was, I don't know. There were little things. Issues, I guess. Red flags, I don't know."

A part of her wanted to tell Cade about the whole V-card thing, but her guard was up too high. Lily craved a drink, just a touch of liquid courage to get everything off her chest.

But what would he think if I asked for a glass of wine all of a sudden? Dressed in his clothes?

"You're better off," Cade said. His deep voice broke into her internal struggle.

"You think?" she asked. Lily looked up at him.

His hazel eyes bored into hers. *Does he know?* Could he guess about the whole virgin thing?

"Sure," he said. "The guy sounds like a total loser. Besides, you're hot enough to bag any guy you want."

Lily bit her lip and looked back down. *He thinks I'm hot?*

"You think?" she asked again.

"Absolutely."

She willed herself to look up at him again. Before she could think or second-guess herself, she tilted her head up and closed her eyes. Lily couldn't tell if she closed the distance or he did, but when his lips were on hers she eagerly opened her mouth.

She felt Cade's hands move to her waist, the heat of his palms against the sliver of flesh between her skirt and t-shirt. Lily let out a moan into his mouth as he easily hoisted her onto his lap.

As she straddled him, she felt his growing hardness as it pressed against the thin material of her underwear. Cade didn't need to do much to inch the short skirt up. She felt the air against the bare skin of her backside and his hands squeeze into her flesh.

Her hands made their way onto his chest, the muscles from hours of firefighter training evident.

"I've wanted this a long time," he whispered into her ear as he bit gently at her lobe.

Should I tell him? she wondered, but already he'd ripped open her panties with a single tug.

Cade lifted up her tight shirt to expose her bra and pulled down the lace material. As his mouth moved down her neck and he took a firm nipple into his mouth, she let out a yelp. She felt her wetness begin to soak into the roughness of his denim.

What if I'm not good at it? she wondered, but pushed that thought aside.

Lily couldn't stop herself from riding him. By the time she heard the sound of Cade unzipping himself, she had an ache deep inside her that begged to be filled.

"You're so wet," he said as he tested her opening with his tip.

Lily braced herself against him and felt just a small pinch as he lowered her onto him.

Soon, she bore onto him, unable to get enough. As Cade kissed and sucked her neck, she felt the wave build up inside her that she'd only ever managed on her own before.

"Come for me," he murmured against her ear, and she had no choice but to obey.

As she climaxed, she felt a rush into her. Cade's hot release filled her with a satisfaction she'd never felt before.

As he gently lifted her off him, a drunken sleepiness washed over her, and in the dark Oregon afternoon it already felt like nearly evening.

"EJ?" she wondered aloud even as sleep overtook her.

"Don't worry," Cade said as he pulled her against him to spoon on the couch—the same couch she'd sat on countless times over the years. "He's gone until tomorrow night."

Lily drifted into sleep with Cade's sturdy arm wrapped around her.

***

Lily fluttered her eyes open to the sound of a steady morning rush of rain. The surroundings were only somewhat familiar.

"Cade?" she asked groggily as the previous day's events began to creep back into her head. Lily groaned and pushed herself up from the couch.

"Cade?" she called again.

She could tell by the stillness in the air he was gone. Her phone, nearly dead, told her it was almost eight in the morning. The heartache she'd felt earlier returned with a vengeance.

I guess that's why EJ and Aiden call him Morningside Manwhore, she thought, her mouth twisting.

The weight of what she'd done, of what she'd let Cade do—wanted him to do—started to dawn on her.

I've had a crush on him for so long, and now what? she wondered. *I'm just another notch on his bedpost.*

"Well," she said aloud. "What did you expect would happen?" In her fantasies, this would always be just the beginning. She'd never imagined what would happen afterward.

Slowly, she picked up her clothes, now dry, and got dressed. A small soreness lingered between her legs.

She used the last of her phone battery to call an Uber, a little glazed over. What really stuck in her mind, though, was how pathetic the situation seemed.

* * * *

CADE

Montana, Six Months Ago

"Here we go," Barron said as he slid into his seat on one of the fire choppers beside Cade. "My guess is cigarette. Got five on it. You?"

Cade shook his head and grinned. "I'm not betting with you

after that last time. How the hell'd you know it was a kerosene lamp anyway?"

Barron shrugged. "Saw it on Facebook before we got there."

"Bastard," Cade said with a chuckle.

Dominguez and Fields each stuck to their sides of the fire rescue chopper, looking down at the terrain below.

"Ain't seen the fire yet, maybe we've been called out for a false alarm," Barron said.

He was the youngest on the repeller crew, just nineteen years old, and came from an all-boys military prep school where he swore up and down he hadn't seen a girl for four straight years.

"Doubtful. I've worked as a hotshot for fifteen years, and this would be my first," Fields muttered.

The helicopter pilot made his way north, and soon enough they could see the smoke and little bits of orange flame here and there in the trees.

They kept going north, almost ten minutes, and Cade's concern level grew. Each minute north they went, the flames were more and more prominent.

"What the hell?" Cade said under his breath. He called to the helicopter pilot. "Hey, Sean, I thought the Captain said this was just a two alarm. This—hell, this is a full-blown wildfire."

"I'll call in to report that," Sean said and clicked on the his radio. "Sean here, you hear me, Captain?"

It crackled, but there was nothing.

"Captain, you copy? This isn't a two alarm, you copy?" Sean clicked it off. "Fuck, man, this piece of shit isn't working."

"It's alright," Cade said as he got ready to rappel out of the chopper. "We gotta go anyway. Just get back as soon as you can manage, and let everybody know. Where's the other crew?"

Sean shrugged. Cade sighed and heaved the door open. The tiny chopper seemed to struggle to stay upright. Dominguez and Fields jumped out, their lines attached to the helicopter still.

"Well, let's get it started. Guys, you know what to do. Barron, you're with me."

"How'd I get so lucky?"

Cade jumped, the feeling of freefall hitting him hard for a few seconds. Then his line caught, and he quickly began rappelling downward. In less than two minutes, he and Barron were on the ground.

The fire was *everywhere*.

Cade led the way into the thick of it, gear heavy on his back. He practiced his breathing without thought. It was built into him. The heat slapped at his face, and from his peripheral vision he could see Barron one step behind him. Twenty feet away, Dominguez and Fields forked off into the brush.

They needed to find someplace to start a firebreak, a big dirt trench that would essentially interrupt the fire, keep it from spreading. He surveyed the land.

This isn't right, Cade thought. *The fire's too hot, it's burning too fast.*

He glanced back toward the chopper, but the air where it had been was vacant. His heart leapt into his chest as the ground began to writhe beneath him.

"Snakes! Snakes!" he thought he heard Barron yell. The com was acting weird, cutting in and out. It made it that much harder to communicate, stuck in the middle of nowhere.

But it wasn't snakes at all, it was a nest of chestnut-colored rabbit kits with no doe in sight.

"Shit," Cade said under his breath. The little balls of fur wriggled in fear, stuck in a nest they'd likely never been out of.

"Fucking hell," Cade said. Everything in him told him to keep going, get that firebreak going before all hell broke loose.

What difference does two seconds make?

He leaned down and grasped the three kits in his gloves and tossed them behind him. On shaky, unfamiliar legs, they raced off away from the fire, freed from the fallen brambles that had pinned them down.

Cade didn't want to see whatever look Barron might shoot him, so he immediately buckled down and started on the firebreak from his side.

But when he got to the point where he thought they'd meet, there was nothing there.

"Barron?" he called and looked up. He was alone, and the fire moved faster than it should have. "Barron!"

In the distance, forty feet away, he thought he saw three yellow figures through the smoke.

What the hell?

Cade grabbed the walkie talkie.

"Barron? You there? Dominguez, Fields?" Like Sean's radio, his walkie talkie cackled, but nothing more. "Shit."

Just like Barron to go running off like that. What, does he think he's some kind of hero?

"Duke, you copy? Cade you copy? The fire's moving fast—" Fields' voice broke through the walkie talkie.

Cade looked around, but the smoke was so thick that he could barely see three feet in front of his face.

"10-4," Cade said, thankful. "Is Barron with you?"

"Cade? The fire's moving your way fast. Cade?"

"10-4!" Cade yelled into the walkie talkie.

"Shit, man, I don't think he can hear—" Fields said, then cut off abruptly.

Cade walked away from the trench, looking around desperately. The smoke shifted and Cade spotted three distinct figures in the gulch below.

What the hell are they all doing down there?

"Hey!" he started, but the fire boxed him in on two sides.

Forwards or backwards, he calculated. *Either way, it was a fifty-fifty shot.*

Cade leapt forward to make it out of the flames, but his heavy boot caught on the edge of the same pit that had entrapped the rabbits. As soon as he went down, he knew it was fractured.

He looked behind him, eyes wide. Somehow, the fire had missed him. It eagerly tore through the grass, brush, and debris behind him.

Cade tried to struggle to his feet, but he couldn't stand on his ankle.

"Cade?" Barron's voice crackled over the walkie talkie. The fear in it was evident. "If you can hear me, retreat. The fire is close, and the firebreak won't stop it."

Cade dragged himself out of the small pit towards the ledge. The high rocky ground was his only chance for cover. He figured it was also his only chance to see the gulch clearly.

"Cade!" Dominguez's voice roared through the radio, all protocol lost. He could hear choking, desperate prayers sent skyward.

Fuck! he thought. *They need me, right now.*

"I'm coming," Cade said into his radio.

He pulled himself forward, but even at the highest part of the ledge he couldn't bring himself to tumble into the flames. The heat kept him at bay. Far below, he watched his crew huddle together.

They no longer tried to escape. Dominguez kept his finger on the walkie talkie, and sounds erupted from it like wild animals.

Cade tried to call for them, but the smoke filled his throat and burned his lungs.

"Dominguez, can you hear me? Dominguez, do you copy? Barron? Fields?" Cade barely had enough in him to get the words out.

I'm going to die. It wasn't an entirely unwelcome thought.

Dominguez's voice roared over the walkie talkie, intermittent and subdued. "... *perdónanos nuestras deudas, así como nosotros perdonamos á nuestros deudores...*"

"No!" Cade cried, even as the smoke almost blinded him.

He watched as the flames circled the three men below like a

playful lover. It licked at their feet, and none of them flinched. *It should have been me.*

"No," Cade said again, even as the darkness hugged him close.

"Amen," Dominguez's voice rang through the walkie talkie.

Cade watched him drop the walkie talkie into the flames. As the fire trailed along Barron's leg, the three men looked up at once, right into Cade's eyes. Into the darkest, inkiest part of him.

Barron let out a keen like nothing Cade had ever heard before. It crashed into his soul and buried itself deep.

I'm sorry.

1

LILY

Current day

*W*hat is it about a missed opportunity for romance that, in retrospect, makes a man so much more attractive?

Lily was wondering that very thing while she worked in the back of at Wilde's Bakery, carefully frosting some petit fours. She wasn't thinking of anyone in particular, but Cade Moore was in the back her head. Cade was always in the back of her head, though.

"Your petit fours are looking much better."

Lily looked up and smiled at Jean-Michel as she finished icing one of the Christmas-themed creations.

"Thanks," she said. Lily had been at Wilde's Bakery in historic Salem since finishing the patisserie course at Le Cordon Bleu in Portland last year. "I think maybe I've finally mastered these little beasts."

"Mastered? No," Jean-Michel said in his thick Parisian accent. "Made acceptable for the sale section, maybe."

"Wow, thanks, boss," she said with an eye roll.

"Is a compliment," he said as he swapped out the register

beside her. "You know how many pastry chefs with a bachelor's in chemistry I hire?"

"Zero. I know, I know," she said as she slid the tray into the display case. "And you know I don't agree with that. What is baking but based in science, anyway?"

"Baking is *art, mon canard,*" he said. "Remember that."

"Right. So, can I do macarons today?"

"No," he said bluntly. "You practice enough today. Back to counter work up front."

"But, Jean-Michel—"

"Your last macarons, they were too dry. Tomorrow, maybe, I show you more and you try again."

"Alright," she said, defeated.

"By the way, you find out more about the... how you say, graphic-y?"

"Graffiti," she corrected. "And, no. I talked to the police again, but they think it's just kids."

"Just kids," Jean-Michel repeated. "Why they graphic my bakery? Who they think is going to pay for that?"

"Maybe you should just stop covering it up then," Lily said as she snuck one of the macarons Jean-Michel had created that morning into her mouth. "I mean, you can't even tell what it says anyway."

"Is French. Or supposed to be," he said.

"Yeah? And what does that last thing they wrote mean?"

"Stop eating. You want to keep French woman waistline or no?"

"Fine," she said as she tried to covertly run a hand along her trim waist. "But only if you tell me what it means."

"*Bâtard Français.* French Bastard. Of course, they spell it wrong," he said with a huff. "Right, French bastard. Those kids probably the ones without parents, running wild in the streets —sorry," he said quickly. "*Pardon,* I didn't mean—"

"It's okay. Don't worry about it," she said quickly.

Lily hated how everyone walked on eggshells around her.

She barely remembered her mom. Lily had been six when she'd died in that car accident. But her dad's death six months ago, that still hurt, of course. Even as Jean-Michel apologized, she felt the sting in her eyes.

What did you expect? He had one of the most dangerous jobs there is.

"Really, it's fine," she said and forced a smile. "You didn't mean to bring it up."

"You watch the front," he repeated. "I need to finish the cake for the ridiculous wedding. Can you believe it? Naked icing, is the most ridiculous trend..."

She smiled as she listened to Jean-Michel tick off the woes of modern-day wedding cakes in the back. She slipped out into the front, dusting off her jeans.

"Hey, Lil."

Lily looked up at Elijah's voice, complemented by the gentle chime of the front door. EJ, as they called her brother, tipped his hat to her.

"Hi. Nice shirt," she said with a wry smile.

"This old thing?" He pulled at the taut new shirt advertising the firehouse's latest fundraiser.

"Yeah. Totally subtle. No girl will fail to realize you are a firefighter, for sure," she said.

"Finally, something to help drop the panties of this town. Not that I really had any problem before, of course..."

"Ew, would you stop?" Lily asked with a fake shudder. "Your sister's here, you know."

"I'll stop for now, but only because you hook me up," EJ said. "Can I get the usual?"

"I'm way ahead of you." Lily started to pour dark roast into large canisters while arranging eclairs in Jean-Michel's trademark pink boxes. "You know, with how much of these pastries you guys eat, you're all going to have to double down at the gym to work this off."

"Do I look like I need extra gym sessions?" EJ asked. "Feel these," he said and flexed his arm.

"Thanks, I'll pass."

The door chimed again, and Lily plastered on her customer smile. Cade strolled in with his matching firehouse shirt and Lily felt the heat rush to her face.

He was the same as ever, big and strong and muscular all over. He still had the broad chest and narrow hips of an athlete, and he was still covered in tattoos, the whorls of ink covering both of his arms to the wrist.

She bit her lip. *And you just happen to know exactly what those tattoos look like up close...*

Fuck, Lily thought as her heart began to hammer. She hadn't seen him, not really, in what? *Three years,* she told herself. As if she needed to think about it. *It's been almost three years since that day...*

"Hey! Lily! Watch it," EJ said. He reached across the counter to pull her hand away from the coffee pour.

"I wasn't going to spill it!" she hissed. "God, Elijah James. You're such a drama queen."

She straightened her apron and fumbled with the to-go box.

"Yeah, *Elijah James*, such a drama queen," Cade said as he approached the counter. "Hey, Lily."

"Hi." She panicked with what to say next, but luckily EJ and his big mouth took over.

"Cade! I thought you wouldn't be here until Monday, dude," EJ said.

Cade shrugged. "Things change."

"Glad to have you back, man," EJ said as he clapped Cade on the shoulder. "Damn, we haven't been on crew together in forever."

"Hey, Lil? Can I get a large latte?" he asked. Her name on his full lips sent a shiver down her spine.

"I, uh. Yeah, right away. Large latte," she repeated, all business.

She couldn't bring herself to look at him directly. It was like looking at the sun. In the past couple of years, ever since *that* day, they'd rarely seen each other.

Almost immediately after *it* happened, Cade had accepted a post in Montana.

She hated to admit it, but that had broken her heart. It was part of the reason she'd jumped on the offer at the culinary school.

Now, he'd lost all his boyishness, save for that grin she remembered obsessing over since she was a kid.

Not that he wasn't hot before, but damn, she thought to herself. *What are they putting in the water out in Montana?*

He was bronzed, a rarity in Oregon. It contrasted perfectly with his chestnut hair, kept clipped close. The perpetual five o'clock shadow was a harsh reminder of the burn he'd left on her neck, her lips, nearly three years ago.

Because like it or not, his searing touch had changed her...

But that was then. This was now. Lily straightened her spine and blatantly ogled Cade in the reflection of the espresso machine's steel body.

He put on some serious muscle, she thought. She'd sworn to herself that the next time she saw him, if she ever did, all traces of her crush would be gone.

I should just be grateful I gave my virginity to someone I'd always wanted, she thought.

But now, seeing him like this? All those feelings rushed back.

"You look good, dude," EJ said as he sized up his brother-from-another-mother. "Healthy. Sorry about what happened with your old company, though—"

"It's fine," Cade said, too quickly. All of them stood in uncomfortable silence, unable to gauge where the sudden attitude change came from.

"Well, you've come to the right place to get an energy jolt before hitting up the station," EJ said. "Lily pours the best in town."

Both of them turned to stare at her as she poured the steamed milk on top of the medium roast. She froze when his eyes caught hers.

Am I imagining this? she thought. In those familiar hazel eyes, she saw nothing but raw animal desire.

"You, uh ... you did something different with your hair," Cade said to her.

She touched her shorn locks, embarrassed. "Yeah, I, uh, I cut it off."

"I can see that," Cade said.

"Calls it a pixie," EJ said with a wrinkle of his nose. "I call it the look of a prepubescent boy."

"EJ!" she exclaimed, embarrassed.

She felt another rush of heat in her face and was suddenly desperate for long strands to cover it.

The last time he saw me, I had hair nearly to my butt, she remembered. *God, Lily. What a time to go for a dramatic new look—*

"I think it looks good," Cade said.

"You do?" Lily and EJ asked at the same time.

"Yeah. Like, Audrey Hepburn or something. Actually, you look a bit like her," Cade said as he cocked his head to the side.

"I do?" she asked.

Part of her body was on autopilot and she reached out the latte to him. His fingers brushed against hers as he took it. Fireworks seemed to explode from between them.

"Yeah. I never noticed it before."

"Audrey Hepburn before her makeover in *Sabrina,* maybe," EJ said as he backed up slightly to take in the interaction.

"EJ, the fact that you even said that is so much worse than the so-called insult you're trying to hurl," Cade said. "What kind of firefighter knows all of Audrey Hepburn's looks?"

"Would you shut up?" EJ asked.

While the guys bickered, Lily couldn't stop remembering the last time she'd been with Cade. It was the same day her breakup with her college boyfriend. The way Cade had looked at her in his shorts and t-shirt in the apartment he'd shared with EJ, the only dry option after her own clothes were soaked in the downpour.

It was the same look he's giving me right now, she thought. And then on the couch, the way he'd kissed her. *Or I kissed him...*

How he'd pulled her onto his lap, kissed her neck. How she'd ached for him, and the feeling when he ripped her panties apart and lowered her onto his cock—

And then he was gone, she reminded herself. She'd woken up the next morning alone and naked on the couch. *What a freaking great way to lose your V-card.*

After that, she'd barely seen him, and she couldn't have been more grateful. Until now. For the most part, she'd hardly thought of him, eager to push that memory into the past.

But now? Now he's back.

" ... open single-handedly," EJ said. "Right, Lil?"

"Sorry, what?" Lily asked.

"God, Lily, where are you today? I was telling Cade how the firehouse is basically bankrolling the bakery with how much we spend here. We're lucky our baby sister is running the show around here."

"You run this place?" Cade asked, impressed.

"Um, well, Jean-Michel owns it—"

"You call me?" Jean-Michel asked as he poked his head out of the back. A dusting of flour covered his face, and his eyes lit up when he saw the crowd. "Ah, firemen! Back again. You boys must keep energy high to save all those kittens in the trees."

"That's not what we—" EJ started, but Cade elbowed him.

"Lily, you hurry with these boys. They have busy, important work. And I need help with cupcake icing back here. At least cupcakes, they are never naked..." he started as he let the door swing shut.

"Naked cupcakes, huh?" Cade asked with a grin. Lily flushed and looked down as she shoved the box of eclairs across the counter.

EJ slapped two twenties on the counter.

"Bye, Lily Flower!" he called. She stiffened at the nickname, what their dad had called her in childhood.

She watched them through the windows as they joked and walked toward the fire house.

I can't believe Cade's back. Or that he's somehow even hotter.

"Lily, come!" Jean-Michel called. "The cupcakes, they do not, how you say, ice by themselves."

"Ice themselves," she said as she walked into the back.

"That's what I say. Who is the new one?"

"Huh?" she asked as she picked up the pastry bag.

"The new fireman." Jean-Michel stared intently at his own cupcake.

"Oh. Sorry, you're out of luck, Jean-Michel. He's straight."

"That is not why I ask," he said. "What you think I am? A whore-man?"

"Manwhore," she said with a laugh. "And no, that's not what I meant."

"Straight, you say. All Americans think they are straight." He raised a brow. "You are interested then?"

She frowned at her perfect pink cupcake. "No. He's EJ's best friend. And I already have two very overprotective big brothers, so he's super off-limits."

"And the floodgates open," Jean-Michel said. "You have many excuses."

She sighed. "I had a huge crush on him back in the day, okay? But I would never act on it. I know he's not interested. And besides, he's kind of a slut. My brothers had a nickname for him. They called him the Morningside Manwhore, actually, because he left so many broken hearts scattered all over the

Morningside neighborhood. So sorry, even though you're not a manwhore, that title's already taken."

"That's not a 'not interested.' That is reason why you *should not* be interested," Jean-Michel said. "Difference, there."

"Aren't you French supposed to be all about free love or something?" she demurred.

"Free love?" Jean-Michel laughed. "Love is never free. Sex, on the other hand. Sometimes free. Sometimes very pricey."

Lily rolled her eyes and went to work icing the cupcakes. That didn't stop her from wondering about Cade, though...

What had he been up to the past three years?

And how in the hell was he hotter than he'd ever been?

2

CADE

*C*ade mindlessly trailed behind the guys as they would their way towards the firehouse. He hadn't thought seeing Lily would jar him so much.

Sure, he knew she worked at Wilde's because of her LinkedIn profile that he stalked. It was the only covert way he knew how to keep track of her without her knowing.

But Cade thought popping in would be a fun little way to fire up his return to Salem. He didn't know Elijah would be there, too. Or that seeing Lily like that, her face flushed from the ovens in the back and the way her chest pushed at the buttons of her crisp button up shirt would instantly turn him on.

Damn, it had been awkward having an erection while Elijah welcomed him back.

Cade was used to the girls in the Montana college town, the Instagram models who looked like perfect plastic Bratz dolls online but tired and haggard in person. Lily was different.

He'd always known that, even before what happened between them. However, she'd flourished since he'd been gone.

Cade couldn't get over it. In the bakery, without a whit of makeup on, she looked at home.

And hot as hell.

The last summer's freckles scattered across her nose and that dark brown hair that whorled in imperfectly fantastic peaks. Those nearly indigenous cheekbones highlighted her heart-shaped face, and it took all the strength he had to look at her eyes instead of that pout with the sharp cupid's bow.

Or those tits, he thought as he pulled into the firehouse.

Fuck. This is Lily, he reminded himself. A sense of shame washed over him. *If either of her brothers had any idea what I was thinking... Hell, if they had any clue that he'd been with her once, they'd beat me within an inch of my life.*

Cade still couldn't forgive himself for what he'd done the morning after he and Lily were together. He'd gazed at her, trusting in sleep beside him, and just couldn't believe it. She'd chosen him. She could have had anyone, and it was him.

Then you went and screwed it all up, he said as he shook his head. *In just a few moments he'd destroyed any chance of them ever being together for real.*

That, and the fact that Elijah and Aiden would love pounding him into the pavement was enough to have him running for the hills—literally. When he'd driven to Montana, across the rolling hills of eastern Oregon, he couldn't move fast enough to outrun the guilt that stuck to him from back home.

He thought three years would be enough. But he was wrong. Even now, at the bakery, he'd struggled to find the words. Any words, something to tell her that he was sorry, but they got stuck and messy in his throat.

Cade shook his head at his past self as he pulled his gear together.

If I'd known back then how precious life is, maybe I could have stopped thinking with my dick for a minute and either not slept with her at all. Or ... or maybe I would have made her mine.

Cade paused, one hand on his duffel bag. *Is that really what I want?*

"Stop it," he said aloud.

Lily made it impossible to think straight. He'd been in a non-stop tailspin every since he'd left. And it didn't help that something about what had happened made him wonder. It wasn't just how tight she was, though he got hard every time he thought about it. There was an innate innocence to it that almost made him stop right there in the moment.

Was she a virgin? But no, she couldn't be. She'd just broken up with a boyfriend of three years. Plus, she was at one of the biggest party schools in the state.

It had to just be how vulnerable she was given the circumstances, right?

Yeah. And that makes you even more of an asshole.

"Get it together," he whispered. He needed a clear head, a head free of Lily, before he walked into his new job.

"Get lost out there?" Elijah asked as Cade walked in. "I know it's been a few years, but it took you long enough."

Cade shrugged. "Where's the fire?" he asked.

"Haha," Aiden said as he tossed Cade's new standard issues at him.

Cade looked around the firehouse. It had been six months since Elijah and Aiden's dad had died in the unprecedented Eagle Creek fires that raged through the Columbia. He thought the firehouse would have taken down his official Captain's photo by now, but it still hung on the walls.

"You get used to it," Elijah said softly. He approached Cade and put his hand on his shoulder.

"It's not just that," Cade said.

There was something about the firehouse that he guessed would always be familiar. It was the same scents he grew up with, that certain cleaning solution that had wormed its way into his hippocampus. The same wooden benches worn smooth after decades of use. But it seemed smaller now. The ceilings felt lower.

Is this just how it works? he wondered.

When he'd been a kid in the foster care system, he'd lucked

out when he befriended Elijah. Cade just didn't know how lucky he'd been at the time. Elijah's whole family had accepted him as one of their own.

One of his few good memories as a child was stopping by the firehouse after school. Elijah's dad hadn't been the fire Captain then, but he was clearly one of the most respected men on the crew. It was the closest thing to a father figure Cade had ever known.

"How's, uh, how's Crane as Captain?" he asked.

"Eldon?" Elijah gave a short laugh. "You'll see. He's an old fucker, that's for sure. Like in his sixties! But doesn't look or act it. Come on, I'll show you your locker."

Cade followed Elijah to the back and tried to hold it together. Being back in that firehouse made him feel like a kid again. He didn't know why. After all, he'd been a recruit here with Elijah right after high school. But those weren't the memories that were seared into his head.

It was the countless hours hanging out here as kids that he remembered. He could still recall all the stories the old crew told. The valiant rescues and the brave measures they took to keep people safe.

There were certainly remnants of those long-ago years, but there were also some major changes.

"Look weird?" Aiden asked from behind him.

Cade nearly jumped.

"Yeah," he agreed.

"Dad had remodeled the whole place six months before ... well, you know."

"Remodeled it?" Cade asked. He slung his bag onto one of the benches as Elijah opened a locker with a flourish. "How'd he get that kind of funding?"

"Dad had been badgering the state for years for a facelift," Elijah said. "Then, of course, when some idiot kid goes and lights the whole Columbia on fire, even more emergency funds came rolling in."

"Damn," Cade said. "Looks good. But it's just, you know, different. Where's the rest of the crew?"

"Special training in back," Aiden said.

"Yeah? Then why aren't you guys there?"

"We had it last week, jackass. We were just picking up sustenance for these guys. Before you randomly popped up at the bakery, that is" Elijah said. "Oh, shit, the pastries! You think they'll care if they don't get dessert?"

Aiden shrugged. "I think one of the guys brought in doughnuts this morning," Aiden said.

"Yeah, but you know how they get about Lily's desserts..."

A loud bark rang through the firehouse. Cade braced himself as a massive dalmation barreled towards them. The dog immediately buried its nose in his crotch as it checked him out. Elijah laughed.

"That's Sparky Number Six," Aiden said. "Or, you know, just Six."

Cade held out his hand for the dog to inspect. "You all get *Stranger Things* questions from civilians now, naming the fire dogs like that?"

"Sometimes," Elijah said with a shrug.

"So, Five, she ..."

"Last year," Aiden said.

There was a quiver to his voice. They weren't supposed to get attached to the dogs, but Aiden had always had a particularly rough time with that rule.

"Well, let's get this over with," Elijah said with a sigh. "C'mon, let's go meet up with the Captain."

As the three of them headed down the hall with its new, crisp white coat of paint, the alarms started to go off. Cade felt the jolt of excitement sizzle through him. Even after all these years in a firehouse, there was something about that alarm that always reminded him of why he did this.

They started to move faster as an unfamiliar voice crackled over the intercom. Captain Crane calmly announced the address, turnout time, and apparatus for the call. Cade could hear the crew as they flew into the firehouse and the truck rumbled to life.

Elijah and Aiden were instantly in rescue mode.

"What a way to start a shift," Aiden said.

"We'll pick this up when we get back," Elijah called to Cade. "Damn, Commercial Street," he said to Aiden.

Cade smiled as their backs retreated.

Change or no change, coming back here is like coming home, he thought.

He nodded at some of the crew that charged past him. A wave of emotion washed over him, and he felt wet pricks at his eyes. Cade blinked away the tears, grateful that the call meant nobody would pay him much attention.

It was stupid, getting emotional over the station, but he couldn't help it. Ever since the Montana fires had taken three of his crew right in front of him ...

Cade wiped his eyes on his sleeve.

"Can I help you?" The deep voice startled him, and Cade looked up at the grizzly new Captain. The man had blue eyes that pierced straight through him.

"Captain Crane, hello, sir," he said. "I'm Cade—"

"I know who you are."

Cade took in the older man, grayed but in peak physical condition. The Captain offered a small but kind smile that wrinkled his eyes and softened his face. "Come on back, we have some paperwork to take care of."

Cade settled into the straightback metal chair across from the rich wooden desk.

"I'll need you to affirm a few details about your company in Montana," Captain Crane said.

"Sure, I—"

"It's where three crew members died, correct?" the Captain interrupted.

Cade nodded, a lump in his throat.

"I'm real sorry about that. It's a terrible thing. I've lost some good men in my twenty years of service," the Captain said as he made some marks on a thick stack of papers.

Cade nodded again.

The Captain pursed his lips and glanced up. "Don't take this personally, but you'll need to get checked out by the company psychologist."

"What?"

"Since I've taken over here, every man and woman on this crew is my responsibility. To ensure that everyone is capable of doing their best, I've brought in Dr. Hersh. Sometimes it's just good to talk to someone when you've seen some of the stuff we see every day."

"So I'm going to see a shrink instead of fighting fires?" Cade could hear the judgment in his voice, but he couldn't help it.

"Hey. Take it easy," the Captain said.

Cade clamped his mouth shut.

Don't give him a goddamned reason to send you to the psyche ward, he admonished himself.

"It's my understanding that you haven't been on active duty since some of your crew died. I just want you to talk to Dr. Hersh tomorrow before you go rushing into a blaze, that's all."

Cade glowered, but stayed quiet. His crew had died, with him watching, and there wasn't a damn thing he could do about it.

But I'm sure as hell not going to let it happen again.

The Captain handed him a ream of paperwork. "Why don't you get started with this today?"

"Yes, Captain," he said, and stood up.

"Close the door on your way out," the Captain called to Cade's back.

Cade stalked towards the break room. A dark cloud hung over his head.

3

LILY

*L*ily pushed her cart through the Milk and Honey grocery store and smiled at the staff. She'd gone to high school with some of them, and even though they'd barely spoken as teenagers there was the small town demand to be polite.

As Lily made her way to the produce section, she began to load up on veggies. Jean-Michel was right. She needed to be better with her diet.

But this low carb, high veggie kick she'd been on wasn't easy. Lily had almost been tempted to forget the whole thing, especially since Jean-Michel had helped her with her croquembouches last night, but her horoscope had kept her in check.

Libra, it's time to work on things of a personal nature, she'd read on her favorite horoscope app as soon as she parked in the grocery store lot. *You'll have a strange encounter, but the outcome will be great.*

She'd sighed.

"October twelfth, smack in the middle of the Libra dates," she'd said aloud. "Come on, Lily, you can do this. It's just carbs, you're not giving up oxygen."

If she was going to work on something of a personal nature, why not make it her diet? Of course the outcome would be great. This diet would fulfill two horoscope messages in one.

Carbs were one thing. But her caffeine addiction? There's no way she was giving that up.

Besides, doesn't that help with weight loss? She made a beeline for the coffee section, and as she turned the corner she nearly ran right into a mountain of a man.

"Whoa," he said as he held the small hand basket aside.

Shit. Of course I'd run into Cade.

"Uh …" Lily searched for her words as she looked him up and down. Her face was inches from his muscled chest, and she could smell the musky scent of his cologne. It was intoxicating.

God, I hope I'm not drooling. Wait, is this *what my horoscope meant when it meant things of a personal nature, strange encounters —and a great outcome?*

Just seeing Cade made her stomach do gymnastics. She should know, better than anyone, that messing with Cade meant she'd get burned. How many girls had she watched him hump and dump over the years?

He had a real reputation around Salem before he left for California. Some girls still talked about him as they bemoaned why they couldn't be the one to make him change.

And with how he looks now, I'm sure he'll be on a whole new streak by tomorrow.

Lily forced herself to stop staring at him.

"Hi," Cade said. A corner of his mouth hitched up.

Does he know what I'm thinking? Lily turned bright read.

"Sorry," she said. "I'm so sorry. I didn't mean—"

God, you sound like an idiot. But once she started apologizing, she couldn't stop. At least it gave her something to say.

Cade laughed.

"I'll let it slide this time," he said.

"I was just trying to get to the coffee," she said awkwardly.

"I'll walk with you, if that's okay."

"Uh, sure?" she said. She was so nervous, she had started to sweat.

Real attractive, Lily.

As they walked down the narrow aisle side by side, she couldn't stop the images of when they'd been together from replaying through her head. It was like she could feel his lips on her again, nipping at her ears.

And how he'd felt when he'd eased her onto his cock. Just the memory instantly made her wet—and even more embarrassed.

Lily couldn't be completely certain why she was so nervous.

Except maybe that he's freaking gorgeous. The very definition of a bad boy. Not to mention my brother's best friend, she reminded herself.

Okay, so there were plenty of reasons to be nervous. And plenty of reasons to not talk to him, to let this crush go once and for all.

And yet here you are in the grocery store with him, she thought.

As they made their way towards the coffee aisle, she noticed every woman in the store checked him out. It didn't matter if they were teenaged girls or middle-aged women in yoga pants.

They think I'm with him, she thought. She nearly gloated. *Did it matter that it wasn't true?*

Lily searched for something to say, anything to talk about, but her mind was blank. All she could think about was how good he'd made her feel.

"You look really good," Cade said.

"Sorry?" she squeaked.

She wished she could just disappear. That the floor would open up and swallow her whole. For a second, she willed it to happen.

How would that be for a strange encounter?

"So, what have you been up to since the last time I saw you?" she asked, a desperate attempt to change the subject.

Of course, when "the last time" came out of her mouth, she

blushed even deeper. It had been three years since she'd seen Cade, five years since he had up and vanished.

One minute she'd been falling asleep next to him after he took her v-card, the next she had woken up to a cold, empty bed.

She bit her lip and tried to focus on his answer.

"Just been in Montana. Fighting fires and taking care of my Aunt Mary."

"How is your aunt?" she asked, eager to be on safe territory.

Cade's face fell. "She passed away almost a year ago."

"Oh, I'm so sorry…"

Lily instinctively reached and touched his arm. She nearly yanked it back as an electric current flowed between them. When his eyes met hers, her mind went blank.

Even in the bright lights of the supermarket, it felt like it was just the two of them. And the connection between them was palpable.

Lily licked her lips and felt her body inch towards him. She couldn't help herself. But the connection was broken when two teenaged boys ran down the aisle towards them. As one of them jolted her cart, the kid sneered at her.

"Excuse you," he said while his friend laughed.

She sensed a shift in Cade. He cracked his knuckles and turned lightning fast on the boys.

"Hey!" he called. Something in his voice made them stop. "Get back here and apologize."

"Cade, stop," she hissed under her breath. "It's not a big deal—"

"It is," he said.

Why was he so riled up over something that most people would just roll their eyes at? Her heart started to pound in her chest.

"Are you for real?" the boy asked who bumped her cart. That teenage confidence he'd displayed was gone, replaced with a touch of fear.

"Apologize now," Cade said.

"Sorry," the kid mumbled.

"It's fine—" Lily started.

"Like you mean it," Cade interrupted.

"I'm sorry! Okay? Can we go now?" the kid asked. He looked around for help, but there was nobody.

"Can you go?" Cade repeated. "No, you can't go. You think you can just do whatever the hell you want and there won't be consequences?"

"It was an accident, dude," the other kid said. He tilted his pointy chin upwards, an attempt to look more grown-up.

"It wasn't an accident," Cade said. "You think that would have happened if you weren't running around the place like a couple of kindergartners? Is that how you think men act?"

"We were just in a hurry," the kid who bumped into her said.

"And where the hell do you have to be that's so important? Shouldn't you be in school, anyway?"

The boys looked at each other and shuffled their feet side to side.

"What are you even getting here?" Cade asked.

"Nothing," one of the kids started to say, but his friend shot him a look.

"What is it?" Cade asked.

The quieter one sheepishly held up a half-dozen box of free-range eggs.

"Eggs?" Cade asked. "You two think you're Rocky or something?"

"Who?" the kid with the eggs asked.

"Nevermind. Just go buy your eggs and get lost."

"So we can go?" one of them asked, uncertain. He looked longingly towards the front of the store.

"Yeah, sure," Cade said. "Just don't be a little shit again, alright?"

"Yes, sir," the kid said, without a hint of sarcasm. "We just... we just want our eggs."

What was that all about? Lily wondered. Sure, the kids had been jerks, but that's what kids do.

But before Lily could say anything, Aiden appeared around the corner.

"Hey!" he said. "There you are. And you found Lily, too."

"We didn't come here together," Lily said quickly.

Aiden gave her a strange look. "I didn't think you did. But I saw both your cars outside."

"Oh. Right," she said. "Our cars. Yeah."

"So... what's going on?" Aiden asked.

"What do you mean?" Lily said, defensive. "We're just shopping, I wanted coffee—"

"Whoa, calm down," Aiden said. "I mean, it just seems like something weird's going on. There's some kind of, I don't know, energy in the air."

"What, are you psychic now?" Lily asked. "We were just shopping."

"Yeah, you said that," Aiden replied.

He looked from one of them to the other. Lily racked her brain for something to say.

Could Aiden tell? Maybe it was written all over her face. Maybe he and Elijah had always known she'd harbored a crush for Cade.

"Just some little jackass running wild through the store," Cade said. "Seriously, were we that wild when we were teenagers? What the hell are they doing in some boutique market, anyway?"

"Probably picking up some bougie asparagus water or something," Aiden said. "Seriously, kids these days don't eat tater tots and crap like we used to. It's all artisanal this and organic that."

"Yeah, well. I don't think it's doing their attitude any good," Cade said. "Hey, man, I need to head out, but we'll catch up soon, alright?"

"Sounds good. See you at the station," Aiden said.

"Vegetables?" he asked as he examined Lily's cart.

She watched Cade's broad back retreat.

Yeah, I know exactly what that "weird energy" is, and it has nothing to do with those kids, she thought.

It was attraction, mixed with a little self-loathing.

If Elijah ever found out that his little sister was obsessed with his best friend, he'd flip out. She had no doubts about that. Aiden might not be too upset.

Would he be upset? He'd never had the same degree of protectiveness over her that Elijah did. But ever since their dad had died, both of them had upped their guard over her a little more.

"Why are you getting all these vegetables?" Aiden asked. He wrinkled his nose.

"What do you care?" she snapped. "You're not eating them."

"You got that right," he said.

4

CADE

*I*t took everything he had not to slam the door behind him. Dr. Hersh was nice enough, but he got straight to the point.

The older Asian man peered over a pair of rimless glasses and made Cade feel like he could read Cade's darkest secrets.

"Tell me about the incident with your team in Montana," Dr. Hersh said within two minutes of Cade sitting down.

"Crew," Cade had corrected.

"Alright," Dr. Hersh replied. He leaned back in his camel-colored chair and waited.

Cade shrugged. "There's not much to say. I'm guessing you have the reports from it."

"I do," the doctor said. "But I want to hear what you have to say about it."

"Not anything new that isn't in the reports." Cade looked around the office. It was clinical and sterile.

"Can you tell me the emotions you're feeling now when you think about it?" the doctor asked.

Cade looked at him bluntly. "Sad," he said.

"Sad," the doctor repeated. He held Cade's gaze and didn't make any notes. "Anything else? Anger? Confusion? Guilt?"

"Why should I feel guilty?" Cade snapped.

"I don't know. I'm just giving you some options. Why don't we talk about another subject for awhile?"

Yeah. Why don't we?

"Is there anything in particular you'd like to discuss?" Dr. Hersh asked.

"No."

"Alright. How about your romantic life? Many people have strong feelings about that. Is there anyone special in your life?"

Cade barked out a laugh. "Hardly."

"You seem upset about that."

"Why should I be upset?"

"I don't know. Why don't you tell me?"

Cade sighed. "You just started working with the firehouse, right?"

"That's right."

"Ever had a firefighter ... patient before?" Cade asked. He hated to use that word.

"Not before my contract with the firehouse, no."

"Then maybe you don't know, but firefighters don't really have a problem getting women."

"I see." This time the doctor did make a note.

Cade shifted. That wasn't the response he'd expected. "So ... if you're asking if I'm hard up for a date or whatever, the answer's no."

"That wasn't what I asked," the doctor said. "Why do you think that's what you inferred?"

"I don't know," Cade said, exasperated as he crossed his arms.

"So, I'm led to believe you've had a generous amount of sexual partners," Dr. Hersh said.

"Yeah."

"Do you think you're afraid of intimacy?"

Cade glared at him. "Didn't I just tell you that I've slept with a lot of women?"

"That wasn't what I asked. Sex and intimacy can be mutually exclusive. And I'm getting the message that you lean heavily toward the sex-only side."

Cade seethed below the surface, but he gritted his teeth and refused to say anything more.

"Do you have any interest in returning to the subject about your team's deaths in Montana?"

"No," Cade said coldly. He didn't bother to correct him this time.

"Alright. Mr. Charles, I'm going to recommend medical leave for you." Dr. Hersh began writing notes quickly on his pad.

"Medical leave? What? But I haven't even started at this company yet!"

"Mr. Charles, let me make this clear. You can either continue to see me, or you can rethink your position with the company. It's your choice."

"You really think they're going to pay for me to sit around and do nothing but talk to some shrink about my feelings?"

"Actually, that's exactly what the fire captain has told me he's willing to do. And I prefer the term psychiatrist."

Cade let out a heavy breath as he carefully clicked the door shut behind him. "Mr. Charles?" the receptionist asked. "Would you like to schedule your next appointment now or—"

"I'll call you," Cade said as he grabbed his jacket. He felt the dark storm that brewed inside him begin to grow.

As Cade slammed his car door and started toward his new, tiny apartment, he spotted Lily across the street burdened with three shopping bags. Something about seeing her lifted his spirits. She nearly tripped on the uneven sidewalk, stopped and glared at the ground.

"Hey! What's up?" he asked as he rolled up beside her.

She made a face. "My car crapped out again, so I'm walking home."

"Walking? In those?" he asked and looked pointedly at her heels.

"Oh, yeah," she said. "There was a special event at the bakery today, and you know French men. 'A woman should always be in heels.' At least when they're representing Jean-Michel's croissants, at least."

"I actually don't know French men that well. But can I give you a lift?"

She looked skeptical and shifted her weight to the side.

"Come on," he said. "It's on my way, anyway."

Lily sighed and nodded. As Cade leaned over to push open the door, he noticed the top button of her blouse had come undone from carrying the bags. Beneath the ironed white shirt he could see the top of a light pink lace bra.

Kind of like the one she was wearing when we hooked up, he thought.

He could still clearly imagine the pinkness of her nipple, how it had hardened instantly when he wrapped his lips around it.

Cade took the bags from her and set them on the small bench seat in the back. As she climbed in, he tried his best not to stare at her long legs that jutted out from the fitted black skirt.

Lily looked at him, embarrassed, as she realized her top was undone and tried to discreetly button it while she buckled herself in.

He stared straight ahead and clenched the wheel tightly.

"Where to?" he asked.

"Oh. Right. You don't know where I live anymore. Southeast Hoyt," she said.

"Fancy."

"Not really," she said. "You'll see."

Lily chattered nervously as he made his way toward the Richmond neighborhood. She talked about the events coming up at the bakery, Jean-Michel's obsession with cleaning up the graffiti on the building, and plans for Easter brunch with friends, but Cade couldn't find anything to contribute.

"Well, this is it," she said.

"You live at a mechanic shop?" he asked.

"No! I live in the apartment above it."

"Oh. Isn't it noisy?"

"During the day, probably. But by the time I get home they're usually done."

Cade reached back for the bags, uncertain whether to offer to carry them up or not. It would be the polite thing to do, but would she think he had ulterior motives?

"Would you like to come up?" she asked so quickly it sounded like a single word.

"What?"

"I mean, I was going to order some Chinese takeout. So..."

"Didn't you just get a bunch of groceries?"

"Not really. This is all stuff to practice patisseries at home."

"What happened to the veggie and coffee kick you were on?"

She blushed slightly. "It's a cheat day."

Cade was hesitant. "I don't know..."

"Oh, come on," she said, suddenly insistent. "We can order from that place you used to love. Yan Yan, right?"

She remembered that?

"Okay," he said. "You know I can't say no to Yan Yan's."

It's not like you have anything else to look forward to at home besides a microwave dinner.

He followed Lily up the narrow staircase, the smell of grease in the air. Her ass was right in his face, swaying rhythmically side to side. When Cade realized he'd started to stiffen, he forced himself to look at his feet.

When she opened the door, it was to a warm, cozy apartment worlds away from the dark stairwell. And it was totally her.

She tried to tidy up as she ushered him toward the kitchen.

"It's not much," she said. "Just a one-bedroom."

"It's great," he said as he set down the bags, and he meant it.

The main room was set up as a combination kitchen, living room, and dining room with an ornate round wooden table painted and distressed in white. A makeshift chandelier hung overhead, a circle of faux crystals that encased the bare lightbulb on the ceiling.

"Creative," he said.

"Jean-Michel calls it 'French shabby chic,'" she said as she kicked off her heels.

"You two are pretty close, huh?" he asked. Cade felt a tug of jealousy.

"Yeah, I guess," she said. "I mean, he's teaching me how to actually bake like a French chef."

"You didn't get enough of that in culinary school? You went up to Portland, right?"

"Ugh, it's nothing like what he knows."

Over her shoulder, he could see her bedroom. The canopy bed was covered in fluffy white down comforters with oversized knit baby pink throw blankets.

"Want me to look up the menu and call it in?" he asked. Anything to stop thinking about what could happen in that room just a few feet away.

"Sure. I'm going to change. Be right back," she said, and disappeared into the bedroom.

He pulled up the menu, happy to see his favorite combination was still there.

"Hey, Lily? You know what you want?" he called.

She poked her head out of the bedroom door. "Uh, some kind of spicy shrimp and noodle something," she said.

"Okay."

She reemerged just as he'd placed the order, drowning in a huge Le Cordon Bleu sweatshirt and tiny shorts that could pass for underwear.

"What do you call that outfit?" he asked. He had to work to swallow the lump in his throat.

"Comfy clothes," she said. "You try working in a starched shirt and heels all day. Wine?"

"Uh... sure."

He watched as she hunted for a bottle in the cupboard. As she stretched on her toes, the shorts hiked up even higher. Cade could see the swell of her cheeks as they peeked out from below the lacy trim of the shorts.

"I have red and white. But the white's not cold."

"Either," he said. "Doesn't matter."

Lily opened the red and poured two glasses.

"How much do I owe you for dinner?" she asked as she took a generous swallow.

"What? Nothing, don't be weird."

"I'm not! Come on, you already gave me a ride home."

"Lily, it's Chinese takeout. It's hardly dinner at the Joel Palmer House."

She wrinkled her nose. "I'm not some damsel in distress, you know. I know you're used to rescuing helpless women from balconies or whatever, but—"

"Hey, sit down and behave or I'll cancel the order."

"Fine," she said with a fake huff and draped herself across the couch.

They sat side by side on the loveseat, the only seating option besides the two chairs at the dining table. She was silent, but her eyes stayed lit with defiance.

Cade was drawn to that rebellion more than he'd like to admit. "So, tell me. What's Lily Hammond been up to since 2015?"

She tucked a stray lock behind her ear and took another sip of wine. "Finished up at Oregon State, went to culinary school, then came back here. That's about it."

"Why back here? Portland doesn't do it for you?"

"Honestly? I missed Elijah and Aiden."

"Really?"

She laughed. "I know, right?"

"I'm guessing the Salem party scene has livened up though. Or at least I hope so."

"You're asking the wrong person," she said.

"You get all your partying done at OSU?"

"Sure," she said with a laugh. "But no, if I'm being honest I don't have much going on with my social life."

"Yeah. Me either," he admitted.

"Yeah, right."

"I'm serious!"

"Okay, Mr. Morn—never mind."

"It's okay, I know what you were going to say. So. No boyfriend?"

She blushed. "I used to have one, but—"

Cade leaned toward her. "Yeah?"

"Yeah. But it ended. Actually, he dumped me as soon as he, um..."

"He what?"

"It doesn't matter. Never mind."

"It does now. You have to tell me. You can't leave me hanging like that."

"Well, I sort of... refused to have sex with him? And as soon as I did, he broke up with me. And—God, I don't know why I'm telling you this? Anyway, like two days later I saw him out with another girl."

"Well, that sucks," Cade said. "He's an asshole. Want me to kick his ass?"

Lily laughed. "No! It was awhile ago, anyway. And there... well, there hasn't been anyone serious since."

"No? No one?"

"No one," she repeated as she stared into her glass.

A sharp knock came at the door.

Lily pulled the small coffee table forward as Cade opened

up the food. He handed her a pair of chopsticks and they started eating.

"So," Lily said as she dug into the shrimp lo mein, "what's your deal?"

"My deal?"

She blushed. "Your deal with dating."

He felt a warm tightness in his chest.

Is she still interested in this topic? He stole a glance at her amazing legs, taut and slender.

"Well, there's been no one serious since ever, really."

"Ah. Too bad."

He could feel her eyes on him. Cade saw his own desire reflected in them.

What would it be like to just grab her, wrap those legs around my waist? Press her up against the wall, kiss her neck?

Would she moan his name? If he reached for those tiny shorts, would they be damp?

Cade snapped himself out of the fantasy. That couldn't happen, for a number of reasons. Her brothers would beat the living daylights out of him, and that didn't even touch on the destruction of their friendship. Cade cleared his throat.

"Do you have some water?"

Lily hopped up to get it. As she bent over and leaned into the refrigerator, he couldn't stop staring. As she returned with the glass, he reached for it too quickly. Cold water spilled down his shirt.

"Oh my God, I'm so sorry!" she said. "Here, I'll go get a towel."

She raced to the kitchenette and back, then started to blot at his chest. It was innocent, but her touch was too much for him to take. Cade leaned forward and kissed her.

She wasn't expecting it, but her body responded instantly. Just as she began to open her mouth, she froze and stepped back.

"What are you doing?" she asked.

"I'm... shit, I'm sorry," he said. "I need to go."

Lily looked startled as Cade jumped up and bolted toward the door.

As he started up the truck, he berated himself.

Fucking stupid! Now she'll tell her brothers... God, what if she tells them everything? There's a lot to tell...

He'd made a mess and he hadn't even been in town a week. He cursed as he pulled away and sped toward home.

5

LILY

"*Y*ou guys want lamb or beef?" Lily called from the kitchen.

Elijah called for beef and Aiden for lamb, and Lily rolled her eyes. "Fine, I'm the tiebreaker. Lamb it is."

"Lamb's disgusting," Elijah yelled back.

"Yeah, well, then don't eat it," Lily replied.

"Hey, Lil?" Aiden asked. He appeared in the doorway just as Lily began to layer the lasagna. "Cade just texted and he's coming over. There gonna be enough for four?"

She blushed at Cade's name and nodded toward the dish.

It had only been a couple of days since the kiss, and she could still taste him on her lips. Lily slid the dish into the oven, squeezed into the tiny kitchen of Elijah and Aiden's shared apartment, and set the timer.

Maybe the kiss was totally out of the blue, she thought to herself as she put away the ingredients. *But I can't say I haven't been wanting it ever since he showed up at Wilde's.*

Hell, she'd wanted it since she was thirteen years old and the first hint of that crush blossomed.

Until he'd freaked out, of course. She couldn't deny the look of shame that had spread across his face. Cade couldn't get out of there fast enough.

You should have said something, she thought as she loaded the prep utensils into the dishwasher. But at the time, it had all happened so fast, and no words came.

Lily sighed as she slumped onto the couch, a handful of shaved gourmet parmesan in her hand. Slowly, she slid the slivers into her mouth and pressed the rich sharpness against her tongue.

At the opposite end, Elijah was glued to the television. Aiden scrolled through his phone as he hunched on the old wingback chair that used to belong to their mom.

"Can't we watch something else?" she groaned as a cricket match slowly unfolded on the screen. "You're not even Indian or English or whatever."

"Go home if you wanna watch something else," Elijah said, though it was an automatic reply.

She knew he was joking, but Cade coming put her on edge. "I just cooked for you guys!" she snapped.

"What's your problem?" Elijah asked as he finally tore his eyes away from the television. "Fine, if you care so much, put on *The Great British Baking Show* or whatever it is you watch."

"Nothing, sorry," she mumbled.

"Thanks for lunch," Elijah said, his form of an apology. "Even if it's gross sheep. Glad to know you don't have a problem, though."

She laughed and threw a piece of the parmesan at him. "I have a problem with *you*," she said.

Lily was grateful that Cade didn't arrive before she could busy herself in the kitchen. She heard him enter and the slaps on the back as the men greeted one another.

Even the sound of his voice, deep and steady, turned her on. As she started to plate their lunch, she caught herself taking extra care with the presentation. Lasagna was messy by design, so it took a little additional care. But it was worth it.

Pretty food tastes better, she remembered Jean-Michel always told her.

"Smells good." She glanced up as Cade poked his head into the kitchen.

Lily offered up a smile, but quickly turned away.

"Hey, Lil? Let's eat outside. A warm March day in Oregon is unprecedented," Aiden called.

"Sounds good," she yelled back.

"Here, let me help you," Cade said.

Before she could argue, he took two of the plates and headed toward the back patio with them.

Lily wrapped herself in a thick shawl as they gathered at the wrought iron table on the apartment's small balcony.

"Let's have a toast," Elijah said, just as Lily picked up her fork.

She set it back down, acutely aware of how loud it sounded against the iron.

"To?" Aiden asked as he picked up his glass of red.

"To having us all in one place again."

"Hear, hear," Cade said as they clinked glasses.

Lily took a swallow, and couldn't stop herself as she sneaked a glance at Cade. His eyes immediately caught and held hers.

Has he been staring at me? She felt her face go red and tilted her head down to focus on the food.

"So, Cade, I heard you're suspended until the shrink clears you," Elijah said.

Always the blunt one, she thought. But she perked up at the news. *Suspended? For what?*

"Medical leave. It's different than suspension," Cade said.

"I dunno, dude. Remember when you got suspended in eleventh grade? For what, getting caught fingering that cheerleader in the handicapped stall?"

"Damn, Elijah," Aiden said. "Nice dinner conversation."

"It's lunch. It's more informal," Elijah said. "Besides, that's what happened."

"Yeah, well. That's not what happened this time," Cade said.

"Well, medical leave or suspension or whatever, I think it's bullshit," Elijah said.

Cade frowned and shook his head.

"I'm just trying to do my job," he said. "I don't know why that ass Eldon Crane won't let me."

"Crane's alright," Elijah said as he dug into the food.

Nice to see the lamb doesn't bother him, Lily thought wryly.

"But yeah, I don't know why he's standing in your way either. I mean, why hire you and bring you here if he's not even going to let you do anything? Dude, like he won't even let you be a desk jockey, right?"

"Nope," Cade said as he took a generous bite of the casserole. "Man, that's good. Lily, did you make this all by yourself?"

"What, you really think we helped?" Aiden asked with a laugh.

Before Lily could reply, they heard a woman scream in the front yard.

"What the hell—" Elijah started, but all four of them had already pushed their chairs back and raced toward the front door.

Lily smelled the fire before she saw it. One block away, a small apartment building was engulfed in flames. They ran toward it while people emerged from the front door crouching. Some climbed out of windows from the first floor.

"Oh my God," she said. "What do we do? What do we—"

She sensed a shift in Elijah and Aiden already.

He-Man mode, she thought. Cade put a hand on her forearm and brought her to a halt. He opened his mouth, concern in his eyes.

"I'll be okay," she said. "I'll—I'll stay here. Go. Do your thing," she urged.

Cade whipped off his t-shirt to reveal a ribbed tank underneath that hugged every inch of his muscles. He tossed the shirt to her, still warm from his skin.

It took everything she had not to hold it to her nose and breathe him in. Lily settled for watching his perfect body as he quickly caught up to Elijah and Aiden.

I'll remember that image forever, she thought.

Cade in silhouette, his big frame as he moved purposefully toward the burning two-story building. *Goddamn, but that is hot.*

Lily shivered and focused on worrying for all four of them. Cade stopped for a second, the briefest hesitation before he jaunted up the cement steps and into the building.

"Are you okay?" she asked a middle-aged man who coughed violently beside her. "Can I get you water?"

The man looked at her, teary-eyed, and nodded.

She ushered the man toward a garden hose as sirens wailed in the distance.

At least Elijah, Aiden, and Cade won't be without backup for long.

As she turned on the hose and held it to the man's lips, she saw Elijah and Aiden emerge from the building. Elijah somehow cradled two large dogs, one under each arm. Aiden held out an enormous cat as it yowled and scratched at him.

Lily breathed out a sigh of relief.

At least all the people got out okay.

Cade appeared on their tail, cradling what appeared to be a hurt Rottweiler. She watched from two houses away as the three of them repeatedly went into the building to check for pets.

A woman screamed desperately for, "My Sugarbear! My Sugarbear!" The distress in her voice made Lily heavy with heartache.

As she turned off the faucet and started to head toward the sea of bystanders, she saw Cade emerge from the building with a massive cage. A parrot squawked in fear.

"Sugarbear!" the woman shrieked and ran toward the bird.

That's Sugarbear? she thought to herself as the fire trucks arrived. A stream of men rushed by, all suited up and carrying a fire hose.

Elijah, Aiden and Cade stepped out of the way and started administering first aid. She couldn't see any major injuries, but there were some tenants bruised and bleeding from falls.

Lily overheard one of the firefighters say "grease fire," and "hot and fast," but it seemed like the fire was also well contained. Within thirty minutes, she couldn't see any flames, but it was clear the smoke and water damage were significant.

The last victim was loaded into an ambulance, although the old woman swore she was "completely fine and didn't want no ambulance bill."

The guys walked toward her, Elijah rolling his eyes at the woman's protests.

"You see those fire-putting-out skills, Lil?" he asked.

"Is that the technical term for it?" she asked with a laugh as she wrapped her arms around her brothers. On impulse, after she released her brothers, she embraced Cade, too.

He let her, and she felt his hand brush against her hair.

It feels good, she realized. Letting him touch her like that. Still, it felt like it lasted a little too long, and her brothers' eyes started to bore into her.

Lily pulled back and wrinkled her nose.

"You all smell like a thousand campfires," she said.

Cade laughed while Elijah and Aiden started to walk back to the apartment. Lily paused.

Should I say something more to him? she wondered. *Try to explain about the other day?*

Cade looked at her curiously, gave a small headshake, and started to follow the guys.

Lily didn't know what to do. She wanted him to talk to her. Hell, she wanted him to kiss her again.

But maybe it's not meant to be.

6

CADE

*C*ade was aware that he shook his knee, his worst nervous tell, but he couldn't help it. Just being in Dr. Hersh's office got to him, even when he wasn't being questioned.

Interrogated is more like it, he thought.

It was always strange to step into the office. It was sleek, modern, and nearly sterile. A sharp contrast to the waiting room with its two lumpy couches and handknitted pillow covers with flowery inspirational sayings stitched across them.

Clearly, two very different people had decorated each space. Cade guessed the office was more Dr. Hersh's style, and that made total sense.

Sterile and unwelcoming, just like him.

"Are you just going to stare at me for the whole hour?" Cade finally barked.

"I could, though it's not my preference," Dr. Hersh said.

Yeah. I could too, if my only job was to siphon money off the Oregon state government.

Cade stared at his boots, a little singed from the fire at the apartment building.

It hadn't been easy to walk into that burning building.

Knowing that his almost-brothers were inside, he almost couldn't do it.

What if I lost them, too?

Every step he'd taken had felt like his shoes had been lined with lead. Now, it was almost worse that the incident made him so aware of how fucked up his instincts were.

Well, that's not quite right, he corrected himself.

His instincts had actually returned to normal. One of the most important things he'd been taught as a recruit was how to turn off natural human instincts. Survival instincts. It wasn't normal to run toward a fire, but that's what firefighters did.

And I'd been damn good at it too, he recalled. Even battling the worst flames, he'd somehow managed to switch off both his survival and fear instincts. *Yeah, and gotten three men killed in the process.*

Dr. Hersh shifted slightly in the hard, contemporary seat that looked like it belonged in a spaceship.

"If you don't want to talk about the incident with the apartment building, that's fine for today," Dr. Hersh said. "But it would help both of us if we talked about something."

"You decorate this office?" Cade asked.

He didn't want to engage with the doctor, but he was curious and needed affirmation.

"Me? No," Dr. Hersh said with a laugh. "My daughter-in-law, she's an interior designer. She did all this."

"And the waiting room?"

"I don't know, that's how it was when we moved into this location. It's technically a shared space, so we weren't allowed to touch it."

So you should know how it feels to be stuck in a place where you can't be yourself, he thought. Cade went silent again, but any time he wasn't actively distracting himself, all he could think about was that apartment fire. At the doorstep, everything in him had screamed to run away.

"What are you thinking now?" Dr. Hersh asked.

"Nothing," he said quickly, automatically.

Every firefighter out there probably has stories like mine, he thought. *It's just nobody talks about them. So why am I stuck in this office while everyone else is out working?*

"Nothing," Dr. Hersh repeated. "I doubt it's about interior design. Look, Cade, I know you don't want to be here—"

"It's that obvious, huh?"

Dr. Hersh ignored the remark. "But you have to be here. I could tell you the reasons why you're here, and I have. However, I'm curious why *you* think you're here."

Cade opened his mouth as a smart retort was already forming.

"And I don't want to hear any of that, 'because the captain is making me' type of excuses."

Cade snapped his mouth shut and glared at Dr. Hersh. The doctor remained straight-faced.

Damn, it really does look like he could just sit there forever.

"I don't know," Cade finally said.

"You don't know what?"

"I don't know why I'm here."

The doctor continued to stare at him. *Does he ever blink?*

"I mean, I guess I'm here because ... you know, I lost three of my crew in a fire. And I guess that fucked with my head, or something."

"Correct me if I'm wrong, but weren't you there? You didn't just lose friends, you were trying to get to them?"

"Well, yeah."

"You weren't the only one in the fire, though. There were other firefighters, right?"

"Yeah, they're not going to send out four guys in the crew to take on Lodgepole Complex."

"I didn't realize that's where you were," Dr. Hersh said as he pushed up his glasses.

"It was only supposed to be a small blaze. At first. I mean, at least when it started ... a two-alarm."

"Two-alarm?"

"Multiple units from different companies," Cade said with a sigh.

"Would you mind telling me more?"

"Oh, why the hell not. Clearly, you're not going to give up."

"I've been told I'm persistent."

Cade crossed his arms over his chest and slouched down into the seat. "You ever been to Square Butte in the autumn?"

"No."

"It's cold as hell. Colder than Oregon in the spring. It wasn't really our busy season and, well, after those two hundred and seventy thousand acres burned in the summer everyone pretty much forgot about this one."

"Except for you."

Cade swallowed.

"We don't ... we still don't know why it grew out of hand so fast," he said. "I mean, the four of us had been on the crew together for almost three years. We'd been in worse situations than that before. Or at least that's what we thought. But when the chopper approached that fire—it was unprecedented. Like rappelling straight into hell."

"So nobody who was on the scene was prepared for how fast it would spread."

Cade shook his head.

"We suspected maybe a campfire had gotten out of hand at first. Or someone's cigarette. I, uh, I left before we got back the official report of the cause, and I never bothered to look it up."

Didn't want to, you mean. He swallowed, willing himself to continue.

"But all the talk afterward, it seems however the fire started, it made its way to an accelerant."

Dr. Hersh scratched some notes in his pad, but didn't say anything.

"Anyway, the three of them, they were in a gulch. We got separated, but at first I wasn't worried."

"And this was standard procedure?" Dr. Hersh asked. "To get separated."

"Yes," Cade said. He bristled at even the hint that his crew was responsible for their deaths.

"I'm just asking," Dr. Hersh said. "I'm still learning about all these things."

"Well, no," Cade admitted.

"It wasn't standard?"

Cade shook his head.

"How so?"

There wasn't any judgment in the doctor's voice, so Cade pushed on.

"It was standard for two of them," he said slowly. "But, and I'm just guessing here, but I think maybe the third, Thom Barron, he might have heard one of them on the walkie-talkie? Or for some reason thought they needed help and broke protocol."

"And where was Mr. Barron supposed to be?"

"With me," Cade said quietly.

"And what did you do? When he went toward the other two?"

"I, uh … nothing."

"Nothing?" The doctor raised his brow. "I find that hard to believe."

"I didn't do anything because I didn't realize right away that he'd left."

"I see. And do you have any guess on how long he was away from you?"

"I don't …" Cade closed his eyes and tried to remember.

That was the one part of the day that was always black. He remembered the heat, the brightness. It was always almost impossible to hear his crew anyway with such a contained fire.

But you should have checked, he thought. *How long did you go without seeing him? Thirty seconds? A minute? Three minutes, five?*

Any of those timeframes could have happened. He just didn't know.

"It was all so fast," he said weakly.

"That's common, for time to get wonky in high-stress situations. Even for professionals who regularly work in traumatic environments," Dr. Hersh said. "But what you need to remember is you're not the one who broke protocol."

"I should have made sure he was there," Cade said.

"And he should have stayed with you if he was able," Dr. Hersh said. "I'm not saying what he did was morally or ethically wrong, especially if he broke protocol to help the other men on your crew. But what you did wasn't morally, ethically, or *technically* wrong."

"You don't understand," Cade said.

"I understand more than you think. Maybe not your specific circumstances, but we all have histories."

We all have histories.

"Are you able to tell me what happened next, from what you remember?"

"I ... it's all so blurry. I don't know. I realized he was gone, but for how long I don't know. And by the time I figured out where he was ..."

"Yes?"

"There was just so much screaming."

"From?"

"*Them*," Cade said. He squeezed his eyes shut. The voices, all of them, echoed through his head. "God, I can still hear it. You know how when you hear a person scream, it's usually in a movie and they're acting. Or if it's in person, they're usually still acting—like on a carnival ride or something. But you don't really ever hear a person scream for their life. Not really. Until they really are."

Dr. Hersh nodded and jotted notes on his pad. "And you knew, without a doubt, in that moment, that all three of them were in that gulch?"

Cade nodded.

"You just know," he said. "You work with someone, live with them a lot of the time, you just know." He looked up and met Dr. Hersh's eyes. "You know when someone you care about is screaming for their life."

"Tell me more."

"They were … they were maybe forty feet away? I'd made it to high ground, but my ankle was fucked up. Got pinned down by some branches, fractured it instantly. At first I couldn't see them. It was just the sounds … but everything was falling apart. I was trying to yell down at them. Tell them it was okay. They couldn't hear me on the walkies. But then something gave way, the smoke cleared for a minute, and I could see them."

"You saw them?"

"Yeah," Cade said quietly. "I watched them die."

"Wasn't it difficult to see clearly? I imagine with the smoke, all the flames—"

"I watched them die," Cade repeated firmly. "I saw their faces. They were looking at me, all three of them. They screamed my name while they died."

"Alright."

"You know, in a fire? Most people think it's the flames that kill you. It's usually not. It's usually the smoke. You suffocate to death way before you're burned. But they didn't even get that. I tried to get to them."

"I believe you."

"But I just … I wasn't strong enough."

"What do you mean?"

"I tried, but the fire … it was just so goddamned hot."

"What did you try to do?"

"I tried—I tried to just power through it. You know? I thought if I could just get to them, get some debris out of the way so they could get back out … but my body wouldn't let me."

"Humans have innate survival instincts. They're what keep

most of us from successful suicides, or repeating dangerous mistakes over and over."

"Not us."

"What?"

"Firefighters override instincts."

Dr. Hersh scribbled wildly on his notepad. "And how did you get out?"

"I was carried out."

"Excuse me?"

"I ... passed out from the smoke. Or that's what I was told, since I don't remember. The last thing I remember was their faces. That look in their eyes, I'll never forget it. And then I was in an ambulance."

"So you would have died trying to save them if you weren't rendered unconscious."

"I should have died trying to save them."

He stopped short of saying that in those last moments before darkness claimed him, he'd welcomed those flames.

There was nothing to live for anyway.

Cade felt a warm trickle lick down his cheek. He jerked up an arm to wipe away the tear and tried to make it look like a scratch.

"Cade—"

He made a fist and slammed his hand down on the table between them. The living edge wooden piece tremored beneath the impact.

"Why did it take them?" he demanded. "Why did it take three good men, two with families and one a brand new recruit —and it didn't take me?"

"Cade, I think—"

"Forget it, I have to go." Before the doctor could interrupt, Cade jumped out of his seat and raced out the door.

In the parking lot, he was too wound up to drive. Instead, he took to the sidewalk for the three-mile walk home. Or at least that's what he'd thought. He was on autopilot, and his feet carried him to the bakery.

I just need a glimpse of something good. Someone who's glad I survived.

He could see Lily through the bakery windows, a frilly apron tied around her waist.

God, she looks pretty, he thought. *Pretty and good. Too good for someone like me.*

Lily's back was to him as she talked to someone outside of his line of sight.

What would she look like bouncing a baby on one hip? he thought suddenly, unaware of where such a thought had come from.

But the way she stood with her weight heavily on one hip, it wasn't hard to imagine.

"There's Daddy!" she would say when she saw him, cooing to the baby. "Say hi! Can you say hi?"

"You're fucking ridiculous," he whispered to himself under his breath.

He didn't even want kids, necessarily. *But maybe, if they were with her ...*

The possibility intrigued him, but Cade immediately rebuked himself. There were so many reasons why it couldn't happen.

Lily turned, spotted him through the window and smiled. He could feel the electricity even from the patio. Even if Lily wasn't his best friend's little sister, he didn't deserve someone like her. Hell, he'd slept through half of Salem's population finding that out.

You should have never slept with her. Never led her on. Never restarted whatever this is.

He turned on his heel and marched toward his apartment.

7

LILY

"Fill it with premium, please," she told the gas station attendant as she handed him her card.

Lily turned off the ignition and tapped her horoscope app.

Libra, today might present some challenges. Tread carefully.

"That's one way of putting it," she said.

She heard the attendant struggle with the gas cap, as usual. Lily glared at the steering wheel. She liked that it was a Mercedes, seafoam green. But it was also a 1979.

It was a beast and expensive to maintain, from the premium gas to the five hundred dollars she'd had to pay just to get it running again.

And I thought living above a mechanic shop would magically make her run like new.

A black Hummer pulled up to the pump opposite her. Tim Criss jumped out and handed the attendant his card. Lily sank as low into her seat as she could. She hadn't seen her college boyfriend since he'd dumped her at the coffee shop three years ago.

What the hell is he doing in Salem, anyway?

They'd met at OSU, but Tim was from Medford and always

talked smack about her hometown. He'd complained every year she'd "dragged him" to holidays.

Lily slipped her aviators on and pretended to be engrossed in her phone. But all she could do was reread the same sentence over and over.

Libra, today might present some challenges.

"Hey! Hey, babe."

Tim leaned down toward her. He still wore the same cologne that he had in college, and it instantly took her back. She felt like an undergraduate again, naively proud to have someone like Tim Criss as a boyfriend.

Lily shifted away from him as best she could and kept her eyes on her phone.

"Damn, cold shoulder, alright I get it," he said with a laugh. "You look good. I'm up here for a meeting with an investor. I was going to text you."

Lily sighed and took off the sunglasses. "What do you want, Tim?"

He bit his lip and blatantly looked her up and down. She was aware that her work blouse probably pulled tight at the chest, but she refused to act embarrassed or try to adjust it.

"We might have broken up, but that doesn't mean we can't still see each other. What are you up to this evening?"

"Work." She had to admit, he still looked good. Not as muscular as he used to be, and his red hair had thinned, but he could still turn some heads.

"Where do you work?"

"Bakery."

"How late are bakeries open? I'm in meetings until probably ten or eleven tonight anyway. Nightcap?"

She was enraged at not just his invitation, but his assumption that she'd be down for a booty call after three years and the way he'd dumped her.

"No."

Tim looked to either side and leaned in closer.

"You're still mad that I dumped you?" he hissed. "It's not my fault that your personality wasn't enough to keep me—or any guy—interested. I know what you did."

She jerked up her head. "What are you talking about?"

He grinned at her reaction. "Whoring yourself out the second you could. Didn't want to let the whole campus know what a slut you were, huh? So you played the good girl with me while you were handing it out all over town up here—"

"Miss? Your receipt?" The attendant appeared, uncertain, over Tim's shoulder.

Anger mixed with shame as she reached past Tim to grab the receipt.

He couldn't know. Could he? Cade wouldn't have told anybody, and there's no way it could have gotten back to Tim. Could it?

"Ah, come on, don't be mad!" Tim said. "I'm the same way, it's too bad there are double standards for girls. So what about tonight, babe—"

For once, the Mercedes roared to life without any trouble. Tim casually stood up and strolled to the front of her car. Lily revved her engine to warn him, but he crossed his arms and smiled.

Frustrated, she threw the gear into reverse and felt a rich satisfaction as the little Mercedes peeled out of the gas station.

She'd been on her way home after the opening shift, but now all she could think about was a drink. And she needed something stronger than wine.

Lily hadn't been into the nightlife scene in Salem since ... well, ever, she realized. But she'd heard Jean-Michel talk about Archive Coffee & Bar where the drinks got a little stronger starting at happy hour. She veered toward Liberty Street and parked in the small lot.

It was only five o'clock, but Archive had already switched into full-on bar mode. Lily sank into one of the iron chairs on the outdoor patio and grabbed the cocktail list.

There was a decadent list of coffee-based cocktails from

Spanish coffee served flambé, to more complicated drinks she'd never heard of. Lily squinted at the menu and tried to figure out what the long descriptions meant.

"Is this seat taken?" a deep voice asked.

Fuck, did he follow me?

"Look, asshole—" Lily looked up to see Cade raise his brows in surprise. "Sorry... I thought... I thought you were someone else."

"Well, I'd hate to be whoever you thought I was. So. Is this where you hang out?"

Lily set down the menu. "Oh! Uh, no, not usually. I just really needed a drink."

"Mind if I sit down a minute?"

"Yeah, of course."

Cade settled into the seat across from her and she handed him the cocktail menu. He scanned it quickly.

"Pretty fancy. What are you going to get?"

"I don't know. I was just trying to get through the menu when you sat down."

"Hmm. What kind of liquor do you like?"

"If I'm going hard, usually vodka or gin."

"How about I order for you?"

Lily blushed. "Sure," she said quietly.

"What can I get you two?" The waitress appeared with a smile. Lily noted her thick glasses and forearm tattoos that poked out from rolled-up sleeves.

"A Moscow mule and champagne spritzer," Cade said as he put down the menu.

"Coming right up."

"So. How's your day been?" Cade asked.

She made a face. "It was okay. Until—"

"Until some asshole ruined it?"

She gave a small laugh. "Until I ran into Tim."

"Who's Tim?"

"You know ... the guy I used to date ..."

"Really?"

"Yeah, he made it really unpleasant, too."

"Unpleasant how?"

"Ugh. It's not worth rehashing."

The drinks arrived just in time to save her from talking about it anymore. She knew Cade probably hadn't figured out Tim was both her college boyfriend *and* the guy she'd mentioned she dated last.

He doesn't need to know everything, like how you haven't dated anyone *since you slept with him three years ago.*

"Which is mine?" she asked.

"Try both, and decide what you like."

Lily took small sips of both, surprised that she liked such different cocktails.

"The spritzer," she said.

"Not a mule fan, then."

"The mug is pretty, I like the copper. And it's good, I just like champagne more I guess." She sighed, the alcohol already doing its job, and leaned back in the seat. "So, is this your signature move? Order two drinks and have the girl choose?"

"No, actually I've never done that before. Why, do you think it works?"

Lily blushed. "Um, no."

"Good to know. Well, cheers to being here. I never thought I'd see this town again, but I have to admit, it's not that bad. It's growing on me."

"Where did you think you'd be?" she asked as she took a long swallow.

"I dunno. Maybe ... living in the Montana wilderness, building a cabin with my own hands. Surviving off of what I could grow or catch—"

"You wanted to be alone." She realized it sounded like a statement, not a question.

"No. Well, maybe. You know my reputation with women ..."

"That sounds horrible. How would you meet someone?"

"Eh, that's not required."

"What about intimacy?"

"Also not required."

"I see. Is that how you prefer it, then? In your dating life, I mean?"

"I don't really date," Cade admitted. "I'm all fucked up, what with Aunt Mary dying and with ... with the loss of my crew. Nobody wants that. And I don't want to put that on someone."

"How do you know? Unless you try—"

Cade rolled his eyes and signaled to the waitress. Lily looked at their glasses, surprised to find they'd already finished one round.

"So, show me your moves," she said, the liquid courage fully arrived.

"Sorry?"

"Pretend I'm a girl that you just met at the bar. And you're trying to pick me up."

"Why?"

"For, you know ... sex."

"I meant why would I pretend that," he said with a smile. "You're cute."

Lily felt her face grow hot, but she persisted. "Come on, indulge me. I've had a rough day."

"Alright. But first of all, you should know I don't have beginning-of-the-date moves. I have *end*-of-the-date moves. I make sure the girl, sorry, *you*, have had a nice time. Plenty of drinks if you're into that. Then I move closer." Cade moved his chair next to hers so quickly and smoothly she barely realized it had happened.

"Round two," the waitress said, and slid the drinks to them.

Cade didn't break eye contact with her.

"And I ask for a taste of your drink, like this." He lowered his voice and looked so deeply into her eyes she thought he could see her deepest secrets. "Can I try your drink?"

Her stomach began to flutter. "Sure, go ahead."

He tried the fresh spritzer. She watched his throat work as he swallowed.

Enjoy it, she told herself. *Just let it be real, just for a moment. Surely there's no harm in that?*

Cade put the drink down and gazed into her eyes. She could sense the fire in him, just below the surface. It matched the flames inside her. His eyes traveled to her lips, which heated up below the smoldering gaze.

She couldn't move as he moved closer, brought up his hand and ran a thumb along her cheek. As he cupped the back of her head, her lips parted in anticipation.

She already knew what his lips felt like, tasted like. As he kissed her, softly at first, her body responded and it escalated to unprecedented passion.

Lily let out a soft moan and he pulled back.

"Lily," he said quietly. "I'm into you. Don't mistake that. But... there are so many reasons why we can't do this. Elijah, and..." Cade let the words trail off while he moved his chair away.

"It's not just about you all the time," she blurted out, irritated. "What if I have my reasons for not wanting you?"

"Good for you, then," Cade said. He stood up and tossed some cash onto the table. "So, we're agreed, then?"

Lily crossed her arms and just shook her head. If she spoke, she was afraid she'd burst into tears.

Cade walked toward the parking lot and never once looked back.

All I do these days is watch this guy's back as he walks away, she thought.

8

LILY

"*H*ey, Jean-Michel, you want to go hiking at Silver Falls?" Lily asked as he rushed past her toward the kitchen.

He wrinkled his nose. "I do not do outdoors. Why you don't ask your friend, that American girl with the French name?"

"Renee's still in Italy," she said with a sigh. "Not only is she my only hiking friend, she's my *only* friend. How depressing is that?"

"When you hiking?" he asked.

"Well, I was *hoping* you'd go with me since we're closing early today."

Jean-Michel shrugged. "Those boys always in here talking with you? Go ask them."

Actually not a bad idea, she thought.

Aiden or Elijah might be up for it. She left Jean-Michel to finish closing and slid into her little Mercedes. In the backseat, her backpack was already stuffed with hiking clothes.

Any day off that was clear and sunny in an Oregon spring demanded to be taken advantage of.

Lily smiled as she pulled up to her brothers' apartment and

saw that Elijah's truck was there. Of her two brothers, he was the most likely to say yes.

"Hey!" she called as she let herself in with the spare key. "Elijah, you want to go to Silver Falls?"

Elijah emerged from the hallway in his firefighting t-shirt.

"Damn, I wish," he said. "My shift's about to start. Heading out. Maybe Cade wants to go."

"Cade?" she asked.

"Yeah?" She heard the hallway bathroom door open. Lily blushed, unaware that he was there.

"Lily wants someone to go hiking with."

"Oh yeah?" Cade asked. She sensed the shared trepidation in his voice.

"It's not like he's being allowed to work," Elijah reminded Lily. "And he's been bitching to us nonstop at the station about how bored he is."

"It's true," Cade admitted with a shrug.

"Uh, it's okay. It was just a random thought. I should probably go home and practice my choux skills, anyway—"

"You two don't be weird," Elijah said as he rolled his eyes and slipped on his jacket. "Cade, I know you love to hike. Don't you even keep your gear in your ride most of the time?"

Cade looked at Lily. "Well, yeah ..."

"Then go," Elijah said. "While the rest of us are stuck at work, make the most of a rare sunny Sunday."

"I mean, a hike would be good ..." Cade said slowly. His eyes searched Lily's for permission.

"Sure!" she said, aware of how fake her enthusiasm sounded. "Sounds good."

"Have some fun for me," Elijah said as he bounded out the front door.

As soon as she couldn't hear his footsteps anymore, Lily turned to Cade. "Obviously I don't expect you to go hiking with me," she said.

"Look, about the other day ... I'm sorry. It was my fault. How about we just pretend it didn't happen?"

"Well ... okay ..." Lily said as she shifted from foot to foot.

"Seriously. We can be friends, can't we?"

"Uh, sure?"

"Good. So, your big brother is right. I do have my hiking gear in the trunk of my car. Where were you thinking?"

"Well ..." Lily mentally scratched Silver Falls off the list. It was too far of a drive, too long of a hike, and too freaking romantic. "I was thinking of going to Hendricks Park. It's close," she added.

"Great. Let me grab my hiking boots and stuff, and we can go."

"Do you mind driving?" Lily asked.

Cade looked at her, amused. "Sure, no problem. Your car still acting up?"

"Yeah, but it's also not as nice as yours."

"Actually, I got a new—"

"I know, Elijah told me. Yesterday, right? A new Mustang?"

"Man, that boy's got a big mouth. Yeah, a convertible."

No wonder I didn't notice his truck in the parking lot.

"What are you doing with the Chevy?"

"Traded it. Not for much, but anything helps."

She held up her backpack. "Just let me change really quick and we can go."

Briefly, as she changed in Elijah's room, she wished she'd brought some cuter hiking gear. Instead, she pulled on the same pair of yoga pants she'd had for four years.

She groaned when she realized which long-sleeved top she had. The cartoon of three burlesque dancers with pasties on their breasts, the fourth holding up macarons and saying, "I thought you said pastries" was cute to her and Jean-Michel.

Probably not anyone else. Lily zipped up her Nike jacket all the way to her throat.

"Ready," she said, and followed Cade down to the sleek,

candy-colored Mustang. As soon as he started the car, Warrant started playing. "I haven't heard this in forever!" she exclaimed as the hook for "Cherry Pie" began.

"Want me to change it?"

"No, I like it."

As Cade maneuvered onto the main road, she turned to him. "So... how many girls have you slept with?"

He was clearly startled, but tried not to show it. "I'm not sure. I've never been very good at math."

"But the number is like, a lot? Right?"

"A lot is subjective, don't you think?" he asked with a wink.

"Okay, like more than one hundred?"

"Why are you asking?" he asked as they pulled up to a red light.

"I dunno. Just making conversation."

"Is this what you consider small talk? You know, when you told me you don't have much of a social life, maybe that's why. Your conversation skills could use some sprucing up."

"I think you're avoiding the question."

"Damn right I'm avoiding the question!"

"Why? Why does it matter if I know?" she asked.

Cade paused. "You're right, I guess it doesn't. So, okay, my answer is a lot."

"A lot," she repeated and nodded. "What's your definition of a lot?"

"Probably similar to yours."

So at least one hundred, she thought.

What the hell? Are there really over one hundred girls in Salem that he would even be into? I mean, after deducting the ones in relationships and everything.

"But none since... you know. The thing in Montana."

"Wait," Lily said. She turned to him. "Seriously? None?"

"Yeah," Cade said with a nod. "I think... you know, it really fucked me up."

"But, Montana. That was like, *awhile* ago."

Cade looked at her, aware that she was about to start a new interrogation. "How about we change the subject?"

"To what?"

She felt a little embarrassed about pushing him, but she'd wondered about his number for most of her life. And having the answer didn't feel very validating. Still, she was surprised that she wasn't jealous.

But did I make the list? she wondered. *Do I count?*

"Let's see," Cade said. "Who do you think looks best from your years in high school?"

Lily laughed.

He's certainly not very good at smooth conversational shifts. But he was right, she'd pushed him enough.

"Honestly, I don't really see many people from high school around. I think most of them left."

"But on Instagram or whatever?"

She shrugged. "I don't really keep up with social media. I think I have an Instagram. And a Twitter? But I'm never on them."

"Yeah, I know," he said.

"What do you mean?"

For a second, she thought she saw him blush.

"I mean, I don't remember really seeing you on there much. Not that I really am, either."

Liar, she thought, but with a smile.

She might not be posting all the time or share anything, but she lurked. It had gotten especially bad right after they'd slept together three years ago.

She'd made an anonymous account to check out his photos, and on Instagram there were scores of girls liking his pictures and commenting.

Lily had slowly stopped her online stalking of him once she'd realized it didn't do any good. If she wanted that crush to die, she needed to stop feeding it every day. She'd never disabled those accounts, just abandoned them.

"What about you?" she asked. "Who do you think looks best from high school?"

"I don't know. Kind of like you, I don't really keep track. You look pretty good," he said, and gave her a wink.

She shoved him playfully. "I wasn't fishing."

"I didn't think you were. I can tell you who doesn't look good, though."

"Who's that?"

"Mr. Stroh."

"Oh God, I forgot about him. As if having him in middle school wasn't bad enough, he had to go and become principal of the freaking high school."

"I had him for homeroom one year," Cade recalled. "I felt kind of bad for the guy."

"Why's that?"

"All these girls were always talking about how he was checking them out, calling him a pervert and stuff."

"Do you ... do you think he did something? Like, hit on them?" she asked. She'd never had him as a teacher, but didn't remember any rumors like that.

"I can't say," he said with a shrug. "All I know is they never gossiped about him actually doing or saying anything. But you know, who knows. He was kind of weird. With that toupee and all."

"Yeah, I remember that," she said. "Well, if he didn't do anything, that is sad. Teenagers are cruel."

They pulled into the parking lot and Cade parked next to a car full of kids in South Salem sweaters.

"Speaking of," he said with a nod.

She smiled at him. "Let's do this."

9

CADE

*A*fter barely a quarter mile on the trail, he could already feel the sweat as it started to pool at the small of his back.

And it's not even that hot out, he thought.

But Cade knew what it was—Lily, just a few steps ahead of him. And how her ass swayed in a hypnotic motion. He couldn't tear his eyes away, and she'd already caught him once.

Or at least he thought she had. When she'd turned around to ask him whether he wanted the longer or shorter route at the fork, he couldn't see her eyes beneath the gold-trimmed aviators.

"Longer," he'd said without pause.

Looking wasn't so bad, right? He could hear the slight tremor in his voice, but she smiled at his response and didn't seem to notice.

" ... especially this time of year," Lily called over her shoulder.

"Sorry, what?" he asked. *Get it together.*

"I said I'm glad we got to take advantage of one of the few sunny days," she said.

"Oh, yeah. It's great," he said.

Cade couldn't help it. His eyes wandered from the swell of her ass, barely contained in the tight black leggings, to her shapely thighs.

She might as well be naked. It didn't take much to imagine.

In some places, the curve of her cheeks and the flare of her hips, he could even see a touch of skin as it shone through the stretchy material. Cade searched for an outline of underwear, but found nothing.

Those gorgeous legs, he thought. *Attached to a gorgeous body, and gorgeous face.*

" ... think so?" Her voice broke through to him, and he realized she'd turned to him again.

Cade cleared his throat as embarrassment flooded him.

"Yeah," he said. He didn't know what he'd agreed to, but she smiled again.

Right answer. You got lucky, he scolded himself. *Can't you keep it together for an hour?*

The path widened, and Lily moved to the edge of the trail to make room for him. Side by side, it was a little easier to avoid the distraction. But here, he could smell her, that familiar perfume or soap that she'd worn even when they'd been together that one time.

"I know I'm from here and everything, but I'm always amazed how beautiful this place is."

"The park?"

"Oregon!" she said with a laugh. "But yeah, this particular trail, too. It's crazy how green it is, even after the winter."

"Evergreen," he said. "That's the thing about the Pacific Northwest. All the pines. It's kind of like Montana, but a different type of green."

He heard that he was babbling, but it was better than getting caught checking out her ass and legs over and over.

It's okay if you want her, he told himself. *Hell, it's even okay that she knows you think she's hot. Just don't cross that line,* he reminded himself.

That seemed simple enough. *But if it's so simple, what am I doing out here in the woods alone with her?*

"I wish EJ could have come," she said.

"Why? Am I not good company?" he asked.

Damn, and EJ. If EJ ever found out about us, or how I think about her ...

"Well, your conversation skills could use a brushing up today," she said with a smirk. "But I'll let it slide since this whole thing was kind of sprung on you. Thanks for coming, though," she added quickly. "I don't want it to sound like your company is a consolation prize or something like that."

"Don't worry about it. I'm glad it was sprung on me. But about EJ, how do you think he's doing?" he asked.

"What do I think?" Lily glanced up at him. "Fine, I guess. I mean, I think we're all handling Dad's death in our own ways, but he seems as okay as could be expected."

"That's good," Cade said. "And what about, you know, the whole love life..."

"I figured you'd know more about that than me," she said with a shrug. "I mean, boy talk and all. It's not like I sit around and compare notes with my brothers."

"That's not what I mean," he said quickly. "Back, you know, a few years ago. He was dating this one girl—"

"You mean Courtney?" she asked sharply. "Yeah, she was a real—well, she crushed his heart for sure. Let's just put it that way."

"Damn, he never told me that," Cade said. "I mean, they were together awhile. And then I left for Montana and on social media at least, one day all the photos he had of her just disappeared. I should have called him."

"You shouldn't have," Lily said. "He was a mess for awhile about that, but you know how he is. Just about spent three hours in the gym every day for a few weeks, and that was it. Actually, EJ's whole breakup wasn't the worst of it."

"What do you mean?"

They reached the crest of a small rolling hill and entered a patch of sunshine that broke through the tree canopies overhead.

"Well, it's not like Aiden's been an angel. He started getting around quite a bit when you left. Maybe he was after your local title, I dunno," she said.

He glanced at her guiltily, but she nudged him playfully in the arm. "I'm kidding. About the title thing, but he did have two pregnancy scares in three days. With two different girls, obviously."

"Are you serious? He never told me that!"

"Well, you were in Montana," she said with a shrug. "And he wasn't exactly bragging about it. He about lost half his hair from the stress."

"And neither were, well, you know..."

"Pregnant? No," she said. "It was actually kind of funny, the circumstances. It was hard not to laugh at him."

"How come?" Cade heard bark chips crunch beneath their feet as ferns brushed softly against his calves.

It really is beautiful, he thought.

But he couldn't tell if it was just that Lily had brought his attention to it, or if it was being here with her.

"Well, one of the girls *was* pregnant. Five months pregnant."

"*What?* So wait, is Aiden—"

"No," she said. "He's not a dad. The girl didn't look pregnant at all, and apparently didn't know she was pregnant. Aiden had only been fooling around with her for about six weeks."

"So whose baby was it?"

"No clue," she said with a shrug. "But he's just glad it wasn't his."

"Yikes."

"Yeah. The whole thing slowed Aiden down, though. Both him and Elijah were off the market for almost a year. It was pretty great, actually," she said. Lily raised her head skyward and let another patch of sun shine down on her skin. "A lot of brother and sister and brother time. That was two years ago."

"I guess your father's death probably had a pretty negative effect on their dating lives, too."

"Yeah," she said softly. "It certainly hasn't been a priority, that's for sure."

He thought she blushed slightly, but couldn't tell.

"I didn't mean you," he said quickly.

"I know," she said with a small smile. "But it seems like dating really isn't our family's thing. Although, I did see Aiden with a girl a few days ago, and I swear Elijah has to be seeing someone. So maybe they're back on the prowl."

She hitched her backpack up higher and rested her hands on either strap.

"Why do you say that?"

"Because he's never home. And when I call him, nine times out of ten he sounds like... like his voice is muffled. You know?"

"Huh," Cade said. Neither Elijah or Aiden had said anything at all about that at the firehouse.

Not like you've really asked, he reminded himself.

He'd been so caught up in his own situation, getting stuck with a shrink instead of actually fighting fires, that he'd taken his friends' support for granted. Cade felt shame wash over him as he thought back over the past couple of weeks.

Why did I think I could come back and everything would be just like it was when I left? They rounded a bend in comfortable silence, and Cade heard a bubbling trickle.

"Hey, you hear that?"

"Oh! We're almost to my favorite waterfall," Lily said. She picked up her pace. "I wasn't sure if it would be active, since we've had such a dry spring. Come on!"

She grabbed his hand and pulled him off the main trail toward a deserted path. Cade held his breath and willed himself not to think about her skin on his. Or how it made his heart start to beat something wild through his entire body.

Lily stopped short at a ledge and sucked in her breath. She rested her hands on a low, stony wall that looked like it hadn't been maintained in decades.

"Look," she whispered, and nodded down. Twenty feet below was a cove framed in moss. Water poured into it from rocks and fallen logs to pool together in a natural swimming hole.

"You aren't scared of getting wet, are you?" Lily asked with a grin.

"Wait, what?" he asked. "Are you crazy? It's—"

"Don't be a baby," she said as she slipped off her backpack. Lily dropped the bag and began to inch her way down the slope with a hand on the ledge.

Cade took off his own pack and followed close behind. Sprays of water to the face were reminders to keep his eyes on where he was going—not on Lily's body that was even easier to admire without the backpack.

"Jesus," he said as he felt a foot slip beneath him. He regained traction and steadied himself.

How was she doing this?

A dozen steps later he reached the bottom, but she was nowhere in sight.

"Lily?" he called. "Come on, this isn't funny."

"I'm in here," she said, and he squinted. The outline of her body was barely visible in the alcove.

"What is this?" he asked.

Inside, it was surprisingly dry. Quaint, even. The stone wall ended in a bench with room for maybe four people.

"My secret place," she said with a smile. Lily ran her hands through her damp hair, but the short locks had already started to dry. She patted the seat next to her. "Cool, huh?"

As he sat, he realized her white t-shirt was almost transparent. Through a pink bra, her nipples were hard.

"Oh," she said, and crossed her arms, embarrassed.

"I'm sorry, I didn't—"

"Jean-Michel got these t-shirts as a joke for everyone at the bakery one year. It's stupid."

"It's fine," he said with a smile. He hadn't even seen what the shirt said, but at least she didn't realize what he'd *really* been staring at. "And yeah, this place is awesome."

She laughed and relaxed. Lily scooted closer and Cade felt himself sit up straighter.

"See there?" she asked, and pointed to the exit of the cave. "In the summer, you can see ..."

Cade tried to listen, but all he could focus on was her. How close she was, how the dampness of her skin made her glow. That she smelled like strawberries, and how she had an adorable cowlick that stuck up on one side.

Before he could stop himself, he reached out to touch the tendril. Lily grew quiet, but she didn't move away.

What will one taste hurt?

Cade bent toward her and she lifted her mouth to his, an offering. Lily's arms wrapped around his waist, pulled him closer. Close enough that he felt her breasts press against his chest and those nipples rub against him. He hardened instantly as a growl erupted from deep within his chest.

As one of his hands cradled her head, the other wandered to her waist. The dampness of her t-shirt clung tight to her skin. As he inched his hand underneath, he was shocked by how warm her stomach was. He made his way to her breasts, grazed a thumb across her nipple through the thin satin fabric.

"Fucking waterfall, dude." The voices of approaching hikers made them both freeze.

In the darkness of the alcove, he couldn't tell if the look in Lily's eyes was fear, embarrassment, or intrigue.

Maybe all three.

"Shit," she said, and tugged down her shirt.

As she scrambled to make it look like nothing had happened, he couldn't figure out if the hikers had just ruined his hookup, or saved him from making a terrible mistake.

Another terrible mistake, he reminded himself.

What the hell is wrong with me? Usually after he'd had a girl, all interest was lost. *So what's the deal? Why does Lily have this hold on me?*

Lily led the way out of the alcove, and he squinted into the sunlight. As they passed the hikers, a group of teenagers, he gave a cursory nod to the one who made eye contact.

The silence lasted fifteen minutes before Lily broke it. "So about what happened back there—"

"Forget it," he said and cut her off.

Something in his voice must have warned her to listen. Neither said a word all the way back to the car.

10

LILY

*L*ily grasped for the door handle and pulled it open with a creak.

"You don't lock it?" Cade gasped into her ear.

"Is that really what you're concerned about?" she asked.

She crawled backward into the cool leather of the backseat. Cade followed and slammed the door behind him.

She could feel the harsh brush of the sequins against the soft flesh of her upper thighs and back, but already Cade had reached for her panties and began to pull them down her legs.

She opened her mouth to protest—the parking lot was crammed full of cars and she could easily see the smokers that lingered by the door—but caught sight of the bulge in his jeans and couldn't wait any longer.

"Fuck," Cade said suddenly as she helped him slide the underwear off her stiletto-clad feet. "I don't have a condom."

"It's okay," she said, and he was on top of her. Crushed together in the tiny backseat, she felt the weight of the little car sway and rock below them. "I'm on the pill."

"Are you sure?" he asked, though the hardness pressed against her center told her *he* certainly was.

"Yeah," she said as his lips trailed along her jawline to her throat.

"I've been tested recently," he whispered, and her eyes shot open.

Don't think about that now. Don't think about all the other women he's been with.

She let out a moan as he released her breasts from the dress. Her nipples hardened in the cold air. As he licked and sucked, she felt them stiffen even more between his lips.

His hand, surprisingly warm in the evening chill, ran upward from the inside of her knee. She spread her legs as much as she could in the cramped backseat, desperate to have him inside her.

"You're so wet," he said as he slipped a finger inside.

The same words he'd said the first time they were together.

Lily groaned and pressed herself against Cade's thick finger. When he inserted a second, she felt her wetness spread across the slick seat. He kissed his way from one breast to the other.

"More," she commanded, and it was as if he'd been waiting for permission.

He slid a third finger into her and began to circle her clit, slippery from her own juices, with his thumb.

She fucked his hand while he pulled gently at her nipple. Lily could see the tops of some people's heads as they walked by and heard snippets of conversation. Instead of embarrassment, she felt a rush of excitement. The idea of getting caught turned her on even more.

"I want you," she said, although she was close.

Not like this.

Cade buried his fingers deep inside her as he quickly unbuckled his jeans. As soon as she felt his warm tip against her opening, it felt familiar. Like home. She wrapped her legs around him and spurred him inside with her heels. Lily's arms pulled him on top of her.

"Cade," she cried out as he reached her depths. Her voice was muffled against his neck.

"Fuck, you feel so good," he moaned into her ear as he began to slowly fuck her. "I forgot... I forgot how good you feel..."

She pulled open his shirt, only vaguely aware that she ripped off the buttons in the process, and ran her fingers along his muscled chest.

Lily dug her nails into the small of his back to force him deeper. Hold him longer inside her. Every inch of him felt so good. Every thrust brought her closer to orgasm.

"You like that, don't you?" Cade asked into her ear. She could hear the grin in his voice.

Lily responded with a lock of her legs around his. She could hear the wetness between them—her wetness.

It turned her on more. Each time he was at her deepest, she felt the pressure against her clit and called out his name. Cade sucked at her neck until it was almost painful, but the near-pain was what made it so good.

She could tell she was being marked by him, and she wanted it.

I want to show the world I'm yours, she thought.

Lily arched her head back to present more of her neck. Cade complied and began to pepper the kisses and sucks along her arch.

"Fuck me harder," she breathed into the darkness.

She could see the outline of her stilettos on his back, the signs for PBR and Deschutes Brewery in the bar windows in the distance.

The car rocked beneath them as the squeaks matched her own calls.

"Shh," Cade said. "Quiet, you're going to get us caught."

"I don't care," she said. "Just fuck me."

"Only if you say please," he said, and stopped suddenly. Only half an inch of him was inside her.

Lily squirmed beneath him. "Come on, this isn't funny."

"I didn't say it was."

"Cade, come on—"

She gazed up into his eyes. Even in the night, she saw something in there, something that hadn't been there before.

"Please fuck me," she said. He immediately sank into her and she rolled her eyes into darkness.

Somewhere far away, she heard the keen of a drunk—or an animal. Something wild and crazed. With her eyes squeezed shut, she focused on Cade's body.

Cade's lips on her jaw. Cade's hand as it caressed and pulled at her nipple.

It wasn't until she felt his other hand over her mouth that she realized the keens were from her. He bore down on her, fucked her deeper, and his length pressed urgently against her G-spot.

The naughtiness of it, his power over her, brought her to the brink. She let her screams go into his hand, forgot about what little control she thought she had over her sounds, as he released himself into her.

"Fuck, Lily," he said as the heat filled her.

His orgasm brought her to her own breaking point. She bucked beneath him and pulled him even closer.

"Don't go," she murmured, but knew he couldn't hear her through the clasp of his hand.

When he finally released his hand, he kissed his way from her neck—already sore and ready to blossom with hickeys—to her chin and finally her lips.

"You're wilder than I remember," he said with a smile.

She blushed while he slowly pulled out of her. Lily felt their combined wetness spill down her thighs.

"Sorry," she said. "I don't know what came over me. I don't... I mean..."

"I like it," he said as he pulled up his jeans. "But I think you put on quite a show for whoever walked by."

Cade lowered himself over her once again and pulled lightly at her lip. The pressure of him against her center made her twitch with want.

"You're still hard," she said, impressed. She reached for his cock, but he straightened up and buckled his jeans completely.

Even in the darkness, she saw the tic in his jaw. It was illuminated by the glowing neon from the bar.

"What's wrong?" she asked. "Unless I'm wrong, we just had totally mind-blowing sex. There should literally be nothing on your mind but when we can do it again."

Cade looked at her, and the look on his face was heartbreaking.

"We can't do that again," he said slowly. "We shouldn't have done it at all to begin with. And we're never going to have sex again, ever."

"Are you serious?" she asked.

Suddenly she wished her hem hadn't hitched its way all the way to her navel, or that her nipples didn't still poke out the top of her dress. She could still feel the wetness of his mouth on hers, his come as it flowed out of her.

"It would kill Elijah. You know that, right?"

"I'm—damn it, Cade, I don't know what to say," she said. Anger began to flood through her. All she wanted was for him to be out of her car. To be out of *her*. "You know that you're an idiot, right? You realize I just gave you a second chance, and you're blowing it so hard."

"Are you seriously asking me to ruin a friendship I've had since I was six? He's my best friend, Lily!"

"Oh, right. Perfect excuse for you, isn't it? 'I can't be with you because you're my best friend's sister, but I'll totally fuck you a few times in secret.' If only you had such a perfect excuse with all the girls you fuck, right?"

She couldn't help it—and hadn't even realized she kind of believed what she said until that moment.

"Is that really what you think?" he asked, aghast. "If it is, then this is definitely for the best. I'm glad we're on the same page."

"Get out of my fucking car," she said coldly.

I will not cry in front of him. I will not cry in front of him.

Without a word, Cade pushed his way out of the car and stalked away. Lily gently pulled down her skirt and reached blindly into the dark for her underwear.

11

LILY

*L*ily opened the doors of the European pastry shop and was welcomed with the scent of the familiar comfort foods.

"Lily!" Renee called from a little table against the window.

"Oh my God, you're so tan!" Lily said as she squeezed her best friend tight.

Renee felt slimmer, tauter. She carried the glow of Italy with her, the hairs on her arm bleached blonde from the foreign sun.

"I can't believe you're back," she said as she released Renee.

"Well, kind of," Renee said with a small smile.

"What do you mean?"

"Two strudels," the waitress said as she slipped the desserts onto their table.

"I mean..." Renee said as they sat down and whipped open the thick white linen napkins, "I'm going back."

"But I thought it was just one term," Lily said.

She slid the hot spiced dessert between her lips and nearly moaned out loud. Jean-Michel refused to have anything other than authentic French pastries in his shop.

Meeting for strudels was her tradition with Renee, and

even after months of not having one it seemed the dessert would always have a hold on her.

"It was," Renee said. "But I met someone."

"What? Are you serious?" Lily leaned forward. "Who? Someone in the program? Or—"

"Ew, no," Renee said. "A local, but *acqua in bocca*, okay?"

"And what does that mean?"

"Keep it to yourself. I'm not telling anyone here."

"Why not?"

"I just don't want all the gossip." Renee neatly put down the fork after just two bites and gingerly sipped at her espresso.

"Since when do you drink espresso?" Lily asked. She noticed that Renee had ordered the usual almond milk latte for her.

Renee shrugged. "Too much fat in lattes."

"It's almond milk."

"Still. Besides, the coffee here is terrible. I didn't realize it until Italy."

"Here, as in this shop? Or Salem?"

"As in America," Renee said. "You should travel, Lily. It's so incredibly eye opening."

"I'd like to think I have a decent palate," Lily said, feeling defensive. "After all, I went to culinary school."

"Yeah, in Portland," Renee said. "One of the guys I dated in Italy? He learned how to make pasta at this *nonna*'s home in Ravenna—that's a town in Italy—"

Lily did her best to keep her eye rolls internal.

If this is what traveling does to you, I think I'll pass, she thought.

Renee had always had a penchant toward snobbishness since they'd met in sixth grade. Lily wasn't sure if it was spending so much time apart with Renee traveling in grad school, or if she'd always been that way and Lily hadn't noticed.

"What?" Renee asked suddenly.

"Nothing," Lily said quickly. She grabbed the latte and took a purposeful long swallow.

"You don't seem very interested in hearing about my trip. Or the new person I'm dating." Renee cocked her head to the side.

"You just told me you didn't want gossip around this mysterious new boyfriend of yours. So how am I supposed to know how much you want to talk about him?"

"Who said it was a boy?"

Lily almost spit out the borderline too-sweet latte, but she held it together.

"Sorry," she said. "I just assumed—"

"People in America are so closed-minded," Renee said. She gave a sad shake of her head. "I mean, who cares? *Chiodo scaccia chiodo*, right?"

"I don't know what that means," Lily said pointedly.

Renee sighed. "It means you'll get over it, okay?"

"I don't have anything to get over. But when your best friend of almost fifteen years has always dated guys, and she casually mentions that she now has a girlfriend, you have to expect some kind of reaction."

And I think a reaction is exactly what you were going for.

"Marco is a guy. Okay?" Renee asked. "I just don't like when people automatically assume that you're straight. In Italy, nobody cares. Love is love. There aren't all these games, people will say *non posso vivere senza di te* on the day they meet."

Lily rolled her eyes, unable to control it anymore.

"Maybe it's for the best that I *don't* visit Italy," she said. "Because what you're saying really isn't impressing me."

Renee crossed her arms and leaned back in the chair. "That's fine," she said bluntly. "Because you're too much of a prude for European tastes anyway."

"And what is that supposed to mean?" Lily was aware of how the coffee had coated her tongue.

She leaned forward and stared into Renee's light blue eyes.

Her best friend looked simultaneously like a total stranger and like the girl she'd ceremoniously buried her Barbies with in seventh grade to declare themselves official teenagers.

"Forget I said anything," Renee said. She uncrossed her arms and became enchanted with her espresso.

"No," Lily said. "You brought it up, I want to know."

"*Non sei capace di tenerti un cece in bocca*—fine. Look, I just meant that you've never been with anyone. You know? Sexually, I mean. You dated Tim forever, and you haven't even bothered to look for anyone since then."

"That's not true!" Lily said.

She was flustered. *How long was Renee going to throw that in her face?*

"I have been looking, but you don't know how the dating scene is in Salem. If you can even call it that—"

"You were in Portland for culinary school. Probably absolutely surrounded by men. And not just men, but future chefs who probably had the exact same interests as you. And nothing? For two years?"

"Do you know what patisserie school is like?" Lily asked. She shook her head.

Of course you don't, because for those two years you didn't even bother to ask. You just loved having a free apartment in downtown to stay at on the weekends.

"Classes started at four in the morning. I was in classes sometimes for twelve hours a day, then working at Voodoo during the graveyard shift to make ends meet. Dating wasn't particularly a priority."

"You always have an excuse. For everything," Renee said. "Ever since eighth grade when you made up that ridiculous reason for not going to the spring formal with Todd."

A flood of words built up in her throat, but Lily commanded herself to stay calm. "I just have high standards. You should try it."

"Yeah, right," Renee said with a little laugh. "Your

'standards' are just a defense mechanism. You don't want *anyone* to get over that hurdle."

"It just so happens that I ... I have a crush on someone."

"Someone real?" Renee asked suspiciously. "Or is this like when you decided Eric from *The Little Mermaid* was your soulmate?"

"Yes, someone real! His name is ... well, it starts with a C."

"Ohhh. Connor? Isn't that the name of the delivery guy at the bakery? You sneaky little slut."

"Connor? Gross, no. And that guy's name was Omar. And no, before you ask, it's not the delivery guy. "

"Christian? Your landlord? Wait, no, Cody. I think you mentioned someone with that name last Christmas? Oh my God, is his name Christmas?"

"You're ridiculous."

"*Lo ami.* So, tell me about him, then."

Lily blushed. She opened her mouth for the big reveal, but realized Renee hadn't ever met Cade. It was the one crush she'd kept to herself even in middle school and high school.

At the time, she'd thought it was because Renee would laugh at her and how ridiculous it was. Now she thought maybe it had been because Renee would have gone after him. "He's one of Elijah's friends."

"EJ always had hot friends," Renee said. "Tell me the physical details. Hair, eyes, height—"

"About six foot two. Dark hair and eyes. He's a firefighter, so—"

"Oh my God, really? Like an actual firefighter? EJ met him at the station?"

"Uh, yeah, like an actual firefighter," Lily said slowly. *It wasn't technically lying if I just fail to mention we met as kids.*

"He must be freaking hot then. But you know what the most important thing is, right?" Renee leaned forward conspiratorially. "Whether or not he's packing heat."

"Renee!"

"See?" Renee said. She leaned back again, smug. "That reaction right there is why you wouldn't do well in Italy. You're such a prude!"

"I can't help it if some of us are more modest than you, Renee. And anyway ... I happen to *know* he is."

"Wait. What?"

"I hooked up with him three years ago."

"Whoa, whoa, whoa. Tell me everything. Do not leave out a single detail. Three years ago? Isn't that when you broke up with Tim—"

"It was amazing," Lily said. She felt not only eager to stop Renee from doing her calculations, but relieved to finally be telling someone about it. "He was amazing," she added. "And he was there when I needed him ..."

"Holy shit! I can't believe you did that! And that you didn't tell me," Renee said.

Lily could hear the hurt in her friend's voice.

She was still in there, the crazy girl who stood up for me in seventh grade when that group of eighth grade girls made fun of me for not having any boobs.

"How could I not know?" Renee asked.

"We were both about to move," Lily said. She grasped for an excuse, any excuse. "And it was around graduation, and your grandparents were coming in and everything. I was going to tell you. I wanted to tell you. But, I don't know. It didn't exactly end the way I thought it would. Besides, it's like ... kind of taboo."

"Because of EJ?"

"Yeah. Elijah loves him like a brother, but ... well, this guy kind of sleeps around. A lot."

Renee wrinkled her nose. "He sounds like a player."

"And he gets into fights," Lily added. "One time, when he was in high school, we were all hanging out at the big library downtown. Waiting for Elijah to return some book. And Cade got into a fight with another dude over a girl. I was freaking out on the inside, but Elijah just shook his head and said, 'That's the shit I'm talking about' to me. 'That's why you're going to be smart, and not date somebody who talks with their fists, right?'"

"Whoa," Renee said. "That's heavy. That's, like, some serious foreshadowing or something."

"Yep. So ... yeah, Cade is off limits."

"I wouldn't say off limits," Renee said. She sipped her coffee slowly. "I would say he's a prime candidate for a secret hookup."

"Right, because I'm such a great liar. And I'm also really good at hiding things from my brothers."

"Is Cade the jealous type?"

"Oh, I don't know. Why?"

"If he's as much of a hothead as you say, you should try making him jealous," Renee said. "Trust me. If he gets all ragey about that, you'll know he feels something for you. Especially since he's such a ho-bag, too. He wouldn't care about just anyone he's been with. But if he gets jealous ..."

Lily laughed. "You can't be serious."

"I totally am! Don't you want to know? Listen, if I learned anything in Italy, it's how to figure out what a man really feels."

"Of course I want to know," Lily said. "But ..."

"Oh! You know what? You should go to Redd's Bar. Make sure to invite Cade. Get nice and tipsy, and get handsy with some random. Make sure Cade sees everything, though."

"I don't know, Renee. I don't like games—"

"It's not a game. It's a strategy. Call it my welcome back party! We can do it tomorrow night. Oh my God, squee! I'm so excited."

"You really will use any excuse to have a party, won't you?" Lily asked. She smiled as she finished the last of the drink.

Renee made a face and stood up. "Come on. We need to take you shopping for tomorrow. Let's go find something that will go with the Manolo Blahniks—only available in Milan, this pair—that I have in the car for you."

12

CADE

"Cade!"

He could hear his crew's voices, desperate and choking, even as the fire roared in his ear. He knew instinctively that when the ground had given way beneath him, his ankle had fractured. But the adrenaline kept him going, kept him moving—moving toward his crew.

They sound like wild animals.

Even through the flames, he could see it in their eyes. It was the same look he'd seen in so many animals trapped in gulches as they waited to die.

The year he'd spent fighting wildfires had infused in him all the fears of the animals he'd watched die.

But these aren't animals.

His crew's voices pounded in his head and mixed with the rush of blood.

You're such a fucking idiot. What did it matter that you had less than a second to decide? Boxed in on either side, it had been a judgment call. *A judgment call that fucked up your ankle.*

"Dominguez, can you hear me?" he yelled into the walkie-talkie. It crackled to life and brought the screams to an unbearable level. "Dominguez, do you copy? Barron? Fields?"

The smoke stung his eyes, and his ankle throbbed all the way to his temples. Cade dragged himself along the charred ground to a ledge that overlooked the gulch. He caught a glimpse of three yellow jackets and heard the wails as they punctuated the night sky. The sounds shot straight up to the heavens.

I'm going to die. The thought was sudden, but not unwelcome. It wasn't even surprising. *I'm going to die now.*

He saw Aunt Mary, first in the kitchen as she stooped over a homemade bearberry pie. Suddenly she was skeletal, bald and nearly translucent. He spooned chicken broth into her mouth and hated himself when he was disgusted by having to mop it off her chin when she coughed it up.

"Cade," a sweet voice purred. He rolled to his side and Aunt Mary was replaced with a Hapa girl whose name he couldn't remember.

"Do you still want to see my hula?" she asked with a laugh.

He couldn't remember her name, or how they'd met, but he suddenly remembered how she'd felt in his arms. How she'd carried the heat of Hawaii within her. Her face shifted and morphed into a blonde, a redhead, another blonde, the girl with the natural afro and the one with the neck tattoo of a rose.

My God, how many were there?

A girl he'd forgotten about, the one who'd used Altoids before she went down on him, was replaced by the first family he'd ever saved. The wife clung to him, held her baby tighter, and the husband let his happy tears fall freely without shame.

"Charles, you get out?" Barron's voice crackled through the walkie-talkie, and Cade realized his eyes had been closed.

He opened his mouth to reply, but the defeat in Barron's voice lulled him deeper into slumber.

"I think Charles's alright," he heard Barron say to the other two.

He no longer sounded scared. There weren't any more

screams. All the fear had been drained, and in the quiet they waited to die.

Cade forced his eyes open and used the last of his strength to hoist himself onto the ledge. In the gulch below, the smoke had cleared. He could see his crew, just one fire shelter between him and them. They huddled together like a family, like loved ones, as the flames lapped closer.

As if they sensed him, all three looked up and directly into his eyes. A flame the size of a small child hugged their feet. Barron let out a keen like nothing Cade had heard before. It shot directly into Cade's deepest, darkest space and wormed in deep. For good, for keeps.

———

" ... STABLE. HE'S STABLE." Cade's eyes opened to see paramedics hovered over him. He tried to speak, but tubes and masks kept him quiet. "We're taking you to the hospital. You'll be okay." He noticed she was pretty, the paramedic. Young and supple with a long black plait of hair.

———

THE NEXT TIME he opened his eyes, he heard the steady beat of a hospital monitor. Cade moaned and blinked away the grit in his eyes. His right forearm was covered in plaster. "What ... what's this ..." he asked as a husky nurse walked in.

"It's okay, baby," she said. "Won't be nothin' but a small scar. You'll still win all them beauty pageants."

———

"JESUS," Cade yelped as he jerked awake.

As he glanced around the room, he remembered where he was.

What the date was.

Montana was over.

He instinctively rubbed the small scar on his arm. He'd received the small burn from a branch that had fallen as he'd dragged himself toward the ledge that night. Big enough to be a reminder, but too small to suggest he'd tried to help.

Cade sighed and pushed himself up. It had been a record week, six straight days without a nightmare. But this one had been bad, almost like he was really there again.

"Fucking Hersh," he said as he cranked up the air conditioner. Nightmares were always bad the day before he saw the shrink.

He looked around his mostly empty apartment and nodded. Two boxes of clothes. A small set of dumbbells. A laptop. The mattress on the floor with no flat sheet.

I don't need anything else, he thought. *I don't deserve anything more.*

Cade stood up and turned on the shower. He kept the water cool and delighted in the goosebumps that broke out along his skin. The single towel that he had was still damp from the last shower, a tiny touch of punishment.

As he slipped on a pair of jeans, he thumbed through his phone for Elijah's number.

What's going on tonight? he asked.

Dude, wtf you been? Not answering your calls.

Cade checked his missed calls and saw four from Elijah.

Sorry man, fell asleep. So what's good?

Everyone's going to Redd's at 9.

Redd's? I haven't been there in years, he thought.

The bar where he'd cut his teeth on jack and cokes had the pull of nostalgia.

See you there, he shot back.

He scrolled through his missed texts and saw that Lily had also sent out what was clearly a mass message.

Welcome home party for my bestie at Redd's tonight at 9. Hope you can make it. XOXO.

It might be a mass text, but it's still an invitation, he thought. *Besides, it would be good to see Lily. And in a group, there wouldn't be any temptation.*

He knew the place would be packed before he even walked in the door. The parking lot overflowed, and trucks lined the street. Cade parked at the end of the block, and walked briskly toward the neon lights.

Redd's had been a staple well before the hipsters had migrated south. It was one of Salem's last holdouts.

Country music assaulted his ears as soon as he stepped through the heavy doors. Redd's had changed since he'd last been there. More of a nightclub than a bar, there were bouncers in matching black shirts that stood guard at the little booth.

The hell, they charge a cover now? He couldn't help but be impressed by how jacked the bouncers were as they patted him down.

"You a firefighter?" the girl taking cover charges asked.

"Yeah. How'd..."

"I can tell," she said. "You get a discount, half price entry."

"Cool." As Cade made his way through the crowd, he heard Elijah before he saw him, even through the din of the excitement.

"Cade, you bastard!" Elijah bellowed when he saw him. Cade sucked in his breath at the word, but it was obvious Elijah was already tipsy.

"Grab a beer," Elijah said, and nodded at the pitcher in the middle of the table.

Cade recognized some of the guys from the firehouse, and they gave nods to one another. Nobody except Elijah bothered to be heard above the music.

"These guys you haven't met before!" Elijah yelled. He screamed their names to Cade, but he couldn't make them out.

"Why's it so slammed in here tonight?" Cade asked as the band mercifully quieted down for their break.

He could barely make out some 1990s Garth Brooks as it came onto the sound system.

Elijah raised a brow.

"It's always packed," he said. "This is standard. Being that it's the only real club Salem has."

"Damn. Times change," Cade said as he took a swallow of the beer.

"Hey, guys." Cade smiled before he even turned around at the sound of Lily's voice. Beside her was a towering, willowy blonde. "This is Renee."

"Hot damn, Lily, who? You been holding out on me," Elijah said from across the table.

Lily rolled her eyes. "Elijah, how drunk are you? This is *Renee.* You only met her a million times when we were kids."

"Renee-Renee? My bad. You grew up good, beanpole."

"Thanks," Renee said with a laugh. She eyed Cade with interest.

He gave the blonde his usual half-smile and waited for the old manwhore inside to raise *his* head with interest—but nothing happened. Instead, his eyes traveled back to Lily.

Her gold sequined dress showed off her long legs. Cleavage nearly spilled out of the top, and her toned arm was slipped easily through her friend's.

"Hey, I think I see someone I want to say hello to," Lily said. "Come on, Renee. We'll be back," she told the table.

Cade watched her go and hoped that her skirt would hitch up just a little higher. Elijah's elbow dug into him.

"Feeling the blonde, huh? Old Morningside Manwhore is back at it!"

Cade sipped his beer noncommittally. The DJ turned the lights down low as a Sam Hunt song came on. He could hear Elijah across the table talking shit with the other firefighters.

A waitress came by and Elijah demanded all the shots of

whiskey on her tray. He couldn't tear his eyes away from the dance floor even as the amber liquid burned down his throat. All he hoped for was a glimpse of gold in the darkness.

"You want to dance?" a soft voice whispered in his ear. Cade smiled as he turned to Lily.

"Renee," he said, surprised. She smiled at him.

"Come on," she said. "I love this song."

"Go, go, M and M!" Elijah crowed, his not-so-subtle Morningside Manwhore nickname for Cade.

On the dance floor, he caught a flash of sequins as Renee snaked her arms around him. Lily was making her way through the dance floor, leading a guy he'd never seen before by the hand.

Cade felt jealousy grip him close even as Renee pressed her body against his. Lily slipped her arms around the guy's neck as his hands dipped dangerously low to Lily's hips.

"Dance with me," Renee urged in his ear. He held her closer, but his mind was ten feet away with Lily.

He watched for two minutes as Lily let the guy caress her lower back. She laughed as he said something in her ear. The jealousy was so much, Cade couldn't take it. Before the song was over, he dropped his hands and turned to leave.

"Hey!" Renee said in mild protest.

Before Cade turned away, he saw the guy Lily danced with grab her ass. Lily tried to push him away, but he had too tight of a grip on her. She squirmed and tried to get free, but the guy wouldn't budge.

Cade thundered through the crowd, grasped Lily by the waist, and pulled her free. "Cade—"

He didn't let her finish. Cade punched the groper in the face, satisfied when he felt the bone splinter beneath his fist.

"Fight!" someone yelled gleefully from beside Cade.

"The fuck, man?" the guy asked.

Blood poured down his face. He was disoriented, but tried to fight back. That ignited a rage in Cade. He felt the animal inside him take over as he crushed the guy's nose. Splayed across the floor, Cade kicked him in the ribs.

"Oh my God, stop!" Lily screamed.

"You're out of here." One of the bouncers jerked Cade's arm and dragged him toward the exit. He grunted as the bouncer tossed him onto the ground. "Cool off out here, and don't come back."

"Cade! Cade!" Lily burst through the door and leaned down.

"I'm fine," he said as he staggered to his feet and dusted himself off. His hands were shaking.

"What the hell?"

"I'm sorry. But like hell was I letting him hurt you like that."

"It wasn't that big of a deal."

"Not a big deal? When some guy that I don't know puts his hands on *my* woman—"

"Your woman?"

"You know what I mean," he said, flustered. The alcohol swam in his head.

"No, I don't think I do."

"Goddamnit, Lily. I can't just watch someone else take what I want so badly—"

"So don't. Take it for yourself. If you're brave enough."

He scanned her face for a clue.

Was she serious? His gaze traveled to her lips. *What the hell...*

Cade pulled her close and brought her lips to his. Lily melted against him, held him close. As he walked her backward and pressed her against her little Mercedes, he realized there was no denying it.

Surely, at least for tonight, this was meant to be.

13

CADE

"Charles, come on in here a minute."

Elijah raised his eyebrows at Cade as the captain walked by. The guys had just started to dig into their breakfast of French challah bread with marionberry jam. The newest recruit got his due ribbing the first time he'd whipped up such a show, but after the crew had tasted what he could do they looked forward to his kitchen days.

"Yes, Captain?" Cade asked. Crane sat down at his desk and nodded at Cade to shut the door.

"How are the sessions going?" Crane asked as soon as Cade sat down.

"With Dr. Hersh, you mean? They're going," Cade said with a shrug.

"Thought you had some kind of breakthrough or something," Crane said as he started to methodically peel an orange that he pulled from a drawer.

"Is that ... is that what he told you?" Cade could have kicked himself.

Of course the captain is getting the reports. Why did I have to go and get all emotional talking about what happened in Montana?

"Not in so many words. Actually, his were quite lengthier, but that's what I gathered."

The captain bit into one of the sections and didn't flinch when the sticky juice splattered across the desk.

Cade felt his neck grow hot, but he refused to act embarrassed. He glanced around the office and searched for what would pass as nonchalant.

"I was glad to hear it," Crane said.

"You were?"

"Of course. What do you think I sent you to that doctor for, so you could talk about how your mama didn't love you enough or whatever?"

Cade looked to the floor.

He couldn't know. Could he? Well, maybe, but even if the whole foster care thing was mentioned in my files, I doubt he remembers that.

"Oh, shit. I'm sorry, son. You were—you're the one who was in the system, weren't you?" The captain put down the orange and sat up straight. "I didn't mean nothing by that."

"It's okay," Cade said.

"Well, now that I went and put my foot in my mouth ... you want to talk about it?"

"About what?" *About my mom?*

"How things are going with that doctor. I mean honestly, not just polite conversation."

"Captain, with all due respect—"

"Let me put it this way. It's going to go a lot better for your case and actually getting on crew if you do."

"I thought I just had to see the doctor for that," Cade said carefully.

How many strings are attached to this gig?

"Seeing the doctor is part of it, sure," the captain said. "But I make the final call. If I don't think you're ready and capable of being on crew, you won't be no matter how many of those headshrinking sessions you attend."

Cade felt his heart sink.

So that was it. Dr. Hersh was just one of however many contingencies. And here I am resisting every goddamned session I've been to.

"Alright," Cade said with a low voice. "We can talk."

"Maybe this'll help," Crane said. He reached back into the drawer and pulled out a bottle of Buffalo Trace. "You drink?"

"I, uh—sometimes."

"Good answer," Crane said. "I'm officially off shift in one minute. And I know you just came for the waffles or whatever."

He poured two fingers of the whiskey into glass tumblers he had wrapped in an old purple Crown Royal bag. Crane pushed one of the glasses toward Cade. "Cheers to another goddamned week done," he said.

Cade clinked glasses with the older man, uncertain of what kind of game this was.

If it's a game at all.

"Cheers," Cade said. The burn of the whiskey on his lips raced down his throat and settled comfortably in his stomach.

"So. Those fires."

"In Montana?" Cade took another sip.

He hadn't had a chance to get any of the French toast in his stomach and he hadn't had a bite to eat since the bar food at Redd's last night.

Before the thing with Lily. Before I left her mad as hell in the car.

Well, at least it meant the whiskey would work fast.

"Where the hell else?" Crane asked.

"Well ... I don't know how much you know." *Probably more than you let on.* "But, you know, I fucked up. Three of my men died."

"It was your fault?"

Cade's face burned.

"I don't know," he said. That was a first. Usually, in his head, it was always his fault.

"You don't know," Crane repeated.

"I mean, two of them were a few yards away. When we rappelled out of that helicopter... I'm not sure any of us knew what we were descending into. I'd never seen anything like it, that's for sure. The guy with me, Barron—I don't know what happened."

"He left?"

"Yeah—"

"Of his own accord."

"I mean, I didn't make him. I didn't even realize he was gone until—" Cade brought the glass to his mouth, anything to shut himself up.

"So what makes that your fault?"

"I was boxed in," Cade said. He shook his head. "Looking for Barron, and I don't know. I fucked up, messed up my ankle, and then it all went to hell." *Literally.* "I ... I couldn't get to them after that."

"So, you're telling me, those three men died because one wandered off and you made a snap judgment to get to them that happened to render you immobile?"

Cade looked at the captain. He'd never really put it in those words before. "I guess?"

"Son, you got some kind of martyr issues or something? 'Cause if you do, then you damn sure picked the right line of work."

Cade gave a short chuckle. It was odd, to laugh when he talked about Montana. Actually, it was the first time he had.

"Death wish, maybe," he said. The captain nodded, unaware of just how honest that admission was.

"We all got that," the captain said.

He took a pull of the whiskey, and Cade noticed the yellow gold wedding band.

"You married?" he asked, the liquid courage strong.

The captain raised his brow at the question. "Widowed, actually."

"Oh, shit. I'm sorry, Captain—"

The captain shook his head.

"You can call me Eldon," he said. "But just in here. And don't worry about it. It was... well, it was a long time ago."

Cade nodded.

"You gonna ask how long?"

"I mean, not out loud—"

The captain laughed.

"Almost forty years," he said with a nod.

"Wow."

"Told you it was a long time."

"And you still wear the ring."

"Still wear the ring," the captain agreed. "To be honest, at first it was a big help. You know, feeling like she was still there. Pretending I was going home to her."

"What was her name?"

"Lillian."

"That's... that's a pretty name," Cade said.

"Yes, it is," the captain agreed.

"Do you... do you mind if I ask how she..."

"I wouldn't have brought it up if I minded," the captain said. "We'd only been married one year. Everyone thought we were crazy. She was ten years older than me—that was real scandalous back then. But I just knew. Just bought a house down in Central Point, little white three-bedroom on an acre of land. Heard from the folks who sold it to us that it was an old officer's place from the camp they used to have down there in the forties. All I know is it didn't have any kind of heat, and we used nothing but blankets, space heaters, and a fireplace that first winter."

"That sounds terrible," Cade said.

"It was great," the captain said with a shrug. "Lillian planted rows and rows of vegetables our first summer. Corn, cucumbers, tomatoes—hid our own little stash of reefer plants in those tomatoes. You know how they look kind of the same.

That was before it was legal," he said with a pointed look at Cade. "So don't go telling nobody."

"I won't," Cade said with a grin.

"Then, going into that next winter … we thought she just had the flu. But it kept on getting worse. She was stubborn though, kept saying it was just the change in weather. When she collapsed in the parking lot of King's Table, I drove her straight to the hospital. She woke up on the way, howling and protesting the second she knew where we were going."

"And?" Cade asked as he leaned forward.

"Liver cancer. Doctors gave her three months to live, and she stuck to that guess on the dot. Never even drank an ounce in her life."

"Then how did she—"

"Hepatitis C. Doctors said she must have had it since she was damn near a newborn. Lillian was… well, she was a baby at the Majdanek concentration camp in Poland. Doctors think the needle they used to tattoo her arm was dirty. 'Course it was," he said with a sniff.

"I'm… I'm so sorry," Cade said, though he knew it was inadequate.

"Not your fault," Eldon said. "I'm just … you know, I think I was lucky. We were both lucky."

"How could … why would you say that?" Cade asked.

The captain looked at him curiously.

"Lillian would have been killed had she been in that camp even a day longer," he said. "They'd already killed her mother, father, her whole family. We got a year together. And Lillian, she got thirty-two years of life."

"And you never… dated anyone after, or…"

"That one year was enough for me," Eldon said. "Sure, I would have wanted more. Would have given anything for more. But that one year? I'll always be grateful for what we had."

"I don't know what to say," Cade said honestly.

"Oh, hell. I told you my sob story. It's your turn to say something real."

"I wish it were me."

"What?"

"I wish it had been me to die out there. And not because I'm some kind of martyr. That's the worst part," Cade said. "I mean, if I'm honest, yeah, I think those guys deserved to live more than me. But I... I didn't think I had anything to live for."

"That's bullshit, son."

"You don't know me," Cade said quietly.

"Cade, the past? It doesn't matter," Eldon said. "Let me tell you, if I had a chance to talk to my wife again? Touch her? I'd—"

"I have to go," Cade said. He slid the empty glass back across the table. "I'm sorry."

"Cade—"

Cade raised his hand behind him and blinked back the tears.

"Cade, just answer me this. Because you're not excused yet."

"What?" Cade asked, his back still to the captain.

"You said you didn't think you had anything to live for. And now?"

"What?"

"You used past tense. Do you think you have something to live for now?"

An image of Lily flashed in his mind.

"I don't know," he said. "Maybe."

"Well. A maybe's better than nothing."

Cade walked out into the hall and could hear the guys working on the truck. He made a beeline for the back door.

Maybe the captain's right, he thought. *A maybe is worth something. Maybe I should explore that instead of just screwing things up like I always do.*

He'd always been good at making things go away. It was easy to walk away, to run away, run straight into the flames.

And what good has that done you?

Maybe the captain and Dr. Hersh were right. Maybe he wasn't responsible for what had happened in Montana. Would it have happened the same way, if it had been someone else there and not him?

Probably. Barron would probably have still gone off protocol.

There was a fifty-fifty chance that when he was boxed in he would have made the wrong choice.

Pure luck. And nobody could have gotten through those flames. Messed-up leg or not, nobody could have.

And if they had? They would have just burned up with them. He knew that, he'd always known that, in the darkest part of his heart.

You got some kind of martyr issues? He smiled at the captain's question. *Maybe I did. But not anymore.*

14

LILY

*L*ily pulled up to the new, white Fiat Spider parked in Renee's parents' driveway. She tried not to think about how raggedy her own "vintage" ride looked in comparison, but couldn't help it. As Lily peeked into the Fiat and admired the camel-colored interior, she heard the front door open.

"Nice, right?" Renee asked with a smile.

Her dark blonde hair was finger-raked into a messy top knot that looked effortlessly chic. With just a swipe of red lipstick, perfectly shaped brows, and mascara, everything about her best friend looked flawless—and like she hadn't even tried.

"Yeah, it's great," Lily said. She plastered on a smile and tried to swallow her envy whole.

"Come on in. My parents are in Bend for the weekend, so we have the house to ourselves."

"How is it? Living back with them?" Lily asked as she loped up the familiar front steps.

"Ugh, it's alright. I mean, I can't complain. Free rent and all. But I can't wait to get back to Italy. I swear, if I could, I'd just have my own little place here for homecomings. Like you! I'm super jealous that you have your own cute little space."

Renee handed her a glass of wine and settled onto the plush couch in the sitting room.

Lily sat carefully, acutely aware of how much damage could be done with a glass of red wine on a white suede couch.

"My place is okay," she said with a shrug. "It's close to work and I can afford it."

Renee nodded and pulled her bare knees up to her chest. In her green and yellow U of O raglan baseball shirt and denim cutoffs, she still looked like the quintessential college student.

"Trust me, you're lucky. My mom's always on my case. 'When are you going to get a job? When are you going to stop running all over Europe?' It's like, relax! I'm looking for a job. It's not like Salem is exactly overflowing with fashion design gigs."

"Salem?" Lily asked. "I thought you were going back to Italy."

Renee's face clouded over.

"I was," she said. "Until my parents decided they weren't going to pay for it anymore. Like, Italy is freaking expensive, you know? I don't know how they thought I was going to pay for rent there on my own."

"So ... fashion design, huh?" Lily asked.

She was surprised Renee was still caught up in that idea. When they'd been teenagers, it had been fun to fantasize. Back then, Lily thought she was going to be some famous, world-class chemist—until she realized how tough it was to make a living with it and not teach.

The idea of standing in front of a room, all those eyes on her as she had the duty to impart knowledge? Just thinking about it made her clam up.

"You know that's what I've always wanted to do," Renee said pointedly.

"Yeah, I know, but ... well, how are you going to make that happen here?"

"My point exactly," Renee said. She sighed. "I don't know. I have a few leads, a couple of wedding dress designers in town who work out of their home shops. I mean, it doesn't pay much —actually, one of them doesn't pay at all. But they do custom, couture, good work. They depend mostly on weddings for the big checks. And if I'm just their assistant or apprentice or whatever? I'm basically getting less than minimum wage."

"Sucks," Lily said. She wanted to ask Renee why she didn't try New York, Los Angeles, or even Portland, but she knew better than to try and help problem solve when Renee wallowed in her own misery.

"I don't know," Renee said with a sigh. "Maybe I should just go for a senior level fashion merchandising position."

"That sounds ... impressive," Lily said.

"Trust me, it sounds a lot more impressive than it is. They have those jobs at pretty much any decent retailer. Even J. Crew has them."

"Oh, well that sounds good. I mean, at least there are some positions available."

"God, Lily," Renee said as she groaned. "I don't want to have come back from Italy and have to tell people I work at like, Cole Haan or something."

"You worked at Victoria's Secret in college," Lily reminded her.

"Yeah, but that was college! That was totally fine. But now? It's like I'm going backward."

Renee stared into her glass and ran one long finger along the rim. For a moment, she looked the same way she had in middle school when she found out she hadn't made it to the state finals for the Junior Miss pageant.

"Hey," Lily said. She reached over and touched Renee's forearm. The Italian bronze had started to fade. "It'll be okay."

"That's easy for you to say. You have your dream job. You have your own place. And what do I have?"

"You have some pretty kickass Instagram stories," Lily said with a smile.

Renee grinned. "I guess I do."

"And you're crazy if you think I have my dream job. I mean, yeah, I work in a bakery. And my boss is pretty cool. But do you really think I went to culinary school to work the front counter at a bakery in Salem? Honestly, anyone could do that."

"You're just trying to make me feel better," Renee said with a sheepish smile.

"I'm not! Seriously, there were zero requirements when I saw Jean-Michel's ad. Yeah, he wanted someone he could teach, for sure. And it helped that I had experience."

"Ugh, false modesty is so not attractive," Renee said as she finished her wine.

"Fine, you want to know something?" Lily asked.

"Always." Renee leaned toward her.

"The girl that I replaced at the bakery? She left because she started school. Her freshman year at Linfield, to be exact."

"Oh my God, no. You took the place of a high schooler?"

"Not my proudest moment," Lily said with a shake of her head. "But if it makes any difference, for the first two months Jean-Michel raved about how fantastic I was. Except for one thing."

"And what was that?"

"Apparently I didn't have the same level of customer service as the kid."

"Well. I could have told him that," Renee said.

"Don't be a bitch!" Lily said with a laugh.

"I'm not, I just know you! I mean, I don't think working with people has ever particularly been your strong suit."

"Well, fortunately even though Jean-Michel said that, he's still happy with me. He's still super French even though he's been in this country for fifteen years. He thinks Americans are too fake happy. So apparently my snobbishness, as he calls it, is an asset in his shop."

"Yeah, I can see that. You'd do well in Paris," Renee said. "Maybe that's where you should be. Italy, though, you have to be really aggressive as a woman."

"What do you mean?"

"Like, when you first get there? As an American, I mean? It's a serious ego boost. The guys are *all* over you. It takes you awhile to realize it's not you. They're just like that with any woman who's even remotely attractive."

Lily nodded. Honestly, it did sound nice. She'd never have to wonder if someone was into her.

"So, no game playing?" she asked. "It's just all out in the open?"

"Oh, believe me, there are games," Renee said with a laugh. "It's just that the rules are totally different than over here."

"Ugh, is it different anywhere?"

"Probably not," Renee said. "But you know what helps? Ice cream."

"From BJ's?"

"Obviously. Hold up, I'll go get it."

Lily listened to the slap of her friend's feet on the hardwood.

Funny, how some things feel the same forever.

Sitting here in the room where she'd spent so many afternoons as a teenager, the sounds of spoons clanging in the kitchen, for a moment everything felt simpler.

"Ta-da!" Renee said in the doorway. She held up two spoons and a quart of ice cream. "Jamaican fudge."

"The one with all the rum? Thank God, I could use it."

Renee jumped on the couch, grabbed the purple furry blanket off the back, and used it to cradle the ice cream between them.

"Alright, I've watered you. I'm feeding you. Now spill," Renee said.

"Spill what?"

Renee elbowed her hard in the ribs.

"You know. Cade. What happened at Redd's? After that shitshow on the dance floor when he knocked down that creep, you disappeared! I mean, what the hell, was he raised in a barn?"

Lily shook her head vehemently. "No, it—he had a rough childhood."

"We all did," Renee replied.

Lily gave her a look. "We're sitting in your parents' half a million dollar house. I think your childhood was fine."

"Point taken."

"But Cade, he was ... he was a foster care kid."

"No shit."

"Yeah, he hung around Elijah a lot, and I think ... you know, I think *my* dad was the closest thing he ever had to a father."

"That sucks," Renee said. "But, I mean, for you—I just hope you're not trying to save him or something. You know that never works out."

"I'm not," Lily said. "It was never like that."

"So, do you think that's partly why he's such a ladies' man?" Renee poked around in the ice cream for the biggest ribbon of fudge.

"What do you mean?"

"You know. Like, trying to make up for the love he never had by spreading it around everywhere he can."

Lily wrinkled her nose. "I never thought about it. But if men sleeping around is caused by them not being loved as children, it seems like there's a hell of a lot of unloved little boys out there."

"True," Renee said. "But still, I don't think you can be a foster kid and not be fucked up on some level. That's got to mess with you, right? I mean, how many foster houses was he in?"

"God, I don't even know," Lily said. "I mean, I was younger

and it's not like he or Elijah ever talked about that kind of stuff to me or in front of me. But I think it was a lot. I remember he seemed to always be living somewhere new when we were growing up."

"You're in a tough spot, Lil," Renee said. "I just ... you know, I hope you're taking care of yourself. Protecting yourself."

"I knew he was ... a player, or whatever," Lily said. "But I thought he and I had a real connection. You know? The potential for something real."

"Yeah, but everyone thinks that. We let our heart get in the way and then we get stupid," Renee said. "Trust me."

"What makes you such an expert all of a sudden?"

Renee sighed. "I'm not just not going back to Italy because of the money. That's part of it, but I could always make it work. It's—well, Marco dumped me."

"What? Renee, I'm so sorry. How—"

"Over texts, even."

"What?"

"He said he's too young to be tied down, and he loved the time we had together, but now it's time for us to both move on to whatever comes next. Fucking coward. I know he had this planned, but he was too much of a freaking baby to say it to my face when I was there. You know he took me to the airport? Gave me this long, drawn-out kiss and made a big show of it."

"Men can be such jerks," Lily said.

"Yeah, but not all of them. I'm still hopeful about that. That's why you should talk to Cade before you call it quits. I mean, it seems like you're really into this guy."

Lily nodded slowly. "You're right. I am really into him. And this has gone on long enough. I mean, talking to him, what's the worst that could happen?"

15

CADE

"Thirty feet, thirty feet!" Cade yelled to the crew. The two newer recruits sweated profusely, eager to show off their strength and dedication. "Rodriguez, does that look thirty feet from the shed?"

The young man stood up and wiped his brow as he tried to calculate the firebreak from the shed.

"I guess?" he called.

"Twenty, at best," Cade said. "Alright, let's break. Grab some water and meet me back here."

He was grateful to the captain for letting him lead and instruct firebreak training, but he was rusty. It had been a long time since he'd tried to herd together a crew that he didn't know.

It didn't help that this particular crew didn't know who the hell he was.

Hell, some of them probably think I'm that guy who's on payroll and doesn't do jack shit but talk to some shrink about my "feelings."

As the men gathered around him, Nalgene bottles in hand, he gestured for them to stoop down.

"Next drill, this is going to be a slope over twenty percent," he said. "So what does that mean?"

They looked at each other, unsure.

"Means the defensible closed-in space is extended to one hundred feet," Elijah said as he sauntered up to the group.

"What he said," Rodriguez piped up.

Cade sighed. "Yeah. Thanks for that, Elijah."

"Unless, you know, we're talking about California chaparral," Elijah added as he showed off. "And the slope is still over twenty percent. Then it's two hundred feet."

"Yeah, yeah, we got it," Cade said. "Are you in this training session?"

"Nope, don't need to be."

"Alright guys, that's it for today. Thanks, good work."

They dispersed quietly and Elijah clapped Cade on the back.

"Captain got you working hard, huh?" he asked.

"I asked for it."

"What do you mean?"

"I asked him if I could be involved. Somehow, anyhow, and this is what I got."

"Damn, dude. That's rough. Most of us can't wait to get out of training the fire virgins."

"Yeah, well, I didn't know this is what he'd give me. When Crane told me, it was all I could do to not roll my eyes. But now that I'm here... I don't know, man. I'm actually enjoying it."

"For real?"

"Yeah. Being with the new guys—or crew, I guess I should say. Shit, Horst hates it when I call her a guy. But you know, it's better than nothing. It's better than being stuck in an office with that doctor while he tries to piece together what the hell's wrong with me."

"So the new recruits are alright?" Elijah asked. "If I'm honest, I haven't gotten to know them."

"They're actually pretty awesome," Cade said. "Seeing that excitement again? How hard they work? I miss that. I remember that."

"Hey, you saying we're old? Jaded?"

"You, maybe. I didn't say we," Cade said with a wink. "But nah, honestly I'm surprised by how much I like teaching them."

"Whatever you say, Professor Charles. My shift's up in an hour, wanna go for a beer then?"

Cade shrugged. "Maybe. Two of the recruits are up then too, and I told them I'd go over—"

"Shit, dude, you're not their babysitter."

Cade laughed. "I know that. But there's something about their dedication that's addictive, you know? It's renewed my own interest in the whole game. Like new growth after a fire's made a landscape barren."

"Whoa. That's like, some Robert Frost shit right there."

The two of them walked toward the firehouse from the practice area. Cade watched as the four new recruits huddled together and stared at Rodriguez's phone.

They burst out laughing en masse, and even from a distance Cade could hear the music from a popular meme featuring a firehouse Dalmatian that had made recent rounds.

"Were we ever that green?" he asked Elijah.

"I dunno, man. They're pretty helpless, though. I guess that innocence is kind of sweet. Hey, you remember that first month we were here? And my dad ordered—"

"—the wrong gear for the event at the fair?" Cade finished with a laugh. "Yeah, I remember."

Elijah shook his head. "His first time ordering online instead of calling it in, and what does he do? Somehow orders his whole crew bright pink everything. Shit, I can still remember the looks we got at that event."

"The girls loved it, though," Cade reminded him. "Remember they kept telling us how 'cute' we looked? And you stole that rodeo saying—"

"Real men are tough enough to wear pink? Fuck yeah, I stole it," Elijah said. "Think I told some girl I was trying to hook up with that we were doing it as part of breast cancer awareness, too. I thought for sure that was going to work, until she told me both she *and* her mom had breast cancer."

"Oh, shit," Cade said. "I didn't know that. But wouldn't that work in your favor? I mean, if she thought you were supporting breast cancer—"

"I don't know, dude. I felt kind of bad about lying then. And then I started to think, well, what if she doesn't have any tits, you know?"

Cade burst out laughing. "I mean ... couldn't you tell?"

"Hell, by then I didn't want to just blatantly stare at her chest. I mean, I think she had them? But what if they were fake?"

"That's never stopped you before."

"True. But what can I say? I'm a purist. I like 'em natural."

"Hey! There you guys are."

Cade looked up and saw Lily as she approached from the firehouse. In her work clothes, black slacks and a white blouse, she was covered in flour dust.

"The hell happened to you?" Elijah asked. "You know you're supposed to get the cake mix inside the bowl, right?"

"Ha ha," Lily said with an eye roll.

Cade bit his lip. *How is it possible that even covered in flour, she still looks this sexy?*

"I came by to see if you guys are interested in getting coffee."

"I'm still on shift another hour," Elijah said. He punched Cade lightly on the shoulder. "But Cade is free. He's been relieved from babysitting duties."

"Babysitting?" Lily asked, confused.

"Nothing," Cade said as he glared at Elijah.

Lily made a face. "Actually, I'm—"

"Oh, come on, Lil," Elijah said. "Why you gotta always be so unfriendly? You really miss hanging out with your big brother that much? Go on, consider Cade my stand-in."

Cade watched as Lily's face grew even more sour, and tried not to laugh.

"Your brother's right, I'm not that bad," he said.

"Shit, I gotta go," Elijah said. "I forgot, Crane wants to meet with me about something, and if I'm even a minute late he'll tar and feather my ass." Elijah ran toward the firehouse and left Cade with Lily.

"How about a grown-up drink instead?" Cade asked. "I could use something a little harder than coffee."

Lily scowled, but grabbed his arm and pulled him around the side of the building to the parking lot.

"Have you literally forgotten what happened a couple days ago?" she asked, teeth clenched. "Or is it that you think I've forgotten how you shut me down after we banged?"

"Jesus, Lily, calm down," he said. "You know your brother could walk around the corner any second? And no, I haven't forgotten. Believe me. And I'm sorry that I froze you out. Okay?"

She probed his eyes.

"It isn't enough to just be sorry," she said. "It's not like this is a one-time screwup on your part. Our part."

"I'm really sorry. I just ... you know that we can't be a thing. You know that."

Lily sighed.

"And yet, here you are, inviting me out for 'something harder than coffee.' What the hell kind of message are you trying to send? You know, I didn't come here to ask *you* out. I came to hang out with Elijah because he's freaking never home anymore with these shifts he's been working. So if you think this is some kind of ploy I've cooked up just to see you, you've got a serious ego—"

"Hey! Calm down." Cade ran his hand through his hair and let out a frustrated growl.

"I'm sorry to make things so impossible for you," Lily said. "It must be really hard."

She turned to walk away, and he saw the smear of a flour handprint on her ass where she must have wiped away the dust at the bakery.

Cade couldn't help himself. He grabbed her by the waist and whirled her around. With her pressed against his chest, he leaned down.

"You don't have the slightest idea, Lily. You don't know how much I crave you. It—fuck, it keeps me awake at night. You're in the back of my mind all the goddamned time. If I could have you without Elijah freaking out, I'd do it in a heartbeat."

He watched Lily's gaze travel to his mouth. It was clear what she wanted. What he wanted. Lily tilted her head up, an invitation he couldn't resist.

Cade lowered his lips to hers, and the taste was familiar, intoxicating. He couldn't get enough of her.

You can't do this. You know one taste won't be enough. But her mouth was sweet as honey...

"Hey. Hey! What the fuck do you think you're doing?"

Cade pulled away from Lily at the sound of Aiden's voice in the distance. In sync, he turned with Lily toward the parking lot as Aiden slammed the door of his truck shut. He stormed toward them as his gear bag trailed on the pavement behind him.

"Aiden, I can—"

"Shut the fuck up," Aiden growled as he approached.

"Aiden—" Lily started.

"Lily, I swear to God," Aiden said. His voice shook, the rage below barely contained. "You do not want to test me right now."

"Aiden, it was nothing—" Cade broke in.

But before he could continue, come up with some kind of excuse, pain raced through his jaw. It was so acute, so sudden, that it didn't register as real pain but instead just paralyzing shock.

He realized Aiden had punched him, and somehow the asphalt clawed into his cheek.

"Aiden!" Lily screamed, somewhere far away.

He felt fists as they battered his chest, and one solid punch into his throat that stole the breath from him. Cade tried to look up, tried to explain to Aiden, to say he was sorry, but the words wouldn't come out.

"Aiden, stop!" he heard Lily scream.

Overhead, she eclipsed the sun that blinded him. He watched as she inserted herself between him and Aiden.

Lily, move, he wanted to say, but all he could do was try and curl into the fetal position. There was no way he'd hit Aiden back.

You deserve this. Just stay down and take it.

"Stop it!" she yelled. He could hear the tears in her voice.

"Fine," Aiden said finally. Cade could feel the warm trickle of blood from his nose and mouth. "I'll stop. For now. But you're coming with me, Lily."

Cade squinted upward as Aiden glared down at him.

"And you," Aiden said to Cade as he leaned down. "You just wait until Elijah hears about this."

"Aiden—" Cade choked out, but his voice was cracked.

Aiden stormed off with Lily gripped by the arm.

You're a fucking idiot for kissing her. And in such a public space —at the fucking firehouse.

Cade craned his neck and tried to see the entrance to the firehouse. But all he could make out were the new recruits, silent and shocked as Aiden dragged Lily toward the firehouse. Their mouths were open and they took a step back as Aiden charged forward.

"Elijah!" he could hear Aiden yell. "Where the hell are you?"

16

LILY

*C*ade heard a flurry of knocks at his door and knew it was Lily. He picked up the ice pack he'd held to his face all morning and pressed it to his jaw.

"Are your brothers around?" he asked when he opened the door.

Lily's eyes grew wide.

"Oh my God," she said. "It's bad."

"Thanks."

Cade knew he looked pretty rough, but seeing Lily made him feel instantly better. It didn't hurt that she was also in a skintight racerback tank, a thin scarf, and jeans that were so worn through they were about to fall apart.

"I, um, I came to see how you were doing."

"Well, you can see," he said, and held out one arm to showcase his battered body.

"Can I come in?"

He sighed. "Lily, I don't think that's a good idea. Especially after yesterday."

"I brought Napoleons with Chantilly cream," she said, and held up a box. "And Tylenol."

Cade groaned. "Fine, but just for a minute."

He saw the look of surprise on her face as she surveyed his apartment.

"Sorry for how the place looks," he said. "The interior designer doesn't come until tomorrow."

"It's fine," she said quickly, and put the pastry box down on the unopened box of his summer clothes he hadn't unpacked yet.

"Lily," he said as peeked into the box of pastries. "I don't think it's a good idea for you to be here."

"Why? Do you think your couch is going to tattle on me? Oh, wait, you have exactly zero furniture."

She leaned against the wall, cutely awkward as she tried to figure out what to do with her hands.

"I have a bed."

Lily rolled her eyes. "Why am I not surprised? Anyway, I came to tell you that I managed to calm Aiden down. He even promised not to tell Elijah. Of course, you'd know that if you hadn't scampered away like some dog with its tail between its legs after he'd whaled on you."

"Yeah, like you wouldn't have booked it to your car if you just got your ass beat."

"You're welcome," she said, and rolled her eyes.

"You're right, thank you. But how?"

"Let's just say that everything I had on him, for our whole lives to this point, has been called up. I blew all my secrets on this one. And you're damn lucky that Elijah was in the office with Crane and didn't hear Aiden bellowing for him."

"Thank you," Cade said quietly. "You didn't have to do that. But I'm thankful you did."

"I did it for both of us. Aiden did say one thing that resonated with me, though."

"What's that?"

"He asked me if you were worth it."

Cade rubbed the back of his neck and looked away. "Yeah?"

"And I said that you were."

Cade looked at Lily and searched her eyes for the truth. "You did?"

"Well ... yeah. There's something that keeps bringing us together, like objects in a magnetic field or something."

"Lily—"

She silenced him by taking a step closer. Lily was so close he could feel her sweet breath as it washed across his skin.

"Don't you want to know why? Don't you want to see if this works? We already know that we're explosive together in bed ... or maybe saying my car would be more correct," she said with a smile. "Don't tell me that was just me?"

Cade looked down at her.

God, what I'd give to have her. But if it goes bad, though...

"At least we'll know," Lily said, as if she could read his mind. "At least I won't be asking what if, what if, what if... we'll know if this is—"

Cade reached up and cupped her face in his hand. Neither of them flinched as he dropped the ice pack to the ground. As he lowered his mouth to hers, he watched her eyes flutter shut.

She welcomed his tongue into her mouth and let out a moan as he squeezed her waist.

Cade lifted her up with ease. He heard her shoes drop to the hardwood floors while she clenched her legs around him.

"Show me this bed," she whispered to him between kisses.

He started to walk with her wrapped around his waist toward the bedroom. Her smell was pure addiction, the scent of berries that poured from her hair unlike anything he'd ever known.

"Hold up," he said.

"Cade, seriously—"

"Here," he said, and bent down as she still clung tightly to him. "Take the pastries."

She grabbed the box he handed her with one hand and held tight to his neck with the other. "Why?"

"You said there was whipped cream, right?"

She threw her head back and laughed as he walked them to the bedroom, but she held tight to the box. Cade tossed her onto the thick mattress on the floor. The box spilled open while she landed and she bit her lip.

"This is a mattress, not a bed," she admonished. He reached down, unbuttoned her jeans with ease, and whipped them off.

"Same thing."

"It's not," she said and giggled.

He crouched down between her legs, grasped either ankle, and began to kiss his way up her calves. Sunlight streamed through the window, and for the first time he realized he could take his time with her.

Enjoy her.

Spend however long he wanted exploring every inch of her.

Lily propped herself up on her elbows and let her head hang back as his lips made their way to her inner thighs. Cade made his way to her center and could see the wetness through the baby blue silk panties.

He pressed his hands into her thighs and opened her legs wider. As he peppered a series of kisses across the underwear, she shuddered. He could smell her scent, sweet and wanting, through the fabric.

Cade kissed and nuzzled her clit insistently through the material until she started to press herself to his mouth.

"Don't tease me," she finally said, and he pulled the material to the side.

She was pink, wet, and fully engorged. He flicked his tongue against her clit. Lily gasped out his name and lifted herself closer to his mouth.

His tongue dipped into her folds, lapped up the juices that flowed steadily from her middle. When he tasted her opening, he couldn't get enough.

He buried his tongue inside her while she raked her fingers through his hair and held him close.

"I want you," she whispered. It was all she had to say.

Cade pulled her underwear off, stood on his knees and removed his own shirt. As he crouched over her, he rolled up her ribbed tank top to expose bare breasts and hard nipples.

"You knew this was coming, didn't you?" he asked with a smile. "No bra ..."

"I just hoped," she said with a blush, but his mouth was already on those firm nipples.

He sucked as they grew harder in his mouth and he felt his own hardness rage as she mewled and called his name. He tested her opening with his finger, shocked at how wet she was.

How wet she always was for him.

As he made his way to her neck, he pulled gently at the scarf.

"What's up with this?" he asked.

"I, um..." she said, and shyly removed the scarf. He was shocked to see the array of hickeys that lined her neck. It looked like she'd been choked.

"Jesus. Is that from me? From the car—"

"Of course it's from you!" she said.

"Damn, I'm sorry."

"So then make it up to me."

He smiled and kissed her neck gently. Cade slid a finger into her and felt her muscles grasp it tight.

"I'll make it up to you," he said quietly as he kissed her mouth and flicked his tongue against hers. "You may have brought the dessert... but how about I serve it to you?"

She smiled up at him as he rose to his knees and pulled her up with him. Lily reached for his jeans, eager to release him, and drew in her breath as she saw him. Cade glanced down and saw precum generously coated his tip.

"I want to taste you," she said. "Like this."

She leaned over and took one of the pastries. Lily wiped off the cream and trailed it along Cade's length. On all fours, she leaned down and took his cream-coated tip between her lips.

The heat of her mouth and the stickiness of the sugar gave him a jolt of pleasure like he'd never known.

"Fuck, Lily," he said, and grasped her tiny waist between his hands.

As she worked her way along his length, as her tongue shot waves of pleasure through him, he willed himself not to come. With her short pixie cut, he had an unprecedented view.

He could see how much pleasure she took in it, heard the moans as it vibrated along his cock, and couldn't wait any longer.

"I need to be inside you," he said.

She released his length slowly. Cade grabbed her, leaned back on his heels, and positioned her to straddle him. Her breasts were at his mouth, and as he lowered her onto him, she shuddered while he pulled softly at one nipple.

Lily rode him hard and delighted each time her clit rubbed against him when he filled her up entirely. Cade grasped her ass and pulled her cheeks apart to bury himself even deeper inside her. As she bounced, he slapped her ass to hear the little yelps of pleasure she let out.

"I want you to come for me," he commanded. A stream of her wetness licked its way down his leg.

"I'm close," she said. "God, I'm close."

In a swift movement, he flipped her onto her back and lowered himself on top of her. Instantly, her nails were in the small of his back.

Just like in her car.

She held him close to her while he started to fuck her to his own rhythm.

"Cade," she called out into his ear. "Make me come. Please, make me come …"

Her words got him close. He felt the release build up inside him. *Not yet.*

"I want to come with you," she whispered into his ear. "Make me come when you let go inside me. Fill me up—"

He nipped at her neck and she let out a gasp. She was so wet he heard the slap of their skin against each other. The hardness of her nipples pressed into his chest.

"You make me so goddamned hard," he said between kisses on her neck.

He'd never felt this way before, been so hard. It took everything in him not to explode inside her.

"Cade," she purred. "Let go. You want to come inside your friend's little sister, don't you? I've wanted it for so long—"

He heard a groan erupt from deep inside and the release as he exploded inside her.

"Fuck ... Lily," he cried quietly.

She cried out with her own orgasm. He felt her inner walls as they clenched and massaged his length, squeezed every last drop from him. And the warmth, the heat. It was so intense he never wanted to leave.

As his breathing slowed, he kissed her gently. He could taste the cream on her lips and felt the stickiness on her cheeks. Lily's face was flushed, her short locks wet with their combined perspiration.

"I love feeling you inside me," she said. He pulled out of her and felt their come spill out of her.

Cade rolled over onto his back and let out a cry as he crushed the half dozen cold, creamed desserts. Lily laughed and buried her head in the single pillow.

"You're crazy," he said.

For a moment, he thought about getting up and cleaning himself off. *But why?*

He wanted this, to remember this. He wanted to remember how Lily looked, naked and happy in his bed.

17

CADE

*T*hey had sex two more times, until both were soaked and exhausted. Cade fell asleep with Lily in his arms, her steady breathing more soothing and powerful than any kind of sleep tricks he'd tried.

For the first time in months, he slept completely through the night. No nightmares, no dreams, just peaceful darkness.

He woke up with the morning sun, and felt unexpectedly light. His face barely hurt from Aiden's attack, and even after the day before with Lily he felt refreshed.

As Cade looked down, he felt a warmth wash over him. She looked so innocent, so peaceful, in his arms. The little amount of makeup she'd worn yesterday had worn off, and he could make out the faint freckles across her nose and cheeks. Her hands curled in beneath her chin and her lips were slightly parted.

How different this one was than the last couple of times they were together. He still burned with shame when he thought about the first time three years ago.

Even then, he'd felt like a coward when he'd snuck out and left her in his apartment. For four hours, he'd huddled in his car and watched the front door. When it had finally opened, he'd ducked down into the seat. She looked slightly hurt, but more confused than anything else.

I wasn't even man enough to watch her leave, he remembered.

Instead, he'd distracted himself and scrolled through his phone until he'd heard her get into a taxi.

And the last time they were together? In that little old car of hers? It had been explosive, sheer magic—until he'd fucked it all up. He'd nearly still been inside her when it had all gone to hell.

So what was so different about this time? Is it the fact that at least one of her brothers knows, even if it's not EJ? Is this what it could be like?

She murmured in her sleep and he stroked her hair.

I won't make the same mistakes I did before, he promised her and himself. *Not if she makes me feel this good. Hell, just for her, I might even get a couch.*

"What are you staring at?" she asked, groggy. Lily squinted up at him.

"You," he said with a smile.

"Hmm. I must look like hell," she said and nuzzled into his arm.

"Far from it. In fact..." He took Lily's hand and directed it to his cock. He was already half hard, but her touch brought him to full attention.

"You're insatiable," she said with a laugh.

"Only for you."

She raised her lips to his and he kissed her, slow and deep. Inch by inch, she made her way on top. Lily straddled him, but grasped his hardness in her hands.

She maintained eye contact as she held his length against her clit and rubbed against him.

"Now who's the tease?" he asked.

"So tell me what you want," she said. "How am I supposed to know?"

"I want to be inside you."

She raised up slightly and positioned his tip at her opening.

"Like this?" she asked. She lowered herself so that just an inch was inside her.

"More," he said, and sucked breath through his teeth.

"Like this?" she asked with a smile, and lowered herself halfway.

"Like this," he said. With one swift movement, he put his hands on her thighs and forced her down. Lily's eyes rolled into the back of her head, but she didn't give in to riding him just yet.

"Tell me what else you want," she said. He could feel the wetness building in her.

"I want you to rub your clit while you ride me. Slowly," he instructed.

She started that rhythm, the one that drove him crazy, but it was slower this time. More controlled than last night. Lily looked down and watched as she drove his length in and out of her.

She circled her clit with her middle finger. As he watched her drive herself closer to orgasm, it took all his willpower to not throw her onto her back and have his way with her.

"Look at me," he said.

Lily lifted her gaze. When her eyes met his, she started to rub her clit harder, but the speed in which she rode him stayed the same.

"Play with your tits now," he told her. "I'll take care of this."

Her hands squeezed and pulled at her breasts while he took over her clit. Lily moaned as she rolled her nipples between her fingers. The wetness from her center coated her clit.

"You like this?" she asked.

"Fuck, yes," he said.

"Are you going to come in me again?" she asked.

"No."

"Why not?" Lily stopped, and her fingers still pinched her nipples but she cocked her head.

"Because I want you to come on my face." She grinned and released him from her center.

As she started to crawl toward him, he grabbed her hips, lifted her and turned her.

"Other way," he said. Cade lowered her onto his face while Lily encircled his cock with her hand. As her sweet wetness slid across his face, he felt her tongue on his tip.

Cade wrapped his arms around her hips and held her close. Lily rode his mouth, his tongue, like she was desperate for it. At the same time, she took him deep into her throat.

Cade licked at her clit and slid a finger inside her.

"Cade," she groaned as she released him from her mouth and slid his length between her hands. "I don't …"

"You're close," he said, and flattened his tongue against her clit. He felt the firmness of her G-spot against his hand and slid in a second finger. "I can feel it. Let go."

"Fuck, Cade, it feels so good," she said. She fucked his face, his hand, with a new kind of eagerness. Intermittently, he felt her mouth on his cock, but it was mostly her hand—slick with her own saliva. Lily called out his name.

"Come on, baby," he said from between her thighs. "Come for me. Right here, come on my face."

"Cade," she cried out. "I'm going to—this feels different—"

"Come for me," he demanded, and flicked his tongue light and fast across her clit.

She let out a cry unlike anything before, and a gush of wetness flooded from her. As he came in her hand, Cade parted his lips and drank her in. Above him, Lily's body shook uncontrollably. When she'd stopped, he kissed and lapped up every last drop of her.

"I don't know what that was," she said, breathless and she dismounted him.

"You squirted."

"I what?"

"It's good," he said with a smile. "And I loved it."

She smiled shyly as she sat beside him. Lily reached for his stream of come that had shot across his stomach. She wiped it up and trailed it along her nipples.

"I have to go to work," she said.

Cade laughed. "The shower's all yours."

"No," she said, with a shake of her head. "I'm going like this. I want to smell you on me all day."

Before he could say another word, she stood up and pulled on her jeans.

"You're serious," he said.

"I'm always serious." He watched her finish getting dressed. Lily gave him a light kiss before she left. "Don't worry," she said with a smile. "The apron will hide the fact that I don't have a bra on."

Cade stayed in bed for an hour after she left until he couldn't wait any longer. It was another day of therapy. Yet when he got up, he was surprised to find that he didn't dread it as much as usual.

Maybe it's finally working, he thought as he hopped in the car and made his way to Dr. Hersh's office.

"Cade—what happened?" Dr. Hersh asked. His mouth was ajar.

Fuck. How did he know?

"Your face ..."

"Oh! Oh, this? Nothing, it, uh, it happened at work."

Dr. Hersh looked at him carefully. "I work with a lot of firefighters, and I've never seen anything like this."

"Fine," Cade said with a sigh. "It happened at work, but it was personal. I just... I kind of got into it with one of the guys on the crew."

He doesn't need to know that I've known the guy forever.

"Cade, I'd like to talk to you today about your anger and where it comes from. This was already on the agenda," Dr.

Hersh said. "It has nothing to do with your face, but I figured it's a good segue."

Instead of getting defensive, Cade sat back in the uncomfortable seat and thought.

Where did it come from?

"I'd like to say I didn't start this fight, and I didn't participate. Which is why I look like I got the worst of it," Cade said. Dr. Hersh opened his mouth, but Cade held up a hand. "But that's an excuse, even if it's true. So, the anger... I think it came from my father."

"Your father?" Dr. Hersh said. "This is the first time you've mentioned him."

"I know. My bio dad... he was an angry alcoholic. He beat me and my mom whenever he felt like it. And then eventually, my mom had enough. Or at least that's what I suspect. She left my dad when I was in foster care. I heard about it through my dad, in this random angry rampage he went on. Tracked me down outside the firehouse when I was about twelve years old, with my friends."

"That must have been hard," Dr. Hersh said.

Cade shrugged. "My mom leaving? I guess I wasn't surprised. And I hadn't seen her in a long time anyway since I was in the system. So it probably wasn't as rough as it would be on some other kids."

"Maybe not as acutely rough, as you put it," Dr. Hersh said. "But it's a major trauma for any child. Were you close with your mother? I mean, when you were in her care?"

"I guess," Cade said. "It's kind of hard to remember. But she was the only person who protected me from him. At least as best she could. Her and Mr. Hammond."

"The former captain?" Dr. Hersh asked.

"Yeah. He was my best friend's dad. He's why I became a firefighter."

"And he protected you from your biological father?"

"Yeah. That time when my dad was on a drunk public

rampage? He came for me at the firehouse, and Mr. Hammond stopped him. Wouldn't let him take me."

"And was there anybody else? Someone else who helped you back then?"

Lily, he realized. She'd been there. She'd held his hand and gave him comfort.

"No," Cade said quietly. "Just Mr. Hammond."

"I see. Cade, I'm going to assign you some homework."

Cade groaned. "Doc, really? Come on, don't I do enough work here with you?"

"This is different," Dr. Hersh said. "And I think it will help. I want you to reflect on your anger. Any time you start to get upset, stop and think about it. What caused the anger? How are you feeling? Are there any common incidents that kickstart it? Any similarities? Write everything down and keep it in one notebook. Can you do that?"

"I can try," Cade said, uncertain.

"Good. And I can give you some strategies to cope with these high-stress times."

Cade cocked his head. "Like what?"

"Well, whenever you feel angry, I know it sounds silly, but take ten deep breaths. Count them, internally or externally. Give yourself a cool-off period."

"Real deep, Doc."

Dr. Hersh smiled.

"It's clichéd because it works. However, if you're in a situation you can walk away from, do that. Go on a walk, at least ten minutes. Get outside, get your heart rate up a bit, and notice what's around you. Again, it's a cool-off period."

"Writing in a diary, deep breathing, and walks," Cade said. "That's your plan to fix me. You must be a genius."

18

LILY

*L*ily finished helping Jean-Michel reconcile the change drawer. She groaned.

"I swear, those chocolate croissants will be the death of me. Why can't we charge a flat price for them after tax?"

Jean-Michel shrugged.

"They cannot be the same price as regular croissant," he said.

"Yeah, well, I don't know how we attract the last people in Salem who actually use cash, but math isn't my strong suit."

"I thought you were chemist."

"Yeah. Chemist, not mathematician. And only on paper, anyway. It's not like anyone's ever paid me for chemistry."

"I pay you for chemistry every week. That's what you say," Jean-Michel said wryly.

"You got me there."

"You want to work double?" Jean-Michel asked.

"Do you really need me?" she asked and bit her lip.

She'd hoped that since she was off early she'd have time to make Cade a fancy dinner.

Or better yet, finally try out some of that lingerie she'd bought.

Jean-Michel sniffed.

"I don't *need* anyone to help with baking," he said. "Just thought you might want some more chemistry money."

She laughed. "Well, if it's not urgent, I'll pass today and help you out in the morning."

"What is this new, how you say, spring in the step you have?" he asked. "You're getting laid."

"Jean-Michel!"

"Tell me I'm wrong," he challenged. "Go on."

"Fine," she said with an exasperated sigh. "You're right, okay?"

"Sex, then. That's all you have to say. You have appointment for sex and I'm keeping you. Go, go! Enjoy the youth."

"Thanks," she said with a smile and squeezed Jean-Michel's arm. "But it's not a 'sex appointment.' It's a date."

"A date?" Jean-Michel asked. "Then that is different. When the heart is involved."

"Why?"

"I let you go on one condition," Jean-Michel said.

She groaned. "I never should have told you that expression."

He grinned. "You tell me who with."

"Um... it's a secret," she said.

"Ooh! A secret affair? Now you must tell. But affairs don't excuse you from work. I might let you go if I approve of who the man is, though." Jean-Michel held up a whisk like it was a paddle. "He married?"

"What? No!" she said. "It's Cade, okay? My brother's best friend."

"The hot firefighter? The new one? I knew it! Get out of here," he said, and smacked her on the butt with the whisk. "Get out of here, go get ready for your date."

"Alright, alright!" she said. "But not a word about Cade to anyone."

"My lips are sealed," he said, and made an exaggerated show of zipping them. "But what you wearing?"

"For the date? I... I don't know yet."

"Harumph. You don't deserve me," he said. "Tell me this, what parfum do you wear?"

"You mean perfume?"

"No, I mean *parfum*. If you tell me you wear the cheap perfume, I swear, you are not my employee."

"I don't wear any?" she said quietly, although she knew it was the wrong answer.

Jean-Michel sighed. "What I will do with you? Sadly, I have no Chanel Number Five—I use it all—but this is almost as good."

He reached into the cupboard below the display case and pulled out the imported vanilla from France. His secret ingredient for the crème Chantilly.

"Really?" she asked in wonder.

When Jean-Michel presented it like it was a jar of saffron, she cradled it delicately in her hands.

"Just one drop here," he said, and tapped behind each ear. "And here," he said as he tapped her inner elbows. "Is all you need."

"Thank you," she said. Lily knew how much the extract meant to him.

"And this, you tell nobody," he said. "I know that *peau de zob* from Pebble and Stone is lurking around here. Always after my recipes."

She laughed. "I'll guard it with my life."

Lily raced to the Mercedes, the little brown vial in hand. When she dropped into the seat, a gust of flour rose up.

God, I really do need a bath.

She texted Cade as she started the engine. *What time you off?*

Two hours. Why?

Can you come over as soon as you're off? Nothing's wrong, but it's kind of an emergency.

What happened? I can leave right now if I have to.

No! she texted. "It's important, but not that important."

Okay, I'll be there right after four.

Lily rushed to straighten up as soon as she got inside, and paid particular attention to the bedroom. The fluffy white down comforter and duvet with the chunky pink handknit throw blanket didn't exactly scream "sexy" but it was what she had.

She draped a red silky scarf over the lamp for instant mood lighting.

Lily put the Ed Sheeran station on Pandora, plugged her phone into the little speaker box, and ran a bubble bath in the clawfoot tub. With candles lit in the bathroom and bedroom, she sank into the warm water and let the bubbles go to work softening her skin.

You have one hour, she told herself.

She grabbed the new razorblade heads and started to meticulously shave every inch of her below the waist. Renee always raved about getting a Brazilian, but Lily couldn't bring herself to do it.

"Doesn't it hurt?" she'd asked, but Renee rolled her eyes.

"It's worth it," she said.

"But then don't you have to wait for the hair to grow out kind of long before you do it again? Kind of seems like a losing battle."

"You just don't get it," Renee said.

Maybe she didn't get it. But Lily had to admit that when she was perfectly smooth, she felt sexier. Cleaner and lighter. And couldn't wait to surprise Cade.

She pulled the plug on the vintage tub and wrapped a towel around her. In the mirror, her face was pink and flushed. She applied two coats of lotion to her entire body. The result was supple, dewy skin that begged to be touched.

Why don't I pamper myself more? she wondered as she ran her hands along her smooth legs. *Wait, because there hasn't been anyone besides me to appreciate it. Until now.*

Lily pulled the selection of lingerie, tags still on, from the top dresser drawer. She'd been too embarrassed to go into any of the shops herself, and the online order just came in yesterday.

A lavender corset, black cupless bra and crotchless panty set, and a virgin-white babydoll with furry trim. She had no idea what Cade would prefer.

First, she tried on the black combination, but she nearly laughed when she looked in the mirror. It had a nearly dominatrix look, and although she was sure Renee could pull it off, it wasn't for her. Still, seeing herself like that—dark and sexy—started to turn her on.

Who knows? Maybe this is exactly what Cade is into.

Next, she slipped on the white transparent babydoll, but it looked all wrong with bare feet or with any shoes she had.

I guess the shopping cart suggestion was right. I should have gotten the matching shoes.

But Lily suspected that even if she had, this look was too seventies porn star.

The lavender corset and matching G-string was, surprisingly, a perfect complement to her figure. It squeezed her small waist in even tighter and provided a sense of comfort. Her breasts spilled out the top and nearly begged for release. Lily's hips flared out, just the tiniest of material from the panties visible beneath the lace trim of the corset.

"This is it," she said and slipped into the silver platform shoes she'd worn on a New Year's Eve years ago.

She kept her face bare, save for a swipe of vanilla-scented chapstick and mascara. Fifteen minutes until Cade would arrive. Carefully, Lily unscrewed the bottle of vanilla extract. Immediately, she could taste the Chantilly crème in her mouth.

The way it had tasted on Cade's hardness, the sweetness and the musk mixed, all of it made her wet.

Like Jean-Michel instructed, she dabbed the vanilla behind her ears and on her inner elbows. However, as she was about to put it away, an idea too deliciously naughty occurred to her. Lily let the extract coat her ring finger and she dabbed it directly onto her clit. A shiver went through her at the touch. She wiped the little excess there was along her inner thighs.

A knock came at the door as she finished pouring two glasses of wine. She took a quick swallow, suddenly nervous, and wrapped the lavender silk robe around her.

"What's the emergency?" Cade asked when she opened the door.

Without a word, she unbelted the robe and let it fall to the floor.

He didn't hesitate. Cade picked her up and kicked the door shut behind him. His lips found hers instantly. She could smell the sweat of the workday on him. The manliness of it made her juices start to flow.

She laughed in his arms.

"Put me down," she said as he carried her to the bedroom.

"Not a chance," he said. "Damn, you taste sweet."

"It's a secret ingredient," she said.

"Yeah, it is." He tossed her on the bed and started to unbuckle his jeans, but she stopped him.

"Wait," she said. "I have a surprise."

"What is it?"

She shrugged. "You'll have to find out."

He grinned, grasped her ankles and flipped her onto her back. "Do I get some kind of prize if I get you out of this contraption or something?"

"Maybe," she said. "A lady never tells."

He reached down and unhooked the first of two dozen hook-and-eye closures on the corset.

"I don't know," he said. "I kind of like you like this.

"Good," she said. "Because that's not where the surprise is anyway."

"No?" he asked. His hands trailed along her neck where the hickeys had started to fade.

"Colder," she said.

He brought a hand to her breasts, encased in the corset, but she felt them harden beneath the material.

"Warmer," she said and rolled onto her side.

Cade's hand moved to her waist, to the side of her hip. He spanked her smartly on the bare skin. "Getting hot," she said with a smile.

He grasped the back of the G-string. With the wisp of material in his hand, he knotted it around his fist. Lily moaned and he made the material slide along her clit.

"Really hot," she said. Cade pushed her onto her back, hooked his thumbs through the underwear, and pulled them to her ankles. "Surprise," she said.

His eyes widened when he saw her. "You ... you did this for me?" he asked.

"I thought you'd be hungry," she said with a laugh. "Honestly, at first I really was going to make you a special dinner. But then I thought..."

"Why not go right to dessert?" he asked with a grin.

"Taste me," she said.

Lily couldn't wait any longer. She brought her hand between her legs and spread open her lips to present her swollen clit to him. Her nipples had made their way out of the corset.

Cade dropped to his knee, gripped her hips, and brought her to his lips. Her legs splayed over his shoulders.

"God, you taste incredible," he said. "It's ... it's fucking intoxicating."

She closed her eyes as the heat of his tongue roamed across her clit. He explored every crevice of her.

"You feel so good," she whispered.

He kissed her clit lightly and raised his head. "I just have one question, though."

Lily opened her eyes and gazed down at him.

"No talking," she said. "Just eating."

"Aren't you eager," he said, and grazed his thumb across her swollen clit. "I'll finish eating this sweet pussy if you tell me one thing."

"What?"

"What is that scent? It's like … damn, it's like no kind of perfume I've known before."

"That's the one thing I can't tell you," she said with a smile. "But I like to call it eau de whipped cream."

Cade's tongue returned to her and she raked her fingers through his hair to hold him close.

*T*here were some scents he'd never forget. They burned into his mind to settle permanent. The smell of his first wildfire when the adrenaline moved his body without thought.

The first time he'd had a beer, with Mr. Hammond offering up a wink as he handed him Terminator Stout. And Lily's scent, now blended with a kind of sweetness that reminded him of the first time he walked into her bakery.

She squeezed her thighs against his head and called out his name. Every taste of her made him want more. Cade trailed his tongue from her slick folds to the softness of her inner thighs.

He wanted to mark her, to claim her as his own. Along her legs, he began to create hickeys that matched those that had started to fade along her neck.

"Come here," she said, and pulled at his shoulders to bring him toward her.

Cade pushed down his jeans and made his way toward her. Already, her face was flushed and her eyes were wild with want. He ran a hand along her chest and watched as her head rolled back.

"Turn over," he said. She bit her lip and pushed herself onto all fours.

Lily's hands gripped the side of the mattress. He bent over her, grabbed her thighs, and in an easy movement spread her legs wider apart. Lily lowered herself onto her forearms and buried her head in the sheets—braced and ready for his entry.

Cade squeezed her round, perfect ass and gave her a smart spank. Her cries were muffled in the sheets. Already he could see the red imprint of his hand on her creamy skin. He was hard, his tip coated in precum for her, but something about her always made him want to draw it out.

With two fingers, he spread her folds apart to see the center of her wetness. Lily pushed her ass back slightly, eager for him to be inside her. Cade slid in just his thumb while his forefinger found her clit.

Lily moaned for more, pushed back insistently, but he wouldn't let her have it that easily.

"Be still," he told her. Her frustration was palpable, but she complied.

Cade released his hand and pressed his tip against her opening. She squirmed slightly, but did as he'd instructed. He wanted to watch himself enter her, slow and steady.

"You can play with your clit," he told her, and Lily's hand was instantly on herself.

The motion as she brought herself closer to orgasm vibrated along his cock. He wrapped his hands around her hip bones and brought her toward him. Every inch deeper he was inside her, he thought he couldn't handle any more. But it felt so good, he couldn't imagine there being an end.

Fully inside her, she furiously worked her clit. He could tell she was bringing herself close.

"That's enough," he said. Lily obeyed and he began to fuck her, controlled and smooth.

The sight of his length disappearing inside her, over and over, made him harder than he'd ever known.

Cade moved his hands from her hips to her breasts. They bounced, nipples hard, to his rhythm. Lily's moans got louder as he pinched each nipple.

"Come here," he murmured against her neck, and lifted her up.

She rode him like a cowgirl, backward, as he leaned back on his heels. Over her shoulder, he could see their reflection in the windowpane. Lily's thighs were open wide, her breasts swayed as she used his length, and her head fell back to rest on his shoulder.

With one hand he circled her clit skillfully. The other gave equal attention to her breasts.

"How do you always get so wet?" he whispered into her ear. He nibbled the lobe and she let out a yelp.

"You do it to me," she said. He felt his hardness as it slid against her G-spot and her wetness as it spilled down his thighs.

"You like this?" he asked. Cade bit her neck and she moved her head to the side to offer up more.

"I love it," she said, breathless.

"You're so fucking tight. Do you want more?"

"I want more," she said.

"Bend over."

He saw the slip of a smile as she repositioned herself onto all fours. Slowly, he pulled himself out, and Lily let out a whimper of frustration.

"Be patient," he said. Cade leaned over to the side table and grabbed the white bottle of lotion.

"What are you doing?" Lily asked, but she didn't get out of her position.

"Just making use of something I've been using to get myself off when I think of you every night." It was true, and he had no shame as he generously poured the lube on one hand.

"Do you really think I need that?" she asked, her voice full of playfulness.

"Trust me, you'll want it." With his forefinger, he traced the rim of her ass. Lily stiffened instantly. "It's okay," he said gently. "Just tell me if it's too much."

Her breath was heavy. Cade's other hand went to her clit for the kind of firm, slow pressure he knew shot her to orgasm fast. He felt the wetness start to build up around his fingers.

"Cade," she whispered, and he inserted the tip of his finger into her ass while he increased the speed at her clit. Lily cried out, a call of pleasure, and leaned back into his hand.

"More?" he asked.

"Yeah," she said, her breath ragged. "I want more."

Cade inserted his finger an inch into her. His cock jumped in excitement. This kind of trust, this kind of vulnerability, it made him not just want to have her. Not just want to fuck her— but to protect her.

"You're so tight," he told her again, amazed at it. "Is this your first time?"

For a second she hesitated. "Yeah," she finally said.

He believed her. It was clear she'd never done this before.

Then why the hesitation?

"How do you want me to make you come?" he asked. He relieved the pressure on her clit and replaced it with the lightest of flicks with his fingertip. Lily growled in frustration.

"On your cock."

"Louder."

"I want to come on your cock," she repeated.

"Louder," he said with a smile. "Say my name."

He flicked his fingertip against her clit faster, harder.

"I want to come on your cock, Cade," she cried out.

"Good girl." Carefully, he released his finger from her ass.

The second she was free, she turned around and forced him down. Lily climbed on top and straddled him with her feet planted on either side of his hips. Knees pointed toward the ceiling, she gripped his base.

Lily positioned his length against her clit and began to raise and lower herself slightly. She used him like a toy against herself—and all he could think about was getting inside her.

"Don't be a tease," he said. "Put it inside you."

"I can do what I want," she said with a smile.

"And what do you want?"

"I want you to come in me, hard."

He reached for her hips, to force her down onto him, but she pushed his hands away.

"You're not always in charge," she said. Lily put her hands on his chest and lowered herself onto him, achingly slow.

"Fuck," he whispered.

She smiled above him. As she started to bounce, he reached for those perfect tits, those tight pink nipples, and let her take control.

Every time he tried to reach for anything besides her breasts, she pushed his arms away. Lily started to pant. The wetness spilled out of her.

"I'm close," she said.

"Are you going to come on my cock?"

"Yeah," she said.

"Do it," he said. "Come all over me."

Cade raised his head and caught a nipple in his mouth. Lily began to moan, to whisper his name over and over. Each time, he got harder. Closer to falling over the edge.

"Now," she called out. "Oh, Cade, you're making me come."

As her muscles tensed around his hardness, he couldn't hold it in any longer. Cade spilled himself into her while her thighs shook uncontrollably. He released her nipple from his lips.

"You're incredible," he said. It was one of the truest things he'd ever told her.

Lily lifted herself up. When his cock was released, he looked down at their combined juices on his groin. "You want me to clean you up?" she asked.

He sucked in his breath, but she'd already started to lower

her head before he could answer. The feel of her mouth, gentle and soft, on his tip was almost unbearable. He felt himself start to get hard again while the sensitivity faded.

"You taste yourself on me?" he asked. Lily ran her tongue along his length.

"Yeah," she said and looked up with a smile.

"How do you taste?"

"Sweet," she said. "So does your come."

He watched as she licked and kissed up everything they'd done.

I don't know if I'll ever be able to give this up.

"You're hard again," she said when she was done, impressed.

"You do that to me."

"So... since you're hard, I was thinking..."

"What?"

She bit her lip. "I don't want you to think I'm too wild or something—"

He gave a short laugh. "I think we're past this point. Tell me what you want."

"Like, what you did with your finger... and that..." Lily pointed to the lube.

"You like that?" he asked, and she blushed.

"I mean, I don't know if I'd like it. But maybe you could, you know, take me from behind ..."

His cock stood at full attention. The idea of actually fucking her in the ass, of being the first in that taboo territory, it was something he'd never really considered a possibility.

"Are you... are you sure?" he asked.

"No," she said with a laugh. "But I'm serious that I want to try."

Cade pushed himself up and Lily immediately moved to all fours. He spread her cheeks with his hands and gazed at that perfect puckered pinkness.

He kissed her ass cheek and brought his tongue to her ass.

He felt her tremble as he rimmed her with the tip of his tongue. When he moved back for the lube, she pushed insistently toward him. Cade laughed.

"You just can't get enough, can you?"

"Not of you."

20

LILY

*S*he felt the coolness of the lubricant as Cade spread it around her rim. She chewed at her lip, nervous but excited. When he'd put his finger in her, it gave her a feeling of fullness that she didn't even know she craved.

Lily had wanted to ask him to fill her entirely, for his cock or hand inside her wetness, but a wave of shyness had washed over her.

Cade's finger found its way back to her clit and she felt herself grow wetter.

"You ready?" he asked.

"Ready," she said—though she didn't know if she was.

She felt his tip press against her ass and Lily squeezed her eyes shut. He worked her clit just the way she liked it. A little hard and in small circles. Lily felt herself open to him and an almost unbearable feeling of fullness. She gasped out.

"Are you okay?" he asked.

"Yeah," she said. "Keep ... keep going."

Inch by inch, he buried himself into a part of her she'd never known needed his touch. There was both pleasure and a touch of pain, but the little pain there was took the pleasure to another level.

Cade kissed her shoulder. "You feel so good," he said. "I'm going to release it, okay?"

"No," she said, and shook her head.

"No?"

"Fuck me," she said. "Like this."

She hadn't even known that's what she wanted until the words were out.

"Slow," she added.

Cade continued kissing her shoulder, her back, as he slid out of her. The vacancy he left behind demanded to be filled.

"Fuck me," she said again, more demanding. She felt the cold wetness of the lubricant again, and he filled her up once more.

Lily brought a hand to her breasts and pulled at her nipples while Cade continued to expertly play with her clit. After just four slow thrusts into her ass, she knew she was close. It was a different kind of orgasm than she'd ever known before. Even more intense than the time she'd squirted.

"I'm ... I'm close," she said.

"Really?" She felt his hardness jump inside her. That small movement made her squeeze her eyes together tighter.

She answered with an orgasm harder and stronger than she'd ever felt before.

"Cade," she said between gritted teeth.

The waves rocked through her while the wetness poured down her thighs. Lily could hear her heartbeat as it pounded through her body.

When he released her, she fell onto the mattress, drenched and satisfied. But as Lily turned to face him, she saw how hard he was.

"You didn't come," she said.

He grinned. "I figured what we just did was kinky enough without me adding to it."

"But I want you to come again," she said, and reached for his cock.

He shook his head and laughed. "You really can't get enough."

"Come on," she said. "Tell me something you want to do. Something you've always wanted to do, and never have."

"Lily, I'm not that—"

"There's got to be something."

"Alright." Cade grabbed a towel. "No judgment?"

"No judgment," she said, her interest piqued.

"And just so you know, this isn't something I've always wanted to do. It's not like that. But... since you brought it up ..."

"Anything," she said.

"I'm going to go take a shower. And when I get back, we're going to pretend it was five years ago."

"What?"

"It's five years ago and you're in your old bedroom. The one with the pink wallpaper and that white desk in the corner."

"Okay?"

"And your brothers are in the room next door. I'm staying the night, but they've already fallen asleep."

Lily grinned. "Got it. See you five years ago."

She listened to the steady fall of the shower in the next room. Lily pulled out the duffel bag of her old clothes stuffed in the back of her closer.

I knew I kept this for something. She pulled out her cheerleading uniform from her senior year of high school. The scratchy material was instantly familiar, and it still carried the scent of the perfume she'd worn that year.

She positioned herself at the little vanity table in the corner when the shower water turned off and pretended to write in a notebook.

"Hi, Cade," she said when he opened the bathroom door. A towel was wrapped loosely around his waist. "What are you doing in here?"

Lily watched his eyes widen at the cheerleading uniform.

"I, uh, I couldn't sleep."

"Oh. You want to hang out or something?"

"Actually, I thought maybe you could help."

"Sure. How?" He walked toward her and she turned in the little wooden chair to face him.

"I can't sleep because I keep thinking about you," he said. She could see his hardness through the towel, inches from her mouth.

"About me?"

"Yeah. About you ... in that little cheerleading uniform. You know, I've always wondered, what do you wear under that?"

"I... I'm not supposed to tell."

"Oh?"

"I mean... technically there's this special underwear we're supposed to wear? But I don't like it."

"So what do you wear?"

"You want me to show you?"

"Show me."

She smiled up at him and spread her legs. The short material lifted to reveal her perfectly smooth skin. "Now you show me yours."

Cade let the towel drop to the floor. His cock sprung forward. It took all her willpower not to immediately bring him to her mouth.

"Wow! I've never... I've never seen one before," she said. "Can I touch it?"

"I don't know ... you just turned eighteen, right?"

"Last autumn."

"I guess it's okay, then."

She gripped his base and felt her wetness spill onto the seat. "My brothers would kill me if they knew," she said.

"Then we better be quiet. You want to taste it?"

"Like this?" She brought her tongue to his tip and heard him suck in his breath.

"Yeah. That's real good. You sure you've never done this before?"

She shook her head. "But I've always thought about it. With you…"

He bent down, scooped her up, and set her on the desk.

"Hey, that's my homework—"

"Fuck your homework." He entered her with ease and she immediately wrapped her legs around his.

"Cade," she started to moan.

"Quiet, they'll hear," he said.

She clamped her mouth shut and focused on the waves of pleasure that rolled through her with every thrust. The rough material of the uniform scratched against her skin.

Cade pushed her legs up until she rested her feet on the edge of the desk. With her legs spread wide, he leaned back.

"I want you to watch," he said.

They both looked down and took in the view of his cock as it slid into her. Cade's thumb went to her clit, and as he started to rub she groaned. "You have to be quiet," he reminded her.

"Cade, come on—"

"You don't want to get grounded, do you?"

"No," she said with a grin.

Cade stopped suddenly. "Do you hear something?"

She lowered her voice. "Are you being serious?"

"I think someone's awake. Be quiet, come here."

He lifted her up and she bit her lip so she wouldn't laugh. He carried her to the bed, lowered her gently, and got in beside her. As Cade spooned her from behind, he pulled the blanket over them.

"Be still," he said. "And don't make a sound."

He kissed her neck from behind and let his hands travel beneath the top of the uniform. She delighted in the feel of his hands across her breasts.

With her eyes closed and the scent of whatever detergent the dry cleaner had used back when she was in high school, she could almost believe it. Lily felt like she was a senior again, and that Cade was hanging out in the room next door.

His hand moved to her thigh. Slowly, he hitched up the cheerleading skirt. She felt the press of his hard heat behind her. Lily lifted her top knee skyward and two of Cade's fingers slipped inside her.

"I've always wanted this," he whispered into her ear. "I've always wanted you."

She opened her mouth to reply, but he slid his cock inside her and she gave a small moan instead. As he fucked her from behind, the heat built up beneath the covers.

Cade had one hand on her clit, the other on her breasts, and somehow Lily was both eighteen years old again and in her twenties.

"Tell me you've always wanted this, too," he said.

"I did. I do," she moaned.

"I see the way you look at me."

"What?"

"You've always wanted me as much as I've wanted you."

"Yeah," she said. "God, you're going to make me come."

"Not yet," he said into her neck. "Not yet."

Lily closed her eyes and let his voice and the feel of her uniform take her back to the first time she got herself off.

She'd been eighteen and the pressure was so intense inside her, she had to find a release.

Lily had taken the new vibrating toothbrush she'd gotten for Christmas and held it against her clit. The jolt of instant pleasure it gave her was mindblowing—and all she could picture was Cade's face.

"The first time I ever masturbated, I thought about you," she said.

Cade slowed. "Are you being serious? Or is this part of the game?"

"Both."

"Tell me about it." He started to fuck her faster.

"It was in the spring, like now," she said quietly. He pinched one of her nipples and she mewled. "You were a new recruit, you'd stopped by the house in your uniform. And it was just so fucking hot. I... I got my new toothbrush, the kind that vibrates."

"Yeah ..."

"And ... I locked myself in my room. I didn't know what I was doing, but ... I held it to me. There," she gasped as he flicked her clit in a new rhythm. "And I just... I thought of you."

"Keep going."

"When I got close, I put it in me."

"Yeah? You fucked yourself while you thought about me?"

"Yeah," she said. "Fuck, Cade, I'm close."

"Almost. Tell me how you made yourself come."

Lily let out a groan. It was getting hard to breathe underneath the blanket. "At first I was scared. I'd, you know, never... had anything in there before. But it felt so good."

"Tell me how hard you came."

"Really hard. I... everything was so wet."

"Just like you are now," he said. "Tell me more."

"I said your name when I came." She'd never even fully admitted that to herself before, but she remembered all of it. The surprise, the feeling of relief after years of the buildup. And then the disappointment that it wasn't real.

"How good did it feel?"

"Amazing," she said. He fucked her harder and she felt herself arrive at the edge. "I didn't know it at the time, but ... I wanted you to come in me. That's all I wanted."

He let out a groan and she felt the rush of his release into her.

"Cade," she called out, and reached behind to keep him close. His orgasm rocketed into her and made her come against his cock.

"Just like this," she said.

Cade kissed her neck and slowly rolled onto his back. She could smell the combined mixture of their sweat, sex, and the scent of her last year in high school all rolled up into one.

"Hey," Cade said. She turned to face him, and he grinned. "You think anyone heard?"

She laughed and slapped his arm. Cade motioned for her to come closer, and she spooned into his chest.

"I could do this all day," she said.

"Let's do it. We both don't work again until Tuesday, right?"

21

CADE

*B*y the time morning came, Cade was sore and exhausted—yet it was still almost impossible to pry himself from her arms.

"Do you really have to go?" Lily murmured, sleepy, into the pillow.

"Unfortunately," he said. "I have a day full of all kinds of things you'll be jealous of."

She narrowed her eyes. "Like what?"

"Oh, like go to therapy. Go home and put on some clean clothes. Wash the dishes."

She wrinkled her nose. "Sounds like a blast."

"Besides, don't you work today?"

"Yeah, the evening shift. And trust me, all anybody orders during that shift are slices of cake and espresso. Not exactly the most challenging of jobs."

He leaned down and kissed her. "I'm sure you'll still knock it out of the park."

Lily buried herself further into the blankets while he stood up and pulled on his jeans. As he stepped outside, the morning fog still clung tight to the ground.

Cade slipped into his denim jacket and raced down the

stairs. He got a few looks from the guys in the mechanic shop and one thumbs-up. He nodded to them briefly and made a beeline for his car.

"Hey! That your ride?" the guy who gave him a thumbs-up called.

"Yeah..."

"Nice. Bring it by any time if you want a tune-up."

"Thanks." He felt a strange levity as the Mustang ushered him home. It was like his soul was lighter.

It probably doesn't hurt that for the past week I've had the most incredible, intense sex of my life followed by dreamless sleep, he reminded himself.

It was better than exercise in that respect. Was the sleep so heavy because he was drained and exhausted, or was it something else?

Cade pulled into the parking lot of his apartment and bounded up the steps. As he pulled out the keys, a neighbor from a few doors down ran past him with tears that streamed down her face.

Shit. What was her name? Victoria? He couldn't remember. Cade's mouth dropped open in tandem with his keys that hit the welcome mat outside his door.

"Hey!" He turned to watch a man barrel down the narrow passageway toward the woman.

Cade heard the woman scream from behind him, and all he saw was red. It didn't take much to intervene. All he had to do was take one outward step.

"Get out the way, asshole," the man said as he came to a halt in front of Cade's barricade. "This doesn't concern you."

The man was in his thirties, shorter than Cade. And his fists were already bundled up ready to attack.

He heard the woman sniffle behind him, and watched as his own fist shot from his shoulder directly into the guy's jaw. A perfect jab.

"Oh my God!" the woman screamed as the man hit the floor.

"What the hell?" the guy asked, astounded as he wiped the blood from his hand.

He leapt up, powered by an unnatural kind of energy. Meth, coke, Cade didn't know. But he could tell the guy felt no pain, only surprise at getting knocked to the ground.

However, the guy didn't know how to fight. He swung at Cade wildly and landed a weak fist on his shoulder. Cade bobbed out of the way and raised up with an uppercut to the other side of the man's jaw.

"Stop! Stop!" the woman yelled. "I'm gonna call the cops!"

"You call the cops, you're dead," the man hollered at her. "You know what we got in there—"

The man struggled to stand up straight, but was clearly disoriented. Blood poured from his lip onto the floor. Still, he lunged for Cade again and wrapped his arms around his waist.

Cade bore his elbow into the man's back and aimed for a kidney. He felt the wind get knocked out of the smaller man and watched as he crumpled to the floor.

"You're killing him!" the woman screamed. He felt her nails start to claw at his back.

"You're both fucking crazy," the guy wheezed.

He managed to get to his feet. Somehow, he pulled together whatever strength he had and bolted toward the parking lot.

The woman had used the last of her strength to try and drag Cade off of him. When he turned to her, her face was red and blotchy. She gasped for air between her sobs.

"Are you... are you okay?" He reached toward her to console her, but she jerked away from him. "Hey, I'm not going to hurt you. I'm... I'm sorry I lost it like that."

"It's not your fault," she said finally as the sobs began to slow. "He's... he can get like that sometimes."

"Are you alright, thought? Did he hurt you?"

She sniffed and attempted to straighten her shirt. "I've had worse."

"Do you want me to call the police? You should—"

"Look, thank you. Alright? For intervening and all. But you should really mind your own goddamned business."

"Excuse me?"

She stomped away from him, back to the apartment she'd flown out of. Cade followed behind, unsure of whether she was safe to go back in there.

"Didn't you hear what I just said?" She turned on her heels at the door. Her steely blue eyes shot up a wall between them. "Mind your own fucking business." With that, she slammed the door in his face.

"What the hell?" he asked quietly to the closed door. Cade slowly made his way to his own apartment.

I have to get out of this neighborhood.

As Cade turned on the water in his bathroom, he replayed what had just happened in his head.

Was there anything different I should have done? I mean, the guy was clearly going to keep going like some kind of meth machine. No matter how Cade spun it, he didn't know what else he was supposed to do. *Let's just add that to one of several past incidents of adjacent woman abuse.*

He shook his head as he splashed the lukewarm water on his face. It was too much, all of these incidents. *Triggering,* Dr. Hersh like to say. But he couldn't help it. Every time he saw a woman being assaulted or attacked by a man, he was three years old all over again.

"Mama?" He remembered searching for her throughout the house. It was close to Christmas, and for once his parents had put up a tree. It had big, multicolored lights on it. The kind meant for outdoors, but it was all they had.

And beneath the tree? Three presents. One for each of them. Cade had spent days shaking his present and trying to figure out what it was. "Mama? Where are you?"

"Go back to bed, Cade." His mom's voice was strong in the kitchen, but there was a whisper of a waver.

He raced toward the kitchen where the bright lights shone overhead. "Mama! Is Santa coming—"

He remembered how the words fell out of him when he walked into the kitchen. His dad, seemingly eight feet tall, stood over his mom with a belt in his hands.

"Why don't you ever listen to your mama?" his dad slurred.

He staggered toward Cade, but nearly lost his balance. His dad grabbed for the heavy kitchen table to steady himself.

"Cade, I said go back to bed."

His mom was crumpled on the floor and she held one hand over her right eye. Her lip was split and blood pooled in her collarbone.

"Mama, you're bleeding—"

"I'm okay. I just... I fell when your daddy and I were playing."

"Hell, Dolores, how the hell long you gonna keep pampering this kid? Turning him into a goddamned faggot—"

"Don't—"

His dad turned and slashed the belt across her head again. He heard the ring of where the metal belt hit her jaw.

"Don't you dare talk ... talk back to me."

"Mama!" Cade cried.

He wanted to run to her, but his legs were frozen. His mom swayed on the floor. She looked drunk, just like his dad. A noise erupted from her, scared and small like an animal. Suddenly, his legs started to work.

He rushed at his father and dropped his blanket in the process.

"Don't hurt Mama," he yelled. But when he ran against those tall legs, big and strong as tree trunks, his dad didn't move. Instead, he laughed.

"Well, looka that!" his dad said. "Maybe there's a man in there after all."

Cade didn't know why, and he didn't like it, but those words brought a rush of pride through him. Then he felt the metal against his back. Any strength he had drained out of him and he fell to his knees. When he looked up, tears in his eyes, his dad smiled with the belt securely in his hand.

"Might be a man in there," his dad repeated. "But you still ain't got nothin' on me. You come at me again, boy, I'mma kill her. You hear me? I'mma kill your mama. And make you watch."

———

CADE PRESSED the towel firmly against his eyes at the memory. Every time. Every time he saw a woman getting abused, he was three years old again.

As he got dressed, he remembered what Dr. Hersh had said about those techniques.

Did I try breathing? Did I stop, remove myself from the situation? No—but was there even a chance to?

What was he supposed to do? Just excuse himself while a woman was running for her life so he could take a leisurely stroll around the block?

"Fucking Dr. Hersh," he said. He slipped into some new jeans and pulled a t-shirt overhead.

Yeah, those are great techniques when you've got all the time in the world. It was fucking stupid.

Still. Maybe the next time he could do something, catch himself before he flew totally out of control. After all, he hadn't needed to beat that guy as badly as he did.

He clearly didn't know how to fight, and he was high as hell. Would it really be that hard to disarm someone, even if all they had were their own fists, when they were in that kind of state?

Cade mulled it over as he got into his car and headed toward his appointment. Maybe he could ask Dr. Hersh for some more realistic tips and techniques. After all, he couldn't blame the doctor.

Who the hell lived in the kind of place where men went running after their girlfriends, hellbent on beating them? Probably not Dr. Hersh. That didn't really seem to be his scene.

As Cade pulled up to the office, he realized he was early. He sat in the car and gripped the wheel tightly.

Breathe. He counted to ten and focused on fully filling and emptying his lungs. By the time he finished the first round, he felt a bit lightheaded but also calmer.

Hell. Maybe these things really do work.

Cade glanced at his watch. Ten minutes until his appointment. He got out of the car, pulled his jacket on, and started to walk down the block. It was a part of town he'd never been to before.

Once he turned the corner, he noticed a park across the street. Canadian geese squawked and chased after little kids who held big bags of bread when they got too close. The parents took photos and laughed as they perched on the benches.

When he turned the next corner, he saw a bakery. It filled the street with an aroma that reminded him of Lily. Baguettes lined up in the window like soldiers. By the third corner, he looked forward to whatever he might find next.

Maybe those walks worked. Maybe what Dr. Hersh has been saying would really work.

*H*er heart fluttered when she heard his knock at the door. Lily pulled the Alsatian bacon and onion tart out of the oven and set it beside the tarte Tatin she'd whipped up earlier that day.

"Glad you could make it," she said as she opened the door.

"Well, this isn't quite as sexy as the lavender robe... and what you had, or didn't have on, underneath, the last time..." Cade said as he pulled playfully at her apron generously covered in flour and oil stains.

Lily blushed. "I made you dinner."

"Yeah, but last time, dinner—well, dessert was code for something else." Cade stepped into her living room and took off his jacket. "Can I help with anything?"

"You're not disappointed, are you?" Lily asked. A flurry of worries gathered in her stomach. "I mean, I thought actually making you dinner, you know, it would be—"

"It's great," he said. Cade leaned down and kissed her lightly on the lips. "I was just teasing. And it smells amazing by the way. My offer to help is probably a bit empty. I'm pretty useless in the kitchen."

"I don't know. I could probably think of a few uses for you," she said with a wink. "But actually, if you want, you can open the white wine on the table. I couldn't get it."

"That I can do."

Lily rushed into the kitchen and picked up the casserole dish. In the little makeshift breakfast nook, she scooted over the salad full of seasonal ingredients she'd picked up that morning.

"Damn, that looks professional," Cade said. "What do you call it?"

"It's just a kind of quiche," she said. "Jean-Michel has been working on it with me."

Cade's face clouded for a moment.

"A Parisian man who can bake," he said. "Tough to compete with that."

"What, you're jealous?" she asked. Lily whipped off the apron and hung it on the hook overhead. "Do you think Jean-Michel is attractive?"

"I don't know if I'd say that," Cade said quickly as he sat down across from her and filled their wine glasses. "I mean, I only saw him once, that first time I went into the shop. I wasn't exactly checking him out. I was kind of busy checking you out."

Lily felt her face turn even pinker as she sliced the quiche.

"Well, it'll break his heart, but I'm going to have to tell him the feeling isn't mutual." Lily slid a slice of the quiche—perfectly baked, she noted—onto Cade's plate.

"What do you mean?"

"Well, Jean-Michel was certainly checking *you* out. I had to tell him not only are my brothers straight, but so is their best friend."

Cade nearly choked on his first bite. "Oh. You mean—"

"A Parisian man that can bake? Yeah, sometimes it's called a cliché for a reason."

"Well now I feel kind of stupid," Cade said. "Thankfully, the most amazing dish ever makes up for it."

"You really like it?"

"Before just now, I could honestly say I don't like French food, but I think you just converted me."

Lily smiled and dug into her own slice. She was aware of the happy little bubble they'd created around themselves. Ten days.

It had been ten days since they'd gotten together with no walls up. And she was scared to death that any minute it would come crashing down. She could feel how shaky and vulnerable it was.

Of course it can't last, she reminded herself every day. It made her grateful for every moment of happiness they did have together.

Just don't mess it up, she told herself.

"Don't fill up," she said. "There's still dessert."

Cade's ears perked up at that. "And by dessert, you mean—"

"Tarte Tatin. Come here, I'll show you." She stood up, finished her wine in a single swallow, and pulled him into the kitchen.

"You made this?" he asked.

"Don't act so surprised. I do work in a bakery."

"Yeah, but—"

"Don't talk, just taste," she said, and plucked a pinch of the sweet dessert out of the dish.

When she brought her fingers to Cade's lips, she truly intended to leave it as a sweet flirt. But as soon as she felt his lips on her fingertips, when he took her wrist and held her hand close—sucked her finger slowly—she knew the tarte would have to wait.

"It's sweet," he said. "But not as sweet as you."

He hoisted her onto the counter and shoved the prep dishes out of the way. The sounds of the clang of them hitting the floor shrouded the groan in his throat.

Cade reached up her thighs and searched for her underwear. All he found was her wetness, her want, and her heat.

Cade cradled her jaw and leaned her head back.

"Sneaky girl," he said.

Lily laughed. She heard the rattle of his belt. He squeezed the flesh of her thighs and brought her toward him. Just when she thought she was about to slip off the edge, he slid inside her.

Lily wrapped her legs around his waist to hold him closer. She felt a tug at her chest followed by a series of pops as her snap-button shirt came undone. The air was cold on her breasts just long enough to harden her nipples, and then his mouth was on them.

His tongue flicked across her nipples while she rode him as best she could perched on the counter.

"You know you can see the shop from here," he said into her ear.

Lily's eyes popped open. She tried to twist around to look out the kitchen window, but Cade held her close. Below, she saw broad backs clad in denim bent over vintage cars.

"Shit," she said.

"Don't be shy," he said. "How about we give them a good show?"

She knew if they were caught, she'd regret it the next day. The guys would give her knowing looks, and the loudmouthed one might even say something. But he felt so good.

Damn, he just feels so good.

Suddenly, Cade lifted her up. She squealed. "What are you doing?"

"Changed my mind," he said. "Decided I don't want to share you."

With every step he walked her toward the bedroom, she held on tighter. With every step, she felt him sink deeper into her. Cade laid her on the bed and never exited her. He was on top of her, all-consuming, the only thing she could see or breathe. At that angle, he hit her G-spot just right.

Lily moaned into his ear.

"You've got me close," she said.

"Let go," he urged. "Just know that when you do, I'm not going to stop. I want you to keep coming for me..."

Lily felt the first orgasm build up at her center. She exploded onto him and called out his name the entire time. Cade slowed and worked every last layer of pleasure out of her.

She was sensitive, but didn't want to stop. As soon as she thought she could handle more, she whispered in his ear. "Hey. Where's that second round you promised me?"

Cade increased his pace, and Lily couldn't tell if her first orgasm was still going or if it was a new one that built inside her. This time, when she reached her peak, he came with her.

"That wasn't the dessert I spent three hours making," she said as he lay heavy on top of her.

He laughed and pushed himself to one side. "Sorry. But I'm starving again now. Tarte in bed?"

Lily walked to the kitchen, naked and not caring if the people below saw. She grabbed the entire dish and brought it to bed. Cade scooped out a piece with his fingers and popped it in his mouth.

"Damn," he said. "I never thought I'd think the whole Suzy Homemaker thing was so hot—"

She smacked him playfully. "I'm not a homemaker," she said. "Trust me, I wouldn't have the calluses I do if I were."

"I didn't mean it as an insult," he said. "I'm just saying. You know, if we're *official* or whatever ... I've just never had a girlfriend before. And don't think I'm complaining, but I didn't think if I ever did that, you know, she'd be like you. You're better than I could have ever imagined."

"Girlfriend?" she asked, shocked. "Official? What ... what do you mean—"

"Oh," he said. "Sorry, I just kind of assumed. I mean, I thought we were on the same page—"

"Yes! I mean, we are. I just... we didn't even talk about it, so I thought..."

"You thought what?"

"You know, that we weren't putting a label on it. Or whatever."

Cade laughed. "Is that the kind of guy you think I am?"

Lily looked down at the dessert, embarrassed.

"I don't know," she said. "It's not just you. Every guy in his twenties, I thought that was the thing. The whole play it cool until you get married schtick."

Cade laughed harder. "I'd like to think there would be a little more communication between meeting and getting married. I mean, if we have kids, I'd rather it not be a surprise."

"You want kids?" she asked. *With me?*

"I never thought about it seriously, but, yeah. I think I do. One day. Don't you?" he asked. "Although I have to be totally honest. There's a part of me that kind of hopes for a redo of my own childhood. But I guess we all bring our baggage to the kid thing, right?"

"Talking about kids right now is a little too weird," she said. "But, yeah, I agree. One day. How about we just stick with the whole boyfriend-girlfriend thing for now?"

"Okay. So... do we need to pinky swear or something? How do you make it official?"

"I think a pinky swear will work fine," she said. As he looped his finger through hers, she couldn't remember ever being so happy.

23

CADE

My receptionist just sent your clearance to Captain Crane.

Cade stared at the text from Dr. Hersh. *That's it?* he thought. It seemed too easy.

Does that mean I can return to duty? he replied.

You have medical clearance. Returning to duty is up to Captain Crane. Do you have time to talk?

Cade groaned. He was so close and then Dr. Hersh threw in that little question. It was almost like being in a real relationship.

Sure.

Immediately, his phone rang.

"Hey, Doc," he said.

"Good morning, Cade. I trust you're happy with the medical clearance?"

"Well, yeah. Of course."

"Good. I'm sure Captain Crane will have you on the team in no time."

"Crew," Cade reminded him. "So if I'm cleared, what do you need to talk to me about?"

"Well, medical clearance is a big step, but mental health

and managing the kind of trauma you sustained is going to take much longer than the few sessions we've had. It's my strong recommendation—and one that I included in your clearance—that we continue sessions."

"You want to keep seeing me," Cade confirmed.

"Yes, but not necessarily as frequently as we have been. My recommendation is twice a month."

"Huh." Cade realized he didn't hate the idea.

He'd gotten used to Dr. Crane and the strange, sci-fi furniture that didn't fit his personality. "I ... I guess that would be okay."

"Great. I'll have my receptionist call and set up our next few appointments."

Cade hung up and pulled on the most recent firehouse t-shirt.

Might as well look the part when I arrive, he thought.

He grimaced when he saw Aiden's truck in the firehouse lot. Since the incident in the parking lot, he'd largely managed to avoid Aiden without Elijah getting suspicious.

It was clear Aiden had avoided him, too. In order to keep up appearances, he'd asked Elijah out for drinks a couple of times. Both times, Elijah came alone.

"Where's Aiden?" he asked each time.

Elijah always shrugged as he took a pull of beer. "Had something to do."

"The crew's all here!" Elijah crowed as Cade walked in.

The new recruits he'd trained clapped him on the back, but he saw Aiden with his jaw clenched in anger. Before Cade could figure out how to handle it, Aiden turned his back to him and went back to his task.

Well, this is going to be awkward.

"Hey, Aiden—" Cade started as he walked toward him, but his voice was drowned out by the alarm that started to wail.

"All crews head out," Crane's voice boomed over the system. "Including Charles."

Shit. So this was it?

He hadn't had an induction like this since his first day in Montana. As he raced to his locker, he felt the immediate rush of adrenaline mixed with naked fear. That was a first, and he wasn't sure what to think of it. Fear hadn't even been part of the equation before.

Cade suited up and raced to the airfield behind the station. He noticed the recruits he'd worked with stuck close to him.

God, no. Please don't let them be counting on me.

"You six, go," the captain called. Cade's heart fell deeper when he realized he was on a rappeller group with not only Elijah, but Aiden.

If anything happens to either of them, that's it, he thought. *There's no getting over that.*

As the helicopter lifted into the air, he worked on his breathing. Even count in, even count hold, even count exhale.

You're a goddamned firefighter, he told himself. *Dangerous and stupid things are second nature.*

In the past, every time he ascended with a crew, he was always first. He wanted to get the lay of the land, make sure there weren't any surprises on the ground. But now? He was worried. There was no other word for it—and he'd never been worried before.

Below, the small wildfire had just started. It was small, but clean and hot. The chopper raged all around him. It filled his head with vibrations that made it hard to think.

Elijah nudged him hard through the suit. *Fine?* Elijah asked in rudimentary sign language as he tapped his thumb to his sternum.

They'd both signed up for American Sign Language in high school as their foreign language requirement, stupidly thinking it would be easier. It wasn't, but what little they remembered had stuck.

Cade nodded and shrugged. For a moment, he though he saw his Montana crew below. Heard their screams.

They're not there, he told himself. *Breathe.*

The pilot gave the signal to go, and Cade forced everything out of his head. All he saw was white. A soothing, calm white. His body took over, and Cade reached for the harness. Even if his brain couldn't fathom it, his body couldn't handle anything but to rappel out first.

As soon as he hit the ground, he looked up to count the suits that came behind him. Five. Two he knew were Elijah and Aiden. The other three were new recruits.

I got you.

"Trenches, go! Now!" Elijah commanded.

Cade was impressed. When he'd left Salem, Elijah was somewhat on the track to be a leader, but still had that boyishness to him. Now, it was gone. Elijah was all business, and Cade saw a trace of his dad in him.

Cade threw himself into the work. He didn't look up when he started to sweat. He didn't stop when the pain in his back got so severe he wondered if it was causing permanent damage. He kept his peripherals on the boots and suits around him. There were always five pairs. Always.

When he grabbed a shovel, he felt instant blisters blossom on his hands from the heat even through the gloves. Cade refused to flinch. His body was a machine, but it couldn't stop the worry that broke through in his mind. It barreled through the serene whiteness and weighed on his brain.

What if something goes wrong? Five pairs of boots. He checked over and over again without a lift of his head.

For five hours, he pushed through. The trenches were strong, sure to hold.

That's what you thought last time. The worry grew heavier, spread from his brain to his shoulders. The pain in any other moment would have been excruciating, but in the moment it served as a means to ground him.

I'm alive. There couldn't be this much pain if I wasn't.

In the distance, he thought he heard yelling and he paused for a moment.

Nothing. It was just the wind.

Cade went back to work. The walkie-talkie crackled for a moment. He bristled, but there was nothing. He waited for the voice of Barron, of Dominguez, but there was nothing but the whisper of static.

"... hear me?" Cade felt a sharp shove on his shoulder. It heated up the pain and traveled fast down his spine. Finally, he looked up and Elijah stood over him.

"Huh?"

"I said you're on firebreak! Didn't you hear me call you on the radio?"

"Uh ... no," Cade said.

Briefly, excuses flooded through him. Truth, too. *I was too scared to listen.*

"We're done here," Elijah said. Cade scanned his surroundings. Five suits. "There's another crew coming in to relieve us. We just have to hike down to the main road now."

"Oh. Okay." Cade stood up straight, though the pain was almost too much to bear.

Elijah looked at him strangely. He opened his mouth, but snapped it back shut.

We're both too tired for this, Cade thought.

As the two of them started down the trail together, Cade turned back to look at the fire. It had largely burned itself out. Elijah marched ahead of him.

From the back, he looked like his dad. Dog-tired after the fight, but still sturdy and strong. Cade felt like the little boy he used to be when he thought Mr. Hammond might as well be God.

Five suits. There were five suits in front of him.

But that was sheer luck, he thought to himself. *I didn't keep them safe. Elijah did. And so what does that matter?*

He jogged after Elijah as the post-adrenaline rush shakes

started to come on. His gear wasn't that heavy—he worked out more than that in the gym. But it felt like it weighed a ton.

He spotted Aiden's signature bowlegged walk at the head of the pack. He walked alone while the three recruits hung together in the middle. They no longer thought he could protect them.

And maybe I can't. They're on their own now.

Cade had never been happier to see the truck that waited at the main road. Aiden jumped in first and nodded for one of the recruits to sit beside him.

Anything to keep me away from him, Cade thought. But in that moment he was grateful. It wasn't the time to get into it. Especially in a small, confined space.

Aiden had really whaled on him.

Not that I didn't deserve it, he thought as he climbed into the truck.

Elijah was beside him. Cade stared out the window as a ground crew arrived. He watched as they moved in perfect sync together, clearly a crew that had seen some shit—and survived.

Cade wanted that again, he realized. He wanted to work together, to have zero animosity. More than that, he wanted his friends back. Elijah and Aiden had both been like his brothers ever since he could remember.

Hell, I remember when Aiden was still in diapers, he thought.

As they maneuvered onto a paved road, he thought about the years behind them. It was too much to give up.

And why should we? Why can't we make this new dynamic work?

Aiden thought he would hurt Lily, and he couldn't blame him.

But what if he knew how I really felt?

24

LILY

"*L*ily! What is wrong with you, you will burn the kouign-amann." Jean-Michel tsked at her and batted a towel at her to get her to move.

"Sorry," she squeaked. "It's just—"

"The fire, the fire, yes I know. We *all* know," Jean-Michel said as he eyed the pastries. "You are lucky, the perfect timing," he said as he pulled out the tray. "Why you worry? What good will it do? He is a firefighter, he fights the fires."

The bell to the front door rang and Jean-Michel gave her a look.

"Alright, I'm going," she said, and rushed out front.

The last thing I feel like doing is ringing up croissants all day.

When she saw Renee, she broke into a smile. "Hi."

"I heard about the fire," Renee said. She reached across the counter and squeezed Lily's hand. "It'll be fine. He'll be fine."

"I know," Lily said. "Or at least I hope so. It's the first big fire —or any fire—since Montana. And... I mean, I always stress out with Elijah and Aiden out there, but with what Cade went through in Montana... I don't know, it's worse this time."

"He wouldn't be out there if the doctor and captain didn't think he was ready," Renee said.

"Ah, the pretty friend," Jean-Michel said. He emerged from the kitchen armed with trays of perfectly golden kouign-amann.

Renee perked up at the compliment.

"Thanks," she said.

"Don't be so grateful," Jean-Michel scoffed. "You are pretty, yes, but you are also the only girlfriend Lily has."

"Wow, thanks," Lily said, as she rolled her eyes.

"You are welcome. It is truth. So, what can I serve you?" Jean-Michel asked Renee. "Your figure, so slender. Only baguette, then? Coffee black?"

"Actually, I was just stopping by to see how Lily is, what with the fire—"

Jean-Michel sighed loudly. "Ah, yes, the fire. Fires do not pay the bills for me. Baguette?"

"Uh. Sure," Renee said.

"Lily, ring up your pretty friend." Jean-Michel disappeared back into the kitchen.

"He's all business," Renee said under her breath.

"He's just tired of hearing me freak out about Cade all day. I just don't know how he'll handle it."

"I'm more concerned about how you're handling it. Or not," Renee said. "I get that it's a big deal, but all the reports say it's not huge. It'll be okay. I'm sure he'll check in with you as soon as he can."

"I know, but I just can't stop thinking about my mom. And how she'd sit up all night knitting, worrying about Dad." Lily shook her head. "I don't... I don't think I'm up for it."

"For what?"

"Doing what she did."

"Lily—"

"I'm serious! I mean, even if all the obstacles disappeared with Cade and me, even if my brothers didn't care about us being together, then what? Am I just supposed to sit around crocheting a scarf while I wonder if he's burning up in some forest?"

"I think that's a bit dramatic."

"It's not. Firefighting is one of the most dangerous jobs there is. I mean, look at my dad—"

"That Eagle Creek fire was unprecedented," Renee broke in. "And your dad, I mean I'm sorry for saying this, but he was *old*. To be fighting fires, I mean."

"Yeah. I know," Lily said quietly.

Outside, a fire truck pulled up into the bakery. She sucked in her breath as the door opened.

Please be Cade. Please be Cade. But the crew that jumped out were unrecognizable.

"He'll be here," Renee said. She squeezed Lily's hand again. "I promise."

"I just ... I didn't realize that saying yes to Cade meant saying yes to a fireman," she said. "It sounds stupid, but it's true."

Lily boxed up the mille-feuilles that the firefighters ordered. She took solace in their wide smiles.

Surely they wouldn't be smiling if it was bad out there. Right?

"Hey, were you guys with Cade up there?" she asked.

"Who?"

"Cade Charles? He—"

"Sorry, don't know him," the young man with skin dark and shiny as onyx told her. "But we came in from Corvallis, so..."

Just as Lily's heart sank, as her hands were full of boxed opera cakes, the door jingled again. Her eyes shot toward the door, and Elijah led the way while Cade trailed behind.

"Cade," she blurted out, and plopped the box onto the counter.

"Lily, I see that!" Jean-Michel called from the kitchen. "Those cakes are precious—"

She raced around the corner and caught Elijah's eye. He

was dog-tired, eyes bloodshot, and with the flush of fatigue that she remembered from childhood.

"Uh, I'm on a break," she said to the crew.

"What? This is not break—" Jean-Michel started from behind her.

"Sorry!" she called to him. "I need to... get something from my car." She held Cade's eyes and nodded toward the parking lot.

Jean-Michel sighed. "Fine. I take your order," he called to the crews. "Lily, you go home the rest of the day. So scattered."

Elijah moved toward the thick accent that promised strong coffee and sweet comfort.

Lily shifted her weight back and forth as she waited by her car. She felt guilty for not saying more to Elijah, but in the moment all she wanted was Cade.

When he finally made his way out of the bakery, alone, she could hardly wait until they were out of view of her brothers before she barreled into him.

He smelled like campfire, of the woods. As she wrapped her arms around him, she squeezed her eyes shut to hold in the tears.

Cade laughed quietly.

"So, I hear you're off for the day," he said. "You mind driving? I'm beyond tired."

She noticed that he shook slightly. The trembles brought a lump to her throat.

"Are you okay?" she asked. "You're shaking—"

"I'm fine. It's just exhaustion." Cade held up the keys to the Mustang.

"You drove here?" she asked. "You're in no shape to drive."

Cade gave her a tired smile. "I just spent who knows how many hours putting out a wildfire. Side by side with your brothers, which wasn't exactly the most relaxing surrounding. Trust me, I'm lucky that the shakes is all that I'm dealing with."

As Lily started up the car, Cade reclined his seat back and

rubbed his temples. She carefully made her way out of the parking lot, unable to adapt to the smoothness and speed of a car that wasn't older than her.

"You might want to use some gas, Grandma," Cade said.

She pretended to glare at him. "Sorry, it takes awhile to adjust from driving a hybrid dinosaur and boat."

When they arrived at her apartment, she noticed the mechanics' appreciative looks at the car. Lily ushered Cade upstairs and shooed away the questions about the car.

"Sorry for smelling like an animal," Cade said as he kicked off his boots.

"Oh, hush," she said.

She pulled him into the bedroom and peeled off his clothes. Even in this state, smeared in ash and dirt, the sight of him in nothing but his boxers made her heart flutter.

A sheen of sweat remained on his skin. His hands, callused and rough, were evidence of the hours of work he'd endured.

"Sorry," he murmured as she pulled back the duvet and tucked him in. "Just so tired..."

Lily crawled in beside him and gently rubbed his back. She listened to his breath start to lengthen and even. She matched him, breath for breath.

I take back everything I said before. Everything I thought before, she promised to whoever or whatever might listen. *I'd be proud to stay up and wait for him. I'll take him, however I can have him.*

Maybe those nights spent watching her mother fret and worry weren't a warning. Maybe it had been destiny, a means to prepare her. She knew what being with a fireman took—guts and resilience.

Who said being with a hero was easy?

She'd lied to herself before. But those were the last of it. The worries she'd spilled to Jean-Michel and Renee had simply been her sloughing off the last of her trepidation.

I'd stay up waiting forever if he asked me to.

Lily pressed her cheek to his back and let the rise and fall of his body lull her to sleep. As she toed the line between dreams and wakefulness, she felt like she was back in the old living room.

Her mother perched in the brown leather chair while Lily sat cross-legged at her feet. It was dark out, the kind of inky blackness that says it's midnight. Overhead, her mother knit an eternity scarf in the most beautiful shade of red Lily had ever seen. Her mother's fingers moved swiftly with certainty.

Lily crunched through a piece of toast buttered generously and topped with marionberry jam. This was their secret. The click of the needles seemed to only wake Lily.

Rooms away, Elijah and Aiden slept soundly. On these nights, the "fire nights," as her mom called them, if Lily woke up, she was allowed to stay up—as long as she was quiet. And she could have as much toast as she wanted.

"Mama," she whispered up. Her mother glanced down. The lamp overhead made a glowing halo around her mom's wild head of curls.

"What's up, baby?"

"Do you think Dad put all the fire out yet?"

"I'm sure he's getting really close if he hasn't already," she replied.

"And what if... what if the fire's too big? What if he can't put it out?"

"Of course he'll put it out," her mom said. "Don't worry."

"How do you know?"

"Because that's his job," her mom said. "He has to. It's a fire's job to burn, and it's your daddy's job to put them out. It's just as simple as that."

25

CADE

*T*he heat of Lily's back and the gentle drum of her heartbeat woke Cade up. He squinted into the morning light and held her closer. When he woke up in her bed, it had started to feel natural. He'd become used to seeing her there, her back pressed against his chest.

Thank you, Cade thought, the gratitude sent into the universe. *I don't deserve this, I know. So thank you for whatever brought us together.*

He wrapped a hand tighter around her waist and pulled her closer. Her scent, that blend of sweetness baking and a sort of wild freshness, he knew it would always get to him.

"What are you thinking?" she murmured. Her voice was still heavy with sleep.

"I'm exhaling gratitude," he said.

She laughed. "You sound like a yoga teacher I once had."

"That's the point," he said with a smile. "It's part of Dr. Hersh's whole 'don't go batshit crazy' strategy."

"What are you grateful for, then?" she asked over her shoulder.

"You. I'm grateful I didn't die. You know ... back in Montana. I'm thankful that I'm here with you."

"I'm thankful, too," she said. Lily snuggled deeper into the covers and into his arms.

God, I'm really falling for her, he thought. *Fast and hard.*

He felt his hardness jump against the heat of her thigh. "Come on," he said. "Let's shower."

She groaned. "Can't we just stay here?"

"I promise I'll make it worth your while."

She turned to smile and let him pull her out of bed.

The tiny, vintage clawfoot tub had a circular shower curtain that barely encompassed them both. The morning sun that poured through the white curtains hugged every curve of her body. Cade soaped her back and tried to memorize every freckle, every mole, every part of her. There was no telling when it would be the last time.

Elijah still doesn't know. And if Aiden was that pissed off, just imagine Elijah. As he looked at Lily, he knew it was worth it. If it came down to it, he'd give up the only friend he'd ever known, his virtual brother, for what they had. *And what would that do to Lily and Elijah's relationship?*

"My turn," Lily said, and she turned to face him in the small space.

Water trailed down her cheeks and pooled in her collarbone. Cade ran the soap across her breasts and watched the nipples harden at his touch.

She took the soap and began to work his chest down to his stomach.

"Someone's been working out," she said, and grinned up at him.

"That was pretty much all I could do," he said. "See the doctor and hit the gym."

"I'm not complaining," she said. As Lily moved down, she grasped his length with her hands slippery with soap, and he gasped at her touch.

"Turn around," he said.

"But I just got clean," she teased.

Cade gently turned her to the showerhead so the water rained down on her back. Lily grabbed the pipe that gurgled with the rushing water while he braced her hips. When she called out his name, it echoed throughout the bathroom.

The steam from the shower, the water drops that rained down, it made it seem like it was their own world. He didn't want it to ever end.

He spilled himself into her as she pushed herself against him. As Cade released himself, Lily pulled open the shower curtain.

"Too hot," she said as she turned to face him. He rained his own flutter of kisses down on her as he stepped out of the shower and pulled a towel around his waist.

Lily emerged from the bathroom as he sat on the edge of the bed and thumbed through his phone. Her short hair shot up in all directions as she ran a towel through it. "What are you doing?"

"I'm starving," he said. "What are you in the mood for?"

"Pizza?" she asked. "Luis's should be open by now."

He searched for the local pizza joint. "Yeah, they don't deliver."

"That's okay, we can do takeout. It's worth it," she said. Lily jumped onto the bed and crawled toward him. She peered over his shoulder at the menu. "Come on, I haven't had pizza in forever."

Cade kissed her over his shoulder. "Whatever you want."

Lily pulled on his firehouse sweatshirt and a pair of jeans so faded there were parts in the hips and thighs that were nearly transparent.

"I never knew those sweatshirts could look so sexy," he said with a wink as they piled into his car.

"I was kind of going for comfy. But if it doubles as sexy, that's okay with me." She slipped on the sunglasses and began to direct him toward the restaurant.

"Smells good," Cade said as he opened the door for her.

The little mom and pop establishment was stuffed full of the aroma of freshly roasted tomatoes, crusts baking to the perfect thin crispness, and a variety of toppings getting grilled and fried.

Cade took her hand as they got in line. Lily smiled up at him.

"Extra red sauce," she said. "That's the secret."

"Look, either speak English or go somewhere where they can understand you!" Cade bristled at the sheer hatred in the voice. At the front of the line, the cashier leaned across the counter. The woman in line had thick black hair to her waist. She held out a piece of paper to him. Her arm visibly shook with fear. "No, I don't want a freaking letter! Either tell me what you want, in English, or get out."

A small sob emitted from the girl in line and Lily tugged at his arm.

All Cade could see was red. He assessed the cashier without trying. It would be easy to take him down. The stooped shoulders and arthritic hands made him an easy target.

Why don't you take a walk around the block?

Dr. Hersh's voice wormed its way into his brain. *When you feel yourself getting angry, first consider the circumstances and then your options. I always like to remove myself from the situation, preferably to get outside and a little exercise, but that isn't always feasible.*

Cade started to go through the options.

Focus on a calming memory, place, or person that settles you. Elijah when they were twelve years old. After school in Elijah's room where they could watch *Hey, Arnold!* until his dad got home and binge on Hot Pockets and Mountain Dew. He could feel the give of the bean bag chair beneath him and the softness of the throw blankets.

His heart rate began to settle. The blood in his ears subsided. In front of him, he saw the ugly reality—a young Korean girl gestured to an aging, racist, hateful cashier.

"She can't speak anything!" an older woman in line yelled as she rushed up to the counter. "She's deaf, you asshole!"

"Oh my God," Lily said. "What a jerk."

"Is your manager here?" the older woman demanded. "I want to talk to him right now."

"Come on," Cade said. "Let's get out of here."

Lily looked up at him in surprise, but didn't ask any questions. Instead, she let him lead her out of the restaurant. As the door shut behind him, he heard the manager's booming voice as he apologized and offered free pizzas to the young girl for the next month.

"How about Thai instead?" Lily asked.

He smiled as he looked down at her.

This is what I need, he thought. *And it's what I want.*

Someone who could calm and soothe with just their presence. In Lily, he saw the non-judgment of Elijah echoed within her.

Maybe it wouldn't be so bad, he thought. *Maybe Elijah might even be happy about this—at least, once he gets used to it.*

In a Thai restaurant up the block that he'd never noticed before, bells chimed as they entered. Lily pretended to shiver.

"Every time I hear bells like that, I automatically want to welcome someone to the bakery and ask if they'd like to sample the Savarin."

Cade laughed. "If you'd like, you can ask me."

She wrinkled her nose at him. "I'd rather get some khao na pet to go and eat it in bed. With you," she added with a wink.

"That sounds like a plan."

The young woman took their order in halting English, and Lily slipped her hand into his.

"Your first time here?" the hostess asked as she jotted down their order for the kitchen.

"Yeah," Cade said. "I don't know how I missed it. We get Thai takeout at least once a week."

"You like, you come back," she said with a smile. "Here, take this. Coupon for next time."

"Do you deliver?" Lily asked.

"Yes, of course. If you live within five miles, delivery is free."

As the hostess rang them up, Lily pulled him down to her lips.

"We're sticking with delivery from now on," she said. "I'm pretty sure we could have squeezed in another session with the time it's taken us to go out and find sustenance."

"You seriously can't get enough, can you?" he asked with a laugh.

Lily widened her eyes.

"Don't blame me," she said. "You're the one who basically lived in a gym the past few months. And you expect me to control myself?"

She started to dig through the boxes as soon as they got into the car.

"What are you doing?" he asked.

"Looking for the mango pudding." She stuck a white plastic spoon in her mouth and reached into the bottom of the bag.

"Don't tell me you're a desserts first kind of person," he said, and pretended to shake his head in disappointment.

"Desserts always come first," she said. "You're lucky I'm here to teach you the right path." When she found the little container, she dug into it and moaned in satisfaction. "Here, try."

He let her spoon the sweetness into his mouth as she stopped at a red light.

26

LILY

"*I*'m out, Jean-Michel!" Lily called into the kitchen. She poked her head in and found him elbows-deep in fondant.

He muttered into the concoction.

"Ridiculous, these wedding requests for plastic 'frosting'— oh, *mon dieu!*" he exclaimed when he saw her. "Where are you going? More important, what are you wearing?"

She laughed and looked down.

"You don't like it?" Decked out in tiny short shorts, a tight raglan shirt and baseball socks pulled up to her knees, even she'd been impressed that she'd managed to pull the look together.

"Like, it is not a word for it. By the by, it is clear where you are going today." He arched a brow at her and smirked.

"Oh? And where's that?"

"In English, I don't know. We say *faire une partie de jambes en l'air.*"

"Yeah, I don't know what that means. But I get what you're implying."

"And I am not wrong?"

"*Anyway,*" she said, "given that I'm not one hundred

percent on what you said, I'll just tell you maybe. But at the moment, I'm going to play kickball with Aiden."

Jean-Michel snorted. "You disappoint me. Lily, you are the only employee I talk to. Why you cannot, how you say, bring the gossip for me?"

She laughed. "Sorry to disappoint you."

"What is this kickball? Football? Girls, they should not play the football."

"No, it's not football. Or soccer, if that's what you actually mean," she said with a smile. "It's like a game kids play at recess. But now there are intramural leagues so you can play for fun as adults."

Jean-Michel sniffed. "Americans, you never want to grow up. Okay, have fun with your ball kicking."

"Thanks," she said. "See you tomorrow."

As Lily headed toward the parking lot, her phone vibrated with a text from Aiden.

You on your way? You better not bail like the last 100 times! Everyone's waiting for you!

OMW, she replied and rolled her eyes.

For years Aiden had begged her to play in his tournament. And for years she'd come up with excuses. But now that Cade had joined, there was some motivation to actually go.

She pulled up to Riverfront Park and shielded her eyes to gaze up at the carousel as she jogged by. So many childhood summers had been spent at that carousel. One of her favorite pictures was of her and her mom and matching white horses with big brass poles that made it look like they were riding unicorns.

Lily could see the teams in the distances, half of them with bright pink strips of cloth tied around their arms. As she jogged up to the spectator area, she spotted Elijah, Aiden, and Cade huddled together.

Thank God, she thought. It seemed that Aiden and Cade had gotten over the tiff between them.

The one I caused, she reminded herself with guilt.

"Hey! Lily!"

Renee bounded up to the small circle with a thermos in hand. Renee's long golden legs shot out of her bright neon running shorts. One of the neon pink strips hugged her bicep tight.

"Renee! Uh ... what are you doing here?" Lily asked. She crouched down beside her brothers and stuck her phone into her backpack.

Renee shrugged. "Aiden invited me."

"Aiden?"

She looked down at her brother, but he wouldn't make eye contact with her. Awkwardly, she hugged Renee and offered up smiles to everyone else. The last thing she wanted to think about was whether her best friend and brother were hooking up.

When her eyes caught Cade's, she blushed and looked down to hide the grin she couldn't stop from spreading across her face.

Last night in bed, she'd told Cade that he might be a firefighter, but she'd surely kick his ass at a recess game.

"You sound really confident," he'd laughed. "Especially for someone who considers baking their primary form of fitness."

"Hey!" she'd protested. "I'd like to see you carry a five-tier cake without wobbling."

"I stand corrected," he said. "You're super buff."

"Seriously, I bet my team will win tomorrow."

"Okay, okay!" he'd laughed. "I'm sure you will."

"Yeah, but I said I'd bet you."

"Oh, yeah?" he'd raised a brow as he turned toward her. "And what are you going to bet? Because if it's cars, sorry, but no. I have way more to lose."

"Don't be mean to Mariah!"

"Mariah?"

"Yeah, that's the name of my car."

"My bad. I don't want the diva mad at me. So then tell me. What are you going to bet?"

"If my team doesn't win, I'm willing to put a week of blowjobs on the table."

"And if you win?" he asked. "Go on, you have my attention now. Literally, see?" He'd taken her hand and brought it over the sheets to his hardness.

"Don't get cocky already," she'd said. "If I win, the same. A full week of going down on me."

"You act like either of these bets have losers. Or that it wouldn't happen anyway."

"You might be right," she said with a grin. "But this still makes it more fun."

"Hey, so when is the field ours?" Renee asked. Her lilting voice broke into Lily's reminiscing about last night.

"Um, they should have been done ten minutes ago," Elijah said. "So I'm guessing any minute."

Lily squatted down between Elijah and Renee. It took everything she had in her not to let her eyes linger on Cade. Aiden already knew—or at least he knew there was something between her and Cade.

But how much did he know? Maybe he thought it was just a fling.

When Cade stood up and headed toward the restroom building, she watched him out of the corner of her eye.

"I, uh, should go fill up my water bottle before we start—"

"Me too, I'll go with you," Renee stood up to join her, but she shooed her back down.

"It's okay, I'll fill yours, too," she said.

Renee gave her an odd look. "Well, okay. Since you're so insistent on it. I won't say no to being indulged."

Lily trotted toward the small brick building. As soon as she turned the corner, she found Cade leaned up against the building. He pounced on her the second he saw her. Lily let out a squeal and dropped both bottles.

Cade pinned her against the wall and kissed her deeply. She felt the roughness of the brick tug at her clothes. He moved from her lips to her jawline and started to bite gently at her neck. Lily let out a moan and felt the familiar heat spread between her thighs.

"What, you can't even make it through one game?" Cade pulled away from her and they both turned to see Aiden. His face was bright red. The anger made his jaw twitch.

"Aiden—" she started, but he held up a hand.

"Are you two so stupid that you'd do this in public? Where anyone could catch you—like Elijah?"

"Hey—" Cade began, but Aiden just shook his head.

"We're about to start. You know, if you two would like to join us."

As Aiden stormed off, Lily looked up at Cade. She saw her thoughts reflected in his eyes even before she spoke.

"We're going to eventually have to tell Elijah," she said. "It's not fair, Aiden keeping this to himself."

Cade let out a short laugh. "I don't think he's having any trouble letting out some steam. You know, considering the beating he gave me."

"Actually, I think you're kind of lucky," she said. "Aiden's one thing, but Elijah ... I mean, he's been your best friend forever. And they're both protective over me, but Elijah is definitely the worse of the two."

"Yeah," Cade said quietly. "You're right, I know."

"I mean, what if it was Elijah that caught us just now?"

Cade chewed at his lip. "I can't even imagine."

"Let's just ... we need to figure out a plan. A plan to tell Elijah so we can stop all this sneaking around."

"Yeah, but I have to admit, I'm kind of going to miss that."

"Miss what?"

"The sneaking around part," he said. Cade slapped her butt lightly. "You have to admit, it's kind of a turn-on."

"Well, I certainly hope that's not the only thing that turns you on," she said. "You still have a bet to lose."

"We'll see about that."

"You go on first," she said, and gestured toward the field. "I actually do have to fill up these bottles if our flimsy excuse to get away is going to be even halfway believable."

She watched Cade jog up toward the field as she held Renee's bottle below the fountain. With each step he made away from her, she could almost feel the happy little bubble they'd built around themselves start to burst.

Lily followed a few minutes later. Up the hill, she could see her team with bright pink armbands start to warm up as the earlier group dispersed.

The last thing I want to do right now is play a stupid game of kickball.

She joined her team and watched as Aiden offered a shoulder to Renee so she could balance during a stretch. He raised a brow at her and dared her silently to say something. Lily tossed the bottle toward Renee.

"Took you long enough!" Renee said. "Were you sourcing the water directly from Mt. Hood or something?"

"Nature called," Lily said, and heard Aiden let out a bark of a laugh.

"Sorry," he said. "I shouldn't laugh. After all, who am I to say whether or not you should be able to manage your animal urges?"

Renee gave him a strange look as she released his shoulder and swan-dived down to touch her toes. Aiden didn't even try to pretend not to overtly check her out.

Lily's cheeks burned, but she knew better than to say anything.

27

CADE

"*A*lright, let's call it a day," Cade called out to the newest recruits.

They shot him grateful looks as they started to clear out the gear from the practice field. In the distance, he watched Aiden watch him. It had been like that all day.

No matter where Cade was around the firehouse, it seemed like Aiden was never far away. Cade waited until the recruits had everything packed up and were out of sight before he made his way over to Aiden.

With every step closer to one of his closest friends, he felt his heart rate increase.

Keep calm, he told himself. *Remember what the doctor told you.*

"We need to talk," Cade said.

Aiden spit onto the grass. "You think?"

Cade looked to either side, but the captain was nowhere in sight.

"Kitchen," he said as he nodded toward the back entrance. "Now."

The kitchen was spotless as usual. Bags of groceries for that night's dinner were neatly lined up on the countertop. Aiden leaned casually against the industrial refrigerator and surveyed Cade.

"Well? Go ahead."

"I just want you to know my feelings for Lily are real," Cade said. The words came out in a rapid stream. Aiden raised his brows, but he didn't walk away. "I... I've never felt this way about anyone before."

Aiden let out a small laugh. "Honestly? That's not really saying much. I mean, I watched you fuck around with any piece of strange that would have you, for what? Ten years?"

"It's not like that," Cade said, but he dropped his eyes. Aiden was right. *Why should he believe me?* "That... those days are over," Cade said.

"Right," Aiden said with an eye roll. "You know, I used to envy you? I mean when we were kids. When I was a freshman and you and Elijah were seniors... I thought it was awesome, how you pretty much got any girl you wanted. I just... well, I never thought you'd go after Lily. That's another kind of low. And I'm not even Elijah."

"I know," Cade said. "I know how it looks."

A recruit wandered into the kitchen, saw the tension between them, and backed out.

"You gotta get to the point soon if you have one," Aiden said. "Unless you want all kinds of gossip running around the station."

Cade sighed.

"This *is* the point. I'm trying to tell you—I love her, man. It's not some kind of infatuation or drawn-out manwhore phase. And trust me when I say we weren't looking for this. It's not like I've been trying to get her for years or something."

His face burned slightly at those words.

I may not have been trying, but what happened years ago... it probably got the kindling going.

"You're being serious?" Aiden said. "Because I know I don't have to tell you this, if Elijah finds out—when Elijah finds out

—who knows how he's going to react. And if he accepts it, then you go on to break her heart... I just wouldn't want to be you."

"I know," Cade said. "I know I'm risking pretty much everything. My best friend, you, the closest thing to a family I've ever known. My *job*—"

"Hey," Aiden said. He leaned over and clapped Cade's arm. "You really think you'd get fired over it? I mean, Elijah has some serious pull here, sure, but I don't think he'd do that to you."

"Yeah? Not even if I broke Lily's heart?"

Aiden cocked his head. "Well... yeah, maybe. You're probably right."

"Then you know what I'm putting on the table," Cade said.

"I, uh... I never really considered all that."

"It's the truth. I'm risking everything to be with her."

Aiden eyed him carefully.

"You're being honest, aren't you?" he asked in disbelief.

"You think I'd be in here basically begging you if it was a fling?"

A smile crept across Aiden's face.

"Is that what you're doing? Begging?" he asked. Cade saw the smile that twitched at his jaw.

"Don't push your luck," Cade said with a small laugh. "But, yeah. I guess it's something like that."

"Well, in that case. If the Morningside Manwhore has really mended his ways, *and* he wants to be with my baby sister, I guess I might be able to get on board."

"Thanks, man," Cade said.

His voice choked up, and he forced out a cough, though he knew neither of them would buy it.

"I can't speak for Elijah, though," Aiden said. "You know he's always been the overprotective type."

"I know," Cade said. "Will you give me some time, though? To tell him?"

Aiden let out a whistle. "I don't know... if he finds out that I knew and didn't say anything, we'll both be in a world of hurt."

Cade sucked at his cheek.

"I know," he said quietly. "I didn't want to put you in this position."

"Just tell me this, then. Do you really love her? I mean, all the way through. For real."

Aiden searched his eyes, and for once during the conversation Cade didn't need to will himself to maintain eye contact.

"I do," he said. "I really love her."

They were the easiest words he'd ever said.

Then why haven't you said it to her?

"Well damn, Cade. Why didn't you just tell me that from the start?"

Cade laughed. "It was kind of hard to get the words out when you were pummeling me in the parking lot."

"Yeah, sorry about that, man," Aiden said. "I guess I have some anger issues or something."

"You know, I know a doctor who might be able to help you with that."

Aiden wrinkled his nose. "No thanks, man. And no offense. But once you get into the headshrinking game, it's tough to get out."

"It's not so bad," Cade said with a shrug. "He actually taught me some good tricks for it. Anger issues, I mean."

"Well, that's good. Maybe you can tell me a few over a beer sometime."

"Is that a peace offering?" Cade asked.

He realized he'd never intentionally hung out with Aiden before, just the two of them. For most of their lives, Aiden had always been Elijah's little brother. A nuisance when they were really little, then an afterthought as they grew up.

How much do I even know him? The second almost-brother that's been right in front of me?

"Call it what you want," Aiden said. "You'll be the one paying."

Cade laughed. "I see how it is. But yeah, that sounds good. After ... you know, after I tell Elijah and everything."

"Good luck with that," Aiden said. "My advice? Wait until the day before he goes back on shift. The end of his weekend. He'll never forgive you if you screw up his Friday."

"Thanks for the tip," Cade said.

"Hey, where've you two been? The captain's been looking for you." Elijah appeared in the doorway, a greasy towel slapped over his shoulder.

"Nothing," Cade and Aiden said in tandem.

Elijah looked at them curiously.

"Doesn't look that way to me. Anyway, I need one of you to help me with diagnostics on one of the trucks," he said with a shake of his head. "Whole place is going to hell, I swear."

Aiden nudged Cade in the ribs. "Aren't... doesn't your shift not start until tomorrow?" Aiden asked.

"Yeah, well, technically. But these recruits don't know a fuel cap from their own ass."

Aiden looked at Cade pointedly.

"Uh, Elijah," Cade started. "Can I talk to you a minute?"

"What the hell you think we're doing now? Are you going to help or not?" Elijah asked, exasperated.

God, this really isn't the right time, Cade thought. *Just get it over with. Fast and painless. And in public.*

"It'll just take a minute," Cade said hurriedly. "I've been meaning to tell you this, I just couldn't figure out how. So, Lily—"

"What the hell you doing in here?" The captain appeared in the doorway. "Baking pies? Elijah, get going, we need that truck in perfect condition yesterday."

"Yes, Captain," Elijah said.

He gave Cade an inquisitive look as he turned on his heel.

Cade could hear Elijah as he yelled down the hall looking for someone else to help him.

"Sorry, Captain," Aiden said. He tipped his baseball cap at the old man and hurried toward the locker rooms.

"What you waiting on, Betty Crocker?" the captain asked Cade. "Someone to read the recipe to you?"

"Uh, sorry, Captain," Cade said.

He saw a small smile pull at the captain's face as he inched by him.

Cade rushed to the parking lot and slid into the seat. His heart hammered a mile a minute, but he had to admit he was somewhat grateful for the interruption.

Elijah was obviously distracted, but there would be endless excuses at the ready for why it was never a good time.

"You'll have to tell him eventually," he said under his breath as he started the car.

He flipped on the radio to the nineties station. Elijah emerged from the garage doors with one of the new recruits in tow.

Cade hunkered down in the car and watched as Elijah tried, with veiled patience, to show the recruit how to run diagnostics. The way his best friend nudged the kid in the right direction reminded Cade of how Elijah had been with Lily for all those years.

Still is, I'm sure, he thought.

You've gotten yourself in a serious situation, he thought to himself.

He practiced his breathing exercises, filled his lungs up all the way and held it for four counts before a slow release.

Of all the women in all the world, it had to be her. Still, he didn't question if she was worth it or if he was wrong. Everything was falling into place. *But would Elijah accept it?*

28

LILY

*L*ily reached down from the exam table and grabbed her cardigan off the chair. Her toes were frozen, even through her socks.

Why do they always make you get naked and put on these stupid paper gowns if they're going to take forever to come see you?

When the nurse prepped Lily to see her GP, she gave Lily a look when the blood pressure cuff was released.

"That's kind of high for you," the nurse said.

"What is it?"

"It's one hundred eighteen over seventy."

"That's ... that's not, like, bad though. Is it?" Lily asked.

"No, but you've always had low blood pressure according to your charts. Are you under a lot of stress lately?" the nurse asked as she made notes on her tablet.

That's an understatement. "I guess so," Lily said.

"Are you practicing self-care habits?" the nurse asked. "It's important, especially as you get older."

"I'm trying," Lily said. She didn't even convince herself.

"Well, the doctor will be in soon."

Lily sat upright until she heard the door click shut. With a whoosh of air, she exhaled and looked around the room. Every movement made the paper gown crinkle. With the cardigan splayed across her thighs, she thumbed through the apps on her phone.

Don't do it, Lily, she told herself, but she couldn't help it. Once again, she searched "breasts tender symptoms" and watched the internet tell her she was either pregnant, dying, or both.

This is stupid, she thought as she read through the various conditions related to sore breasts. *Breasts get sore! Your period is probably about to start.*

But Lily couldn't stop thinking about her mother. She was too little to remember the worst of it. Any talk about breast cancer and her mom had been veiled in front of her.

However, even as a child Lily had sought out breast cancer stories and early warning signs. Tender breasts were a common symptom.

Yeah, and it's also a symptom of pregnancy and PMS. You're on the pill and you've never had this degree of tenderness with your period—so what else could it be but breast cancer?

A sharp knock came at the door.

"Miss Hammond?" Her doctor appeared in the doorway, short and squat with thick round glasses. "I hear you've been having some tenderness in the breasts."

The nurse rushed in behind the doctor and sat down in the chair in the corner. The gentle tap of her fingers on the screen put Lily on edge.

What is she writing?

"Yeah," Lily said. "I know it doesn't sound like a big deal, but my mom had breast cancer—"

"If you're concerned about anything, it's worth looking into," the doctor said. "Lean back."

Lily leaned against the coolness of the white paper that covered the exam table and let out a little gasp.

"Cold, I know. Sorry about that," the doctor said. The middle-aged   woman   stared   into   the   distance   and concentrated as she palpated Lily's breasts. Lily jumped at the touch.

"That hurts?" the doctor asked.

"Uh, yeah. Kind of," she said.

The doctor shook her head.

"Sorry, I need to press a little deep for a full examination. Your OBGYN did a full exam eight months ago, is that right?"

"Yeah, that sounds right," Lily said.

"And those results were all normal?"

"Yeah." Lily winced as the doctor moved in calculated, sharp movements around her breasts.

"I'm not feeling anything unusual," the doctor said. "You have quite a few cysts, but those are benign and normal for a woman your age. I'm going to order some blood work to rule out some other possibilities."

"Blood work?"

"It'll just take a few minutes. She'll take care of that, and I'll be back in a little while with the results." The doctor nodded toward the nurse who tapped a few more lines into the notepad with certainty. "Any other questions?"

Could it still be cancer? Is it something worse? Just tell me what you think it is!

"No," Lily said with a smile. "I'm good."

"Alright. I'll be back." The doctor swept out of the room while the nurse prepped a needle.

"Just a little sting," she nurse said as she tied a tourniquet Lily's arm and searched for a vein.

"How long will this take?" Lily asked. She watched the vial fill with bright red blood.

"The on-site lab is pretty quiet right now. Not long," the nurse promised with a smile.

"Can I get dressed?"

"Why don't you stay in the gown a little longer? In case the doctor needs to do further examinations after the blood work."

Lily sighed as the nurse disappeared, armed with blood and

a flurry of notes. She replied to all her pending emails, scoured Buzzfeed's LOL lists in an attempt to lighten her mood, and drafted countless texts to Cade that she never sent.

How the hell long is this going to take?

Finally, just as she thought she might die of hypothermia instead of whatever in her breasts was killing her, a knock came at the door.

"Miss Hammond?" the doctor asked as she walked in. "I have your blood results."

"Oh?"

I'm dying. It's some rare blood disease and I'm dying.

"You don't have breast cancer," the doctor said. "Your breasts are sore because you're pregnant."

"I'm... wait, what?"

"I take it you weren't trying?" the doctor asked. "You're in the very early stages. I couldn't give you an exact timeframe without further testing, but definitely in the first trimester. First month, most likely."

"I'm pregnant?" Lily waited for her heart to feel like it was barreling toward the floor, but it never came. Instead, a strange sense of lightness washed over her.

"Yes, you are. Do you have a professional you'd like to talk to? Your OBGYN? If not, we have referrals—"

"That can't be right," Lily said. "I take my birth control pills religiously. The same time I take my vitamins—"

"Miss Hammond, I'm understanding that this isn't a wanted pregnancy. But birth control pills aren't a sure thing. Actually, compared to other options like IUDs, they don't have an impressively high success rate."

"But... this wasn't supposed to happen. Not now," Lily said into her cupped hands. Her body was on fire. Any hint of coldness was long gone.

"I recommend you make an appointment with your OBGYN right away," the doctor said. She patted Lily's hand kindly. "There are options, especially this early on. Don't make a rushed decision right now. The OBGYN we have on file for you is at Providence, is that right?"

"Yeah," Lily said.

Her own voice sounded so far away. *How could I be pregnant? Fuck, what is Cade going to say?*

"I highly suggest you call today to get an appointment. The earlier you see your OBGYN, no matter what you ultimately decide to do about the pregnancy, the better."

"Yeah," Lily said. "Thanks. I'll call them today."

Somehow, she managed to get her clothes back on when the doctor and nurse left. Lily glanced down at her flat stomach.

How is this possible? She tried to come up with ways to tell Cade, but nothing sounded right. *And he hasn't even told Elijah yet. Telling my brother we're together, or whatever, is one thing. But telling him I'm pregnant?*

She couldn't even fathom the fallout.

As Lily walked through the waiting room, she noticed a woman that had to be about ready to pop. *I am so not ready for this.*

She ran through potential ways to start the conversation with Cade as she drove home, but came up with nothing. When she saw his Mustang parked on the street, her heart began to flutter.

Just do it. Just tell him. Get it over with.

Every step up toward her apartment felt like it took all the strength she had. Lily opened the door and saw Cade's back in the kitchen. He was bent over the stove, the scent of grilled cheese all around him.

"Hey!" he said with a smile. "How was your appointment?"

"Fine," she said. Lily tossed her bag onto the couch and moved into the doorway to the kitchen. She watched his broad back as he grilled the thick slices of bread. *I can't believe I messed it all up.*

"So, I talked to Aiden today," Cade said. "Smoothed things over. And Elijah—"

"You talked to Elijah?" she broke in.

"Well, he walked in on Aiden and me—"

"Don't you think you could have told me before you talk to my own brothers? About *us*?" she asked.

He turned slowly and looked at her. "I thought we agreed—"

"Yeah, we agreed that we need to tell them, but not that you were going to take on the whole thing yourself!"

She felt the displacement of her anger, but she couldn't help it. It felt too good, to buy some time. To redirect the rage at someone besides herself.

"Hey, what's the matter?" he asked. Confusion clouded his eyes.

"What's the matter is that you always have to be the freaking hero, and leave me on the sidelines just waiting for you to tell me when to jump. How high, all of that!"

"Lily, calm down—"

"Don't you dare tell me to calm down." Her voice shook with fear, and it sounded just like rage. "You don't get to do that."

She stormed into her bedroom, grabbed her jacket and shoved her feet into her wornout hiking boots. As she stomped toward the front door, she felt his eyes on her.

"Where are you going?"

"Out!" she yelled. "I need to be alone."

"But I made dinner—"

"Oh, eat it your freaking self," she said.

She slammed the door behind her with everything in her and made it all the way to the car before she burst into tears.

29

CADE

*C*ade waited for three hours, but Lily never came back. He'd never seen her like that before—picking fights and freaking out over nothing.

What the hell was that appointment about?

When she'd told him she had a quick appointment, he didn't think much of it. Now, Cade realized he should have dug deeper. It wasn't like Lily to keep secrets.

Had she gone to talk to Elijah?

By the time Cade had given up on her returning, he left the cold sandwiches on the kitchen counter and stormed downstairs to the parking lot. Tucked under the windshield of his car, he saw a yellow note in her familiar scrawl.

Went hiking at Northgate. Needed fresh air. Sorry, L.

Cade slammed the door shut and crumpled up the note.

What the hell is her problem?

His phone vibrated and he scrambled for it. Lily had turned off her phone, but maybe she was finally coming back to her senses. But it was Elijah's name that lit up his screen.

"Hello?" he asked quietly. Cade didn't know what to expect. *What if Lily was with him? What if this was Elijah calling with a death threat?*

"Hey!" Elijah said. His voice was light, happy. "Where are you?"

"Uh... just getting some gas," Cade said as he glanced at the single pump the mechanic shop used.

"You nearby? Want to grab some coffee?"

"Sure," Cade said. The last thing he wanted to do was get some coffee, but at least being around people would keep his mind off Lily. "Where are you thinking?"

Elijah laughed. "Where do you think? The usual. I have a craving for eclairs."

"Uh, okay. See you there in ten?"

The last thing he wanted to do was go into Lily's place of work with Elijah, but there weren't any plausible excuses at the ready. He pulled the Mustang onto the main road and started toward the bakery.

Elijah was already there. He leaned casually against the truck with sunglasses perched on his nose. His eyes were impossible to read.

"Real hog, huh?" Elijah asked when Cade approached him.

"What?"

"The Mustang," Elijah said. He slipped his glasses off. "It's a real gas hog, right?"

"Oh, yeah. It's not too bad," Cade said.

"Come on. I need some caffeine. And sugar."

The bell chimed as they entered, and Cade locked eyes with Jean-Michel at the register.

"Lily's not working today?" Elijah asked, disappointed.

"No," Jean-Michel said slowly. He looked at Cade curiously. "Wouldn't he know—"

"That's alright, we're just taking some stuff to go. Right?" Cade interrupted.

Elijah looked at him strangely. "Are you in a rush? I thought we could eat here—"

"Young love, is always in a rush," Jean-Michel said. "What can I get you?"

"Young love?" Elijah asked with a chuckle. "Sorry, Cade and I are just friends. Uh, half a dozen eclairs, two for here, and two Americanos."

"Americanos," Jean-Michel said with a sigh. "Terrible name. You should try the espresso. Or French press," he said.

"Sure, we'll try that," Elijah said as he took out his wallet.

Cade felt the guilt settle in deeper as he watched Elijah pay. Secrets weighed an enormous lot. He felt the secret he kept from Elijah grow heavier every time they were together. It was almost impossible to keep himself from spilling it right on the spot.

But now? When Lily was freaking out? Obviously she didn't say anything to Elijah, but then what else could it be? Is she having second thoughts?

The last thing he wanted to do was go and tell Elijah when Lily had come to her senses and realized she could do better.

What does she want with a broken guy who's all messed up in the head, anyway?

"What did you say?" Cade snapped out of his thoughts at the tone in Elijah's voice. Elijah stared at Jean-Michel in disbelief.

"I tell your friend, he better treat the young lady right."

"And what the hell is that supposed to mean?" Elijah demanded.

Shit. All this planning, and the fucking Frenchman goes and spills the beans?

Jean-Michel's eyes widened as he realized what he'd done.

"I mean nothing," Jean-Michel said. "Just tease."

Cade turned to Elijah.

"Come with me," he said.

"But the eclairs!" Jean-Michel called from behind.

Cade followed Elijah dutifully out of the shop. The parking lot was deserted. Cars zipped by. Anything could happen here, anything, and nobody would see it.

"You want to tell me what the hell that guy was talking

about?" Elijah demanded. His arms folded across his broad chest.

This is it. Just tell him. Tell him.

"I, uh, I don't know what Jean-Michel knows—"

"I don't give a fuck what he knows or doesn't know. I want you to tell me the truth."

"Elijah… Lily and I, we've been—well, we're together."

"And what the hell does that mean?"

Cade drew in a deep breath. *At least he hasn't kicked my ass yet.*

"I've been trying to figure out how to tell you," he said quietly. "And, please believe me, we didn't plan it—"

"How long has this been going on?"

"A few weeks?"

Elijah nodded. "And what do you mean by together?"

"We—"

"Are you fucking her?"

"Elijah, please—"

"Are you fucking my baby sister?" Elijah dropped his arms and Cade saw the balled-up fists.

"It's not like that." *It is like that.* "I—Jesus, Elijah, I have real feelings for her. Okay? We're in a relationship, and it's pretty serious—"

"Fuck, Cade! The *one* thing I told you not to do! The one thing! And you can't even keep it in your pants. She's my goddamned sister —"

"I know! I know, and I'm sorry! I didn't want to hurt you. I don't want to lose you as my best friend. You're like my brother—"

"Yeah, and Lily's *supposed* to be like your sister! Or at least she was. I can't believe you'd do this to me—"

"To you?" Cade asked in disbelief. "This … our relationship has nothing to do with you."

For the first time, Cade realized that was true. *What does it matter if Lily and I love each other? What does that mean to Elijah?*

"She was the one person... what the fuck? What is wrong with you?" Elijah screamed. He lunged at Cade, who let his body go limp as his best defense.

"Hit me back!" Elijah screamed in his face. "Come on, you fucker, fight!"

Cade dropped to one knee and accepted the fists that showered his back. When Elijah hit his ear, he heard a sharp ringing and felt a sting that shook him to the core.

"What the fuck?" Cade looked up. Aiden raced around the corner. "Hey! Hey, both of you! I don't know what the hell you're doing, but a huge fire just broke out near Northgate."

"Northgate?" Cade was breathless.

"Some idiot let a fire get out of control at the barbeque pits," Aiden said. "You need to finish this shit about Lily some other time."

"How do you know this is about Lily?" Elijah asked. "Shit, Aiden, if you knew—"

"Lily's at Northgate," Cade burst out. Both Elijah and Aiden turned to him.

"Fuck," Elijah said. "Let's go." He reached down automatically for Cade and lifted him up.

"What are the reports?" Cade asked as he raced behind Aiden and Elijah toward the fire truck Aiden had parked at the end of the lot.

"Uh ... up to twenty hikers are trapped," he said. "And it's only going to get worse if it spreads. I didn't know. I didn't know she was there—"

"It's not your fault," Cade said as he jumped into the cab.

It's mine. Whatever happened, it's my fault she's out there. I didn't stop her. I just let her go.

The helicopter was prepped and ready as they pulled into the station. No matter what had happened, as they climbed in they naturally assumed their roles. Cade slipped on his headphones and listened as the reports rolled in.

"Looking like closer to twenty-five hikers trapped at Northgate ..."

"Are you sure that's where she is?" Elijah asked loudly over the helicopter.

"Yeah," Cade said. He gazed down as the helicopter brought them closer to the flames that licked across the park below.

I'm sorry.

The captain's voice boomed in their ears. Cade made eye contact with Elijah. All the anger had drained out of him.

"Sorry," Elijah mouthed.

Cade just nodded. He didn't want apologies, or even Elijah's acceptance. All he wanted was to know that Lily was alright. The chopper hovered above the worst of the fire and Cade gripped the rappelling rope.

As he descended into the heat, the adrenaline flooded him. Any linger of the pain from the beating Elijah had given him was gone. All that mattered was finding Lily, saving Lily.

When his boots crunched into the fallen branches, he looked up and saw Elijah and Aiden above him.

This isn't Montana, he told himself. *Breathe.*

The three of them made their way into the smoke while his radio crackled at his chest. *This is it. Your chance of redemption.*

Maybe saving Lily wouldn't make up for what had happened in Montana. Nothing would. But it was the best he could do.

This time, with Elijah and Aiden flanking him, for once he felt like he wasn't alone. It wasn't him against the flames, it was all of them.

Knowing they loved her just as much as he did, would do anything for her just like he would, Cade felt a safety and security that he'd never known.

Firefighters, we don't run away from the flames. We run straight toward them, embrace the heat. Trust that the smoke won't blind us forever. Lily, we're coming for you.

30

LILY

*L*ily slung the light backpack she kept in her trunk off her shoulders. It was one of her favorite resting points on the gentle mountain. She sniffed at the air.

A campfire? At Northgate?

That wasn't right. The only legal fire areas were down at the barbeque pits, but there was no denying the smell. She focused on steady breathing and climbed up onto the old fallen log that offered the best, but dangerous, view of the surroundings. Lily clung to a sturdy branch and leaned out over the precipice. Below her, flames and black smoke climbed skyward.

"Oh my God," she said under her breath.

Shit, how could I not notice that? Am I really so all up in my own head that I don't notice a freaking fire?

She reached for her phone, though she knew it was pointless. There was no service, and hadn't been for the past two miles. *How many times have I hiked this trail?*

Lily pressed her hand to her abdomen. Even though her stomach was still taut and flat, she could feel the tiny life that grew inside her.

Move. Move! she commanded herself. There were two

options. Descend down the sheer rock face on the opposite side of the mountain, or keep hiking upward.

You couldn't handle the rock face when you weren't pregnant, she admonished herself. Lily had only ever known one hiker who could do it, and he was the guy who trained her at the rock climbing gym.

And how high are you going to hike? she asked herself as she pulled the backpack on.

"What happens when I reach the top?" she asked aloud as she started on the switchbacks.

She was tempted to take a shortcut straight up the mountain, but the life that glowed inside her told her to stick to the trails. *The last thing you need is to get hurt on top of being stranded.*

As Lily picked up her pace, she felt cold sweat pool at the small of her back.

Maybe if I get high enough, there won't be enough vegetation or oxygen for the fire to survive. She tried to remember all the facts her brothers and Cade had memorized when they were recruits.

What would a firefighter do in this situation? she wondered. *Higher it is.*

Part of her knew that she was just taking up time. But hiking upward gave her something to think about—something besides Cade. Something besides their baby.

Where the hell are Cade and my brothers? Are they close? God, what if Cade never got the note?

She'd scribbled it quickly and couldn't remember how well she'd snapped it under the windshield wiper. Maybe it blew away. Maybe some punk kid took it as a joke.

I'm sorry, I take it back. I should have never picked that fight, she thought to herself. *Just keep going. Higher. Higher.*

A part of Lily wished desperately that she'd run into other hikers. Find some sense of hope. But a bigger part of her hated herself for wishing this on anyone else.

She remembered Elijah always talked about how it was the smoke, not the fire, that usually killed a person. *So does that make it a better way to go?*

Lily looked back once, but it seemed like the smoke was thicker. Closer.

Don't turn around, she told herself. As she rounded a switchback, she stumbled over a root that shot out of the ground.

Shit! Already her ankle started to swell. She pushed herself up from the ground, brushed small stones and debris from her palms, and willed herself forward.

What the hell am I supposed to do now that I can't outrun the fire?

She made it a few more yards before even she could tell she was doing more harm than good. A log along the rim of the trail beckoned to her.

So, what? I'm just supposed to wait here to die?

Lily thought she could see the flames as they reached up the trail toward her, but she couldn't be certain. The air was so thick with smoke, she wasn't sure what she was seeing. She pulled her jacket up to cover her mouth and nose and started to cough.

Lily was desperate for oxygen, but with every breath she remembered their baby breathed in the same air. Instead, she took light sips of air through the nose and prayed that it was clean enough.

A crackle filled the air. There was no way to deny it. The flames were visible, and they raced up the trail at a speed she couldn't have outrun even if she hadn't messed up her ankle.

Lily slid the backpack off as tears streamed down her face. She couldn't tell if it was from the smoke, from all the regrets, from the life with Cade and their child she saw falling away, or all three.

She pulled off her jacket and peeled away her sweatshirt to use as a bandana.

Heat rises. Smoke must, too. Lily positioned herself behind the log and lay down flat on a sprawling fern. As she wrapped the sweatshirt around her face as a makeshift mask, she splayed the bright green jacket over her. *If they're looking for me, if anyone's looking for me, please, God, let them see this.*

"I'm sorry," she whispered into the smoky air.

She didn't know if it was to Cade, to their baby, or to herself. She'd barely had time to even process the fact that she was pregnant.

And see what you did when you found out? You ran away—just like you always do.

Her head swam with pieced-together thoughts. Lily remembered her mother, and how good that buttery toast tasted at two in the morning while they waited for her dad. She saw Jean-Michel, a perpetual smear of flour across his face.

"Love is never free."

In the distance, she heard another voice. They all blended together, but this one was soothing, deep and steady. *Cade?*

Lily forced herself up onto her elbows. She coughed violently into the sweatshirt, but when she tried to remove it, that made it worse.

"Lily!" the voice called in the distance.

"Cade," she croaked out. She couldn't make her voice any bigger. "Cade!" she finally managed, from a strength deep inside.

She heard the crunch of boots on hard ground. As the black smoke rose from below her, Lily thought she saw a figure emerge. It was yellow, like the tips of a fire. She couldn't figure out if it was real or her imagination gone wild with the smoke.

You found me, she thought. But in that instant, the figure disappeared again.

You're imagining this, she told herself. *It's okay, let go.*

Lily lay back down and did her best to pull the reflective jacket over her body.

Just get onto the log, she told herself. *If anyone comes by, they need to see you.*

She pulled together the last bit of her strength and hoisted herself onto the log. Deep within, she thought she felt something shift. It wasn't a kick, it was way too early for that. But it was there.

I'm here, it seemed to say. *Don't be scared.*

Lily let her eyes close, convinced herself it was to keep the sting of the smoke away. In the darkness, just like everyone said, her life was showcased as a montage.

She was nine years old and walking home from school with her brothers and Cade. She could feel the weight of her plastic lunchbox in her hand. She was one year older and at the firehouse. Cade's dad was like a monster as he stumbled toward them. She dropped her kite and ran into the firehouse like her dad said.

Minute later, Cade rushed in as blood poured from his nose. "You're bleeding," she said, and took his hand.

She was in high school getting ready for the homecoming dance with girlfriends she hadn't thought about in years. Cade walked in with Elijah.

"I thought you were too old for princess parties," Elijah said, and she shot him a look. But when she saw Cade, she blushed and looked down.

"You all look pretty," Cade said. It made her blush harder.

It was three years ago, and Tim had just dumped her in the most humiliating moment of her life. Her face was streaked with tears and she dug desperately for her keys in her bag. Cade appeared before her.

He took her into his dry truck and drove her to his apartment. She drowned in his sweatshirt that he slowly pulled off of her on that couch. The touch of his lips on her skin shot off fireworks.

It was last month in the bakery. Jean-Michel had a twinkle in his eye when he asked her about the sexy fireman. She wanted to spill it all to him, to gossip and guess and plan an elaborate, ridiculous wedding.

She was on Renee's couch with a pint of ice cream. Lily felt her insides soften as her best friend came back, fully, from her time abroad and attempt at escape.

These are all the things I'll miss, she thought as her dreams began to mix with reality. *These are all the people I've loved.*

But at the top of the list was Cade. He was what kept coming back into her memory.

I'm sorry you'll never know, she thought into the darkness.

But maybe he would. Maybe, somehow, he'd find out about what she'd carried into the flames. And maybe he'd forgive her.

Lily let go of her last grasp of consciousness. It was true what they say. She wasn't afraid. The heat felt good, like a warm blanket wrapped around her. And the smoke, as it filled her body, made its way into her bones so that she was as light as could be. She'd never felt so light in her life.

Don't be scared, the little voice in her center whispered. *I'm here with you.*

31

CADE

*a*s he made his way up the steep incline, he tried to remember what she'd been wearing.

Khaki pants. Those old hiking boots. And the jacket. The bright green jacket. Shit, he thought. *How am I going to find a green jacket in the goddamned Oregon wild?*

Still, he kept on. He heard Elijah and Aiden behind him. Occasionally, he looked back to check on them. But he had no doubts that they were just as committed to finding her as he was.

They came upon the first bundle of hikers, and he saw the internal struggle as Aiden began to help them. Every instinct in Aiden told him to keep on, to look for Lily, but he knew he couldn't.

"I'll find her," Cade called to him as he kept climbing the hillside. "I promise."

By the time he got one-third up the summit, doubts started to creep in.

Maybe she decided to go somewhere else. Maybe she's sitting in some café in downtown, totally unaware of the fire.

But Cade knew those were hopeful thoughts. He felt her here. And she was still alive.

When the smoke became so thick he couldn't see more than four feet in front of him, his radio came to life. The ground crew had a solid head count. They thought they had everyone.

"Charles, you copy?" he heard a voice over the radio. He brought his mouth to the speaker, but stopped.

How would they know if he got the message or not?

"Cade."

He heard her voice, he was sure of it. Even with the fire that raged nearby and the wind that had picked up to carry it, he knew it was her.

"Lily?" he called. "Lily! Where are you?"

He didn't hear her voice again, but her presence drove him onward. He'd already outrun the fire once, near the head of the trail when it whipped around from the eastern side.

But now it was right on his heels. It shot skyward at the same pace as him.

Cade ran up the trail and nearly tripped at a log that was nestled right at the perimeter.

"Shit," he said, and leaned down to stop the fall.

His hands rested on something soft—something alive. He pulled down his bandana and saw Lily. She stared up at him like she'd been expecting him.

"I knew you'd come," she said.

Her voice was weak. Cade felt his heart squeeze. He'd known, all along, that he'd find her.

Lily pushed herself up, and he gripped her under the arms. She held him close, and he wanted more than anything to hug her so tight she'd never slip away again. But there was no time.

"We have to go," he said, brusque. "Here."

He pulled the fire shelter out of his pack and pulled her toward a small clearing near the rim of the mountain. She started to choke back her tears as she hunkered down beside him. "It'll be okay," he said. "I promise. We just have to wait this out."

Cade held the shelter over them firmly as the fire raged on top of them. Her small screams blended with the angry fire outside. For a moment, he wasn't sure if it would be enough. The heat burned into his arms and his hands, through the gear and the shelter, but still he held on.

"Are we going to die?" Lily asked.

He glanced down into her eyes. All he saw was trust.

"No. I won't let you get hurt," he said. Cade sensed an even worse rush of fire coming.

He leaned down and kissed her firmly. Lily's body responded, but he forced her down and covered her with his body. He felt the shelter blanket him, save for one booted foot that jutted out.

Cade gritted his teeth as he felt the searing heat across his ankle. Beneath him, Lily breathed fast and sharp. The ground and rocks that surrounded them had heated up to an almost unbearable degree—and that was through his gear.

He could only imagine how it felt to Lily.

Still, he had to admit that his girl was smart. She'd found a place that was relatively clear and high. Any lower and they'd have been immersed in vegetation. The perfect fodder for a hungry fire.

"Hold on," he whispered into her ear. "We're almost there."

He felt her breathing grow more desperate below him. It wasn't just the weight of his body or the heat of the ground. The fire had sucked most of the oxygen out of the air.

"Small breaths," he whispered into her ear.

She breathed more shallow, and sucked in only what she needed. He wished there was something more he could do, but all they could do was wait. Cade heard the tail end of the fire pass over them and continue up the hill. Not far from where they were, it would start to sizzle out.

"Cade," she whispered.

"Save your breath."

"In case... in case we... just know that I love you," she said.

Lily turned one cheek to the ground and gazed up at him as best she could.

"I love you, too," he said.

It was the first time he'd said it to her, and wildly different than when he'd blurted it out to Aiden.

If secrets were heavy, this was the heaviest by far. The most weighted are those you don't know are on your back. The ones you don't see coming.

It felt like they were under that shelter a lifetime. But Cade wanted more. No amount of lifetimes with her would be enough.

His radio crackled into their little bubble of salvation and gave him the relative clear.

"Charles, where the hell are you? Do you copy? Goddamnit, Cade." Elijah's voice broke into the shelter, and he felt Lily shake with a giggle beneath him.

Cade got to his knees and carefully pulled the shelter off of them.

"I copy," he said. "I have Lily."

"Oh, thank God."

"Is she alright?" Aiden broke into the call. All protocol was gone.

Cade looked at her and raised a brow. She nodded. Dirt was smeared across her face.

"She's fine," he said.

"Where are you?"

"Uh... near the summit," he said. "Rocky terrain, lookout point."

"You have the coordinates?" Elijah asked.

Cade reached for his gear pack and started to shout their location into the radio.

"Copy, ten-four," Elijah said.

As he clipped the radio back on, he surveyed the area. The ground was black and smoking. Around them, trees were aflame but the fire had started to die.

"I can't believe it," Lily said. "I thought... I thought for sure... God, I'm so stupid. I'm sorry, I'm so sorry I left like that—"

"No sorries," he said, and pulled her close. "We're alive. That's all that matters."

Lily's lip shook and tears started to run down her cheeks. She opened her mouth, but all that came out was a gasp.

Cade pulled her against him and stroked her hair.

It was so close. So close, and we made it. And who gives a damn about all the drama before?

It seemed so petty, all of it. He couldn't believe that he'd spend all those weeks, all those years, obsessed with something that didn't matter at all.

"Lily? I know this probably isn't how you imagined this..."

"What?"

He'd fantasized about this moment the past few days, but it was all just that—a fantasy. Cade had thought about taking her to the coast, to a little cave in Florence or Haystack Rock in Astoria.

He'd have a gorgeous diamond ring, maybe even her mother's, and an entire speech prepared that he'd say flawlessly. But now? Now he wasn't even sure if he could get to one knee.

"Lily, I know we haven't had the most traditional relationship. But I can't imagine my life without you. And I don't want to."

"Cade?" she asked, her eyes wide with confusion.

"What I'm trying to say—well, ask—is..." Cade pulled himself onto one knee, and ignored the pain that shot through his ankle. "Will you marry me? I mean, I don't have a ring, not right now. But I'll get one, and—"

"Yes."

"What?"

"I don't want anything more than to marry you," she said.

That bright smile he'd known all his life spread across her face. It was the most beautiful thing he'd ever seen.

"Really?"

"Of course!" She wrapped her arms around his neck, and he kissed her cheek.

"But, Cade?" she asked as she looked up at him.

In the distance, he could hear the helicopter. They were so close, so close to being safe.

"Yeah?"

"There's, uh... I need to tell you something."

His heart sank. *Not again. Not when they were so close to being happy.*

"Don't worry, it's not bad. At least I don't think so," she said.

"Okay." He pulled in his breath. "What—"

The helicopter appeared at the cliff. It drowned out her voice. Cade shielded his eyes and looked in the cockpit. Elijah and Aiden grinned down at them as a ladder released. Cade nodded Lily toward the chopper.

"Whatever it is," he called into her ear as he climbed up behind her, "we'll work it out. Don't worry."

She looked over her shoulder at him and grinned. And he knew it was true. When it came to Lily, nothing was impossible. It had taken him years to figure it out, but now that he knew it, he wasn't about to let anything get in their way.

Lily climbed into the helicopter and Cade watched her brothers hold her close. Neither of them said anything when Lily slipped her arm through Cade's and rested her head on his shoulder. As the helicopter descended into the wide open field, Cade squeezed Lily's hand tightly.

This was it. All I've ever wanted, but never knew I needed.

32

LILY

*L*ily leaned back into the sofa, her ankle propped up on the table. She craned her neck around and watched Cade as he worked in the kitchen.

"What are you making?" she called.

"Firehouse chili," he said. "Protein. It'll help you heal."

"You baby me too much," she said as she popped another piece of caramel popcorn into her mouth.

"I almost lost you," he said, and turned with the spatula in hand. "That means I get to baby you as much as I want."

"The last two days have been wild, right?" she asked.

Lily glanced down at her swollen ankle. It was nothing compared to the burns Cade had sustained on his, but he acted like she'd nearly lost her foot.

Still, I have to admit it's nice.

She'd been thankful that neither of them had been held overnight in the hospital. The smoke inhalation damage had been surprisingly minimal.

"You're lucky," the doctor had said as he released her. "It could have been a lot worse. We have one hiker in here with third degree burns over half his body."

"My God," Lily had said and looked at Cade.

Now, just forty-eight hours later, the whole ordeal seemed like a lifetime ago. Whatever had transpired under that fire guard, it had sealed them together for good. When she'd felt his body on top of her, protecting her, the last of her walls gave way. There was no way she was letting him go—or walking away—again.

"Gotta let it simmer for awhile," Cade said. He dropped onto the sofa next to her. "Cornbread for a starter?" he asked. "And iced tea."

She took a slice and bit into it. The buttery goodness nearly rivaled Jean-Michel's work.

"Oh my God. How'd you learn how to make it like this?"

"Firehouse," he said with a shrug. "The secret is butter four ways, brown sugar—"

She held up her hand. "Please. My waistline doesn't need to know that. Speaking of..."

"Don't tell me you're going to turn into one of those women who worries about her weight all the time," he said. "You're gorgeous, no matter what. Now eat the cornbread your fiancé slaved over for the past two hours."

Lily blushed. "This is serious. I need to tell you something."

Cade put down his slice of bread and looked at her. "What you were going to tell me at the fire?"

She nodded. "I, um... I freaked out because of what happened at my appointment. It was a doctor's appointment."

IIe shoved the plate onto the coffee table. "Are you okay?"

"Yes! I'm fine," she said with a laugh. "We both are."

"What?"

She sighed. "I was hoping the doctors wouldn't let it slip in front of you at the hospital, but now I kind of wish they had. I'm..." she took a sip of the iced tea he handed her and spit it back out.

"What's wrong?" he asked. "Is it bad?"

"Caffeine," she said weakly.

"What?"

"There's a lot of caffeine in iced tea, right?"

"Uh, I guess? I mean, a normal amount?"

"I don't know if I can have this."

All the articles she'd glanced over during her lifetime rushed back at her. No raw seafood, no rare meat of any kind, no caffeine, and definitely no alcohol.

Was a little bit of caffeine going to hurt the baby?

"Lily, don't take this personally, but you're acting really weird. I've seen you down iced tea by the quart plenty of times."

"Hey," she said, and shoved at him playfully.

"Come on. Tell me what's really going on. You know, your dad's the one who taught me to make that tea."

She sighed. "You know that thing I said I needed to tell you?"

"Yeah," he said. "It was quite dramatic. At least until the helicopter drowned you out."

"*Okay*. Don't be upset."

Cade's face darkened, but he didn't say anything. *It's now or never.*

"I went to the doctor because I noticed that my breasts were tender, just as a precaution you know. My mom," she said quietly. "The breast cancer... it's a common symptom."

Cade stiffened beside her.

"No, no! I'm not saying that I have cancer," she said. "God, I'm fucking this up. I went to the doctor and found out that I'm pregnant."

She shrugged and looked up at him. "That's it, all my secrets, laid out in plain sight."

Cade's jaw dropped open. Lily started to count the seconds.

How long until he has a total freak out? Maybe this was a mistake. Marriage is one thing, but a baby? Already? God, a month and a half ago they were virtual strangers.

"I know that maybe you aren't ready—" she began, but Cade grabbed her tight.

His kiss took her breath away. Her stomach fluttered, and for a moment she couldn't tell if it was from him, from what they'd created, or a sweet combination of both. Lily laughed when he let her go.

"I thought you were upset!"

"About a little version of you? How could I be upset about that?"

She bit her lip and watched as he searched her face. After she was released from the hospital, she mulled it over for a full day.

Getting rid of it had never been an option, she knew that. But when that little life inside her had been threatened by the fire, something within her blossomed. She'd grown into fierce protective mode in seconds.

Most women, it takes them months. But I guess I've never been like most.

"It's a little too early to know about that," she said. "Who knows? Maybe it's a little version of you. Honestly, I was completely freaked out. I still am."

"I told you. We'll work through anything, as long as you'll have me." Cade reached up and tucked a wild lock behind her ear. "And I meant what I said after the fire. You'd better damn well be willing to marry me. I've already got an appointment at the jewelry store. I just figured you'd like to walk in and choose your ring, rather than be carried."

She blushed and looked down at her ankle. "Cade—"

"This, right here? This is forever," he said. "And so what if the baby is a little earlier than we might have planned?"

"Early? You mean like years earlier than I would have chosen?"

"I never had a family growing up," Cade said quietly. "Now here you are, and here it is." He placed his hand on her stomach. "The perfect family."

"And what about Elijah?" she asked quietly.

He gave a short laugh. "He was surprisingly easy to win over."

"Seriously?"

"Yeah. I didn't get a chance to tell you, but they're both on board."

"I guess when it comes down to it, you always have been part of the family," she said. "And it wouldn't have mattered, you know. If Elijah or Aiden didn't approve. But, to be honest, I'm glad they do."

"Now I just have to break the news to them that they'll be sharing best man duties," he said.

She gave a laugh. "And from what I saw at the kickball game, my maid of honor just might be Aiden's date."

Cade raised a brow. "You really think—"

"Who knows?" she said with a smile. "And really, who cares? Right now, in this moment, this is about us. All three of us."

"The three of us," Cade echoed. "I like the sound of that. A place to put all my love."

Lily began to tear up. She looked away and tried to discreetly wipe at her eyes.

"Are we going to blame this on pregnancy hormones?" he asked. "Because if we are, you better milk it for all it's worth. You only have a few more months of it, Mrs. Future Hammond."

She laughed and leaned into him. "I'm good with that. But you promise?" she asked. Lily gazed up at him. "Forever?"

"Forever," he said. Cade kissed her on the head as she settled into the crook of his chest. "I promise."

EPILOGUE CADE

Cade stood up as Lily brought the pasta dish to the table, but she shooed him back down.

"You cooked!" she said. "The least I can do is serve."

He put down the flatware he'd been holding on the table and took the dish from her.

"You sit. Rest," he said. "Doctor's orders, remember?"

She sighed.

"Fine," she said. "But this whole getting waited on thing isn't for me. I'm not confined to bed rest, you know!"

For the first five months, she'd barely shown, but in the past week there had been no denying the belly. It was cute, the way she'd deftly learned to work around it.

"When are you going to give Jean-Michel your notice?" he asked as he served her. "You know you don't have to work."

She gave him a look.

"I *want* to work," she said. "As long as I can. He finally graduated me from desserts to more serious dishes, and I don't want to give that up now."

As she leaned over for the bottle of sparkling cider, his eyes roamed to her breasts. They'd grown large and heavy in the past month, and strained at her blouse.

Cade cleared his throat. "You, uh, might want to start wearing some of those maternity shirts Renee got you—"

She looked down and blushed. "Sorry," she said. "I'm still getting used to these."

"Hey, I'm not complaining," he said. "I like it."

"Right," she said with an eye roll. "I'm freaking gorgeous, I'm sure."

"You're still sexy as hell," he said. Cade grabbed her arm and pulled her toward him.

Lily let out a laugh. "You don't always get dessert first," she said.

"Here, taste," he said. He dipped a silver spoon into the side of rich marinara and fed it to her.

"It's good," she said, and licked her lips. "They teach you well at the firehouse."

He shrugged. "It's not gougère, or whatever it is you make at the shop, but it'll do the trick."

"So, speaking of tricks," she said as she held up the envelope, "do you want to do it?"

He eyed the envelope the doctor had given them earlier that day. At first, both of them had been so certain they wanted to know the sex of the baby—but when it came down to it, neither were sure they wanted the element of surprise taken away.

"How about this?" the doctor had said. "I'll put it in an envelope. You can choose to open it or not. A lot of people these days, they're doing that baby reveal cake? You can give the envelope to the bakery if you'd like, and they'll make the inside of the cake either blue or pink."

"That's... weird," Cade had said, but Lily elbowed him.

"I think what he means is, it's not for us, but that's neat," she'd said.

The doctor held up her hands. "I don't judge. I just share the information I know."

"I don't know," Cade said now. He stared at the envelope

across the table. "Don't you have a mother's intuition or something? Can't you just tell me?"

She grinned. "My intuition is all over the place because of these hormones. I don't know, Renee says I'm carrying low, so that means it's a boy. But I don't feel like it's a boy."

"So you feel like it's a girl?"

"I don't know!" she laughed. "I mean, I guess that's what the envelope is for."

"Let's just do it."

"Are you sure?"

He wasn't, but he didn't think he could go another four months without knowing. How would they shop for clothes? Decorate the baby's room? Start realistically thinking about names? They already had a list of over twenty for each gender.

"I'm sure," he said.

"You do it," she said, and pushed the envelope across the table to him. "I can't handle the stress."

"We'll do it together." Cade pushed his chair around the table next to hers. He tore open the envelope and Lily reached inside.

"A girl," they said in unison.

"I knew it," Cade said. "A father's intuition! I told you she was a smaller version of you."

Lily's eyes welled up. "We're having a girl," she said. "I can't believe it. I mean, I can, but—"

Cade leaned into her and kissed her deeply. He felt her body melt into him.

"Why can't we have dessert first?" he asked, a growl in his throat.

He stood up and lifted her into his arms. Lily squealed, "Stop! I'm too heavy!"

"Don't be ridiculous," he said. "You're light as a feather."

As he carried her into the bedroom, he felt her heavy breasts against his chest and his hardness press into his jeans.

EPILOGUE LILY

*S*he fluttered her eyes open as he laid her gently on the bed. Lily was still getting used to this—the gentle touches instead of the raw passion on the bed.

It was different, their lovemaking these days, but good. Cade ripped open her shirt and exposed her breasts.

"It's official," he said with a grin. "This shirt's no good."

Lily smiled and tilted her head up toward him. As he kissed her deeply, his tongue flicked across hers, but she felt a weight at her center she'd never known before.

"What is it?" he whispered to her.

She shook her head. "Not like this," she said.

"Then—"

"Take me from behind."

She moved onto her side as he spooned her. As soon as his fingers traced along her breasts, her nipples hardened and she felt her center melt. She always wanted him, and always had, but these days it was beyond measure.

Lily wanted him, needed him, all the time. Cade pulled at the satin bra at her breasts and released her nipple as he kissed and sucked at her neck. His hand roamed beneath her skirt while she heard the clang of his buckle coming undone behind her.

She felt his heat, his hardness, between her thighs and eagerly opened her knees. As his hand trailed across her clit, his tip paused at her opening.

"How bad do you want it?" he whispered into her ear.

"More than anything," she said as she bit her lip.

She gasped as he entered her, his index finger slowly circling her swollen clit. Cade bit her shoulder lightly and made her cry out. Lily brought her hands to her breasts.

They felt wild and foreign, like they belonged to someone else. That idea turned her on even more. She felt the gush of wetness coat his cock as she pinched her nipples and squeezed her eyes shut.

The orgasm washed over her without warning.

"Cade," Lily burst out. "I'm coming—"

The waves rocked her hard. She felt him spill into her, and it brought on an entirely new orgasm. He clenched her hips and held her to him. She covered his hand with hers, the sensitivity too much to bear. The firm pressure on her clit took her over the edge and into a blissful peace.

As Cade exited her, she felt their juices spill down her thighs. Lily sighed and rolled toward him, her hand on her belly to help shift her weight.

"That was incredible," he said. Breathless, Cade pulled her toward him.

It was different now. Her head was farther down his arm. Her belly pressed against him instead of just her breasts. But it was comfortable, somehow familiar. She never would have imagined this was where they would end up. But every day she thanked her lucky stars they had.

"Promise me one thing," she said as she looked up at him.

"Anything."

"Promise me this will never change? You and me—what we have—no matter what?"

"You and me? That won't change," he said as he bent his head to kiss her. "Promise."

"Forever and ever?"

"Forever and ever. Even with the new additions," he said as he gently rubbed her belly, "they'll make things better. Stronger. But at the core? That will stay the same."

"How do you know?"

"I just know. I was right about her being a girl, wasn't I?"

"Well, yeah. I guess," she said. She could hear his heartbeat. It filled her head with an intoxicating rhythm.

"Some things you just know. Don't you think?"

"Yeah," she said. Lily thought of them, of their past, of all they'd gone through. And yet, at the center of it all, she'd always known.

"Hey," she said. She placed a hand on his chest and gazed up at him. "You want to know a secret?"

He arched his brow at her. "I thought I knew all your secrets."

"All but one," she said. "I, uh... I kind of let you believe that I wasn't a virgin when we... you know..."

"Wait. What?"

She grinned. "My college boyfriend and I? We never did it. That's why he broke up with me."

"So—wait. You're telling me I was your first? And then... when I went to Montana—"

"My first and only," she said.

"Oh my God. Why didn't you tell me? Why didn't you tell me three years ago? I wouldn't have ever... I mean..."

She put a finger on his lips.

"I didn't think it mattered," she said. "It was what I wanted. And I'm happy it all turned out like this."

He shook his head and looked at her with wonder.

"You're amazing," he said.

She laughed. "Okay, that was it," she said. "My last, final secret. No secrets are allowed for a happily ever after, right?"

"No, probably not," he said. "But I'm far from an expert on fairytales."

"That's not true. You're the hero, aren't you? Who rescued the damsel in distress?"

"Maybe," he said with a laugh. "I guess that's one way to put it."

She joined in his laughter, and snuggled down in his arms, truly content.

GET A FREE BOOK!

Join my mailing list to be the first to know of new releases, free books, special prices and other author giveaways.

http://freehotcontemporary.com

ALSO BY JESSA JAMES

Bad Boy Billionaires

Lip Service

Rock Me

Lumber Jacked

Baby Daddy

Billionaire Box Set 1-4

The Virgin Pact

The Teacher and the Virgin

His Virgin Nanny

His Dirty Virgin

Club V

Unravel

Undone

Uncover

Cowboy Romance

How To Love A Cowboy

How To Hold A Cowboy

Beg Me

Valentine Ever After

Covet/Crave

Kiss Me Again

Handy

ABOUT THE AUTHOR

Jessa James grew up on the East Coast but always suffered a severe case of wanderlust. She's lived in six states, had a variety of jobs and always comes back to her first true love – writing. Jessa works full time as a writer, eats too much dark chocolate, has an iced-coffee and Cheetos addiction, and can't get enough of sexy alpha males who know exactly what they want – and aren't afraid to say it. Dominant, alpha-male insta-luv is her favorite to read (and write).

Sign up HERE for Jessa's Newsletter:

http://jessajamesauthor.com/mailing-list/

CPSIA information can be obtained
at www.ICGtesting.com
Printed in the USA
BVHW051426300720
585046BV00011B/1316